THE SOUL OF A STORME

The Storme Brothers
Book One

by Sandra Sookoo

ARE YOU SIGNED UP FOR DRAGONBLADE'S BLOG?

You'll get the latest news and information on exclusive giveaways, exclusive excerpts, coming releases, sales, free books, cover reveals and more.

Check out our complete list of authors, too!

No spam, no junk. That's a promise!

Sign Up Here

www.dragonbladepublishing.com

Dearest Reader;

Thank you for your support of a small press. At Dragonblade Publishing, we strive to bring you the highest quality Historical Romance from the some of the best authors in the business. Without your support, there is no 'us', so we sincerely hope you adore these stories and find some new favorite authors along the way.

Happy Reading!

CEO, Dragonblade Publishing

Dedication

To Pete and Julie. Thank you so much for your unwavering support and love. You'll never know how much it means to me.

CHAPTER ONE

June 4, 1817
London, England

W*HAT THE DEUCE am I doing with my life?*
Not for the first time had Andrew James Storme, the Eighth Earl of Hadleigh asked himself that same question. One of the logs in the grate popped as the fire burned low, but it had kept the spring chill out of the study that even now he didn't find comfort in, for the room would always remind him of his father. No, he had no bloody idea what he was about; he only knew the title, his family, the *ton* expected much from him, and that pressed upon his chest so tight it stole his ability to breathe at times.

The knowledge that he had no blessed clue about how to conduct himself—both professionally or personally—nagged at him day and night, but there was no reason to examine the whys or even where-fores, and little time to do so if he'd wished for it.

Nothing would change. Nothing *ever* changed except the pressure placed upon his shoulders. There had been no guidance, no words of encouragement, no preparation, for even though his father's last illness had been the lingering sort, when they spoke it hadn't been about the title. Mostly his father had wished to converse over memories and things nearly forgotten in the past—happier times perhaps, that hadn't been nearly so for Drew when they'd happened due to the ever-present expectations.

With a sigh, Drew glanced at the letter he'd been attempting to write for the last half hour. Why the devil couldn't he concentrate today? When his brother received the missive, it wouldn't matter after everything that had happened between them, but the weight of responsibility demanded he do something, and this note was two years past due. It was time for everyone to gather at home and fit all the pieces of their shattered lives back together.

If it was possible.

Once more his pen drooped from his lax fingers. Two years. Damn and blast how life had changed in such a short time. For all of them. His hand shook, and a few tiny drops of black ink spattered upon the letter. No, life wouldn't be the same, but would it ever be settled? Would there come a time when he didn't feel like such an abject failure?

The rustle of taffeta preceded his mother's arrival, and he welcomed the distraction, though the task at hand would need completing, and soon. It was the least he could do. He couldn't put his house in order, so to speak, until his brothers had been accounted for and settled. The tightness in his chest went up a notch and he winced while trying to breathe through the pressure.

Yet even that wouldn't erase the scars war—death—had wrought.

Then why is it me who is drowning?

"Good morning, Mother." Drew had seen her at breakfast some hours ago, but when she'd made an attempt to start a serious conversation with him, he'd fled, for he couldn't add another worry to the already precarious pile placed upon his head. It seemed running away was how he handled all the decisions in life, presently, and that stirred the anger that always brewed beneath the surface more than anything else.

Why the devil couldn't he screw his courage to the sticking point and be an earl as his father had been? Poised, confident, nonplussed, congenial had been his sire's outward appearance. All the things he was not.

"We need to talk, Andrew." Her tone brooked no argument even though the words had been couched in a quiet voice with a smile. She crossed the room, the picture of elegant grace, and then sat in one of the leather chairs that face his desk. How many times did he recall sitting in that exact spot waiting for his father's notice? "And when we do, I'd like for you to listen this time." Concern brewed in her hazel eyes and creased her brow. "It's imperative, actually. We can't keep avoiding this." She smoothed a hand over her moss green skirts. There had never been a time when his mother hadn't been the calm rock of the Storme family and though he desperately needed that safe harbor, the storms raging inside him couldn't be soothed with maternal words of affection.

In this, he was quite alone and lost.

God, I'm a failure in every way that matters.

A tendril of cold terror snaked through his gut, but he shoved the thought and the fear away for a later time. Drew rested the pen in its holder. "What is so damned important you've tracked me to earth here? Have I not done enough?" For it was always something that apparently only he could attend to or fix.

Who will take care of me when I finally fall apart?

"Language, dear." She wasted no time in getting to the meat of it. "Your brother arrives home today."

Panic twisted through his gut to mingle with the fear, and he took tiny, panting breaths to stave off an attack of anxiety. They'd come more frequently in the last six months, but he'd not wished to burden anyone with that fact. For what good would it do? Wasn't that what came with being a peer? So, he'd hidden his distress as best he could. "Which one?" he finally managed to ask through a tight throat.

"Phineas. I had a letter from him several days ago." She frowned as she looked at him despite the unabashed excitement in her voice. "I expect you to behave around him."

Bloody hell. "Please, Mother." His brother's imminent arrival made the letter he currently wrote moot. He rolled his eyes heavenward. "Behave? Yes, by all means, let us coddle both of my brothers when they return." He couldn't help his words or the bitterness that propelled them into the air, but he also couldn't stop them. "The heroes of the wars, regardless of the hell I've gone through, and still do."

Why was it that no one cared about the men who hadn't been to the front lines, who'd been left behind due to necessity and responsibility? Why were such men of less importance than the ones who'd seen battle and had the scars to prove it?

"Andrew, not now." The exhaustion in his mother's voice spoke of weary days arguing with him about that very thing.

"When, then? This needs saying, I'll wager." He shook his head and counted to five in his head to stave off an explosion of temper. "I don't matter, for a man who didn't fight has no right to complain. Isn't that correct?" Despite his attempts to ward off the inevitable, anger rose in a hot tide to fill his chest until it threatened to choke him. He fairly shook from it.

"That's not what I meant." A hint of disappointment clouded her eyes, gone with her next blink.

But he'd glimpsed it all the same. "It's implied. It always is." Drew waved a hand. "What's more, I know you blame me for what happened to the boys. How could you not?" His two younger brothers, both returning home from their military careers and both sporting some type of life-changing injury. "I didn't try hard enough to deny their commissions."

I wasn't there to keep them safe.

The vice around his chest tightened. Father's last words to him had been, *Look after your mother and keep your brothers safe.*

Nothing about what he should do in his own life, but he'd failed that simple command. Shame crept in to collide with the anger. What sort of man did that leave him?

"Such gammon." Annoyance snapped in his mother's eyes. "I was grateful one of my sons remained behind to care for your father in his last days."

"As if I had the choice," he muttered. He was the heir, and his first duty was not to his country but to the damned title. A finger drifted to touch the ruby stickpin he wore in his cravat. To him it signified a drop of blood, the terrible wounds his brothers had suffered, so he'd never forget the responsibility placed on his shoulders.

"Please don't be disagreeable. Not today." She clenched her hands in her lap. "I want you boys to put away the animosity and return to how it used to be between you."

"Ha!" Drew snorted. His mother's wishes and the contents of the letter he struggled to write were much the same. "I doubt that's possible." Why was he held to an exacting standard when the others weren't? "Too much has changed." He stood so quickly his chair toppled and crashed against the bookshelf behind him. "If you are *quite* finished, Mother?"

"I am not." She glanced at his chair until he'd righted the piece of furniture. "You've avoided every overture I've made to talk, but two years has been long enough. Things must be settled, least of which is your relationship with your brothers."

The panicked urgency to run away, to find a safe place to hide coursed through him and sent hot, bitter bile into the back of his throat. "Or what?" It sounded as if she'd come to deliver an ultimatum.

"If you cannot work out the details of your life and attend to the title, I shall have no choice but to write to William, request you sign a power of attorney that gives him the authority to oversee the earldom until such time that your mental... faculties are once more clear." There was a hard note to his mother's voice he'd never heard before.

And what was more, she was aware of how he struggled.

Another wave of hot shame invaded his person. "You'd give control of everything I have to my cousin?" William was a year younger than Drew. Viscount Heymont had been the previous Earl of Hadleigh's younger and only sibling. He and William had grown up together and had been as close as brothers until a rift of some sort between their fathers had put an abrupt halt to the relationships. Now, with both their fathers dead, the origin of said rift had been lost to memories—and his mother certainly wouldn't expound on the topic—but the damage was done. Drew had too much pride to ask after the origin of the feud, and if damned William didn't care, well, neither did he. There were also two female cousins, but he'd not been as close to them as he had with William. They'd much preferred his brothers' company.

Rotten to the core, every last one of them. Good riddance.

"I will if you refuse to do what you must." His mother's expression was unwavering. "Your father would be disappointed in you."

"Too damned bad he's not here to ring a peal over my head about it." Disappointing everyone in his life had been a theme for too many years to count. He quickly swallowed and glanced at the doorway. *I need to leave...* it was imperative that his mother not witness one of his attacks lest he appear too weak, but when the butler showed up in the open space, he bit back a curse.

Damn it all to hell. Will I ever know peace? "What is it, Peters?" he asked from around clenched teeth as he worked to regulate his breathing.

The aged butler flicked a faded blue gaze his way. "Major Storme is here, my lord. I've had him settled into the drawing room."

Settled instead of shown, for his brother was unable to walk. Once more, hot embarrassment and anger bubbled up, gathering strength. Soon it would overtake him, as would the crushing bands of anxiety, and he'd lash out in destruction—proving the surname was appropriate.

"Phineas is home," his mother breathed as she rose to her feet. "Oh, I'm so glad." The relief lining her expression grated against his already overwrought nerves.

Drew ignored her to focus on the butler. "The dowager countess and I will be there directly." He glanced at his parent, and a shard of jealousy stabbed through him. She never seemed that glad to speak with him.

"Very good, my lord." The butler withdrew.

"Andrew, please, don't call me the dowager," his mother said with a playful tone. "It makes me seem so old." She patted a tendril of brown hair into place. Though it was streaked with silver, she'd never looked better in his opinion.

"You are as beautiful as always," he conceded in a soft voice. "But until I marry, that's your title and you know it."

Interest lit her face. "Will that be soon? You were always so charming with the ladies before. Is there a special woman—"

"Before Father died and I was free?" He clenched one hand into a fist and then slowly relaxed the fingers. "I haven't found a woman worthy of being a countess." It was merely another responsibility heaped upon the pile. The weight of it pressed into his chest. He staggered from it, obliged to grip the edge of his desk to remain upright.

"Are you well?" She looked him up and down with concern.

"Quite," he managed to gasp out. If he didn't compose himself, the anger and anxiety would win. Would his family diagnose him as insane then? Hand off his responsibilities to William as if he didn't matter? As best he could, he ignored the internal hell he battled with. "Shall we?" When she nodded, they quit the study.

It took all of a minute to reach the sun-drenched drawing room at the opposite end of the corridor. As soon as his gaze landed on his brother sitting in the Bath chair, the anger rushed up anew, threatening to choke him.

Drew fought off the urge to claw at his too-tight cravat as well as retreat from the room like the coward that he was. It was his fault Finn would never walk again and seeing him like that brought back how inadequate he truly was for this position.

For life.

"Phineas. Welcome home," he managed to gasp out. Emotion he could never show raged and grew inside his chest, graveled his voice. Hadn't his father ingrained into him the importance of never allowing such things to show, lest he appear weak before the *ton* or his family? A man—an earl—must be strong at all costs, for it was his responsibility to care for the rest.

Yet, who was there to teach him how to live with the overwhelming feelings that were tearing him apart? Who would be there to make certain the anxiety that told him every damned day that he wasn't good enough would be beaten back? Who would help him manage all he struggled with to live a somewhat normal life?

"Nice to see you again, Drew." His brother lifted his chin a notch. His black hair was a tad longer than fashion demanded, and he wore it disheveled as if he cared not for outward appearances. Unlike Drew, whose hair of the same color had been cut and styled as if he'd meet the Regent tomorrow. Finn's clothes reflected the same attitude as his hair. But then, recovering in hospital didn't require the same attention as a peer about Town. "Being home isn't exactly how I used to imagine it."

"I'm glad you're here." His mother swept across the room. She dropped a kiss on Finn's lean—almost hollow—cheek. "Tell me what you need to make your life easier. How can I help?"

A bitter laugh escaped him. "A new set of legs or a spine that's not busted?"

"I wish I could." She patted his shoulder while throwing Drew a speaking glance. "At least you and Andrew can spend time together now." Her eyes widened with unspoken command. "As well as Brand when he arrives from Ipswich."

"Whenever that is." *So we can be one big happy—unbroken—family.* A fair amount of annoyance crept over him. "Brand's not exactly known for following a schedule." But he needed to, for Drew wouldn't allow him to suckle at the estate's teat. A man should make something of himself.

Finn shook his head. "Cut him some slack, Drew. The man's missing a damned eye now. That should gain him a few months leeway."

Hot guilt and shame welled up to clash with the churning anger inside Drew. His gut knotted with anxiety, which stirred nausea, and he swallowed a few times to stave off the urge to cast up his accounts. "Yes, well, you're here and I trust you'll use the time to figure out the next course of your life." How the hell could he see his brother day after day as he was now and not break apart?

"Time will tell." Finn smiled, but it was a grim affair. "It *is* nice to be home after spending six months in a Bath hospital trying to convalesce." He snorted. "I think the sisters thought that I'd miraculously be healed while taking in the waters. They were a little put out when that didn't happen."

Oh, God. The terrible pressure wouldn't relent in Drew's chest, and the anxiety inside threatened to suck him down into the swirling black depths. He gasped for breath as inconspicuously as he could. It was all too much. "I'd rather you not speak of the war or its aftermath, if you don't mind." Perhaps if he ignored that too it would stem the flood of feelings, for he'd been left behind in London, safe from the French scourge, even though he'd been fighting a war of his own while watching his father die.

"So that's how it is." Annoyance jumped into Finn's expression. The last time Drew had seen his brother—nearly four years before—he'd been an untroubled young man with ideals and dreams. Now, he merely looked tired and hopeless. "War and its aftermath have been my life—Brand's life—for the last handful of years." His Adam's apple bobbed with a hard swallow and shadows flitted through his stormy eyes. "It will take some time for me to adjust to a civilian life, and I'll need to talk about what I've gone through. Especially when Brand comes home."

There would be no escape.

Drew curled his fingers into fists. A blanket of rage descended, fast and furious. It swelled his chest, and one of the buttons on his jacket popped from the garment to ping against a table leg where it landed. The ever-present guilt and anxiety met and a thunderstorm of raw feeling crashed within his being. "It's not been my life, so I would appreciate you not speaking of it in my presence." Even he heard the warning in his voice, but he wasn't sorry for it. They had no idea; none of them knew what he fought with.

"Whose fault is that?" Finn shifted in his chair. Pain etched across his face.

"Boys, please," his mother implored as she stood behind Finn's chair.

Drew took a few steps toward his brother's location. "I had to be here. You know why."

"At least you had a choice to avoid the fighting. I'd never wish that hell upon anyone."

Perhaps it was best to vent some of his spleen and have it done with. "I had no choice. Father was dying. He wanted me here because I was his damned heir, and you certainly never came to say your goodbyes." It had been him at those last terrible days, waiting, listening to every labored breath his father had drawn. He'd endured his mother's stifled sobs. He'd swallowed his own feelings and reactions to appear strong for his parents while he'd hoped for last-minute advice on how to handle the shift in his own life.

Advice that never came.

Dark anger mottled Finn's face. One hand gripped the armrest of his chair so hard the knuckles turned while. "Ah, so I should have asked my commanding officer to pause the battle to return to London so *you* could have a better go of it? Good men died out there, but you don't give two figs about that, do you?" He glared, his voice rising. "Life doesn't pander to your whim and order merely because you're the earl now."

The storm inside him swept through and took away Drew's filter. He tugged at his cravat, his fingers brushing the ruby stickpin nestled in its folds. *Don't forget.* "You don't know how hurt Father was!"

"I rather doubt that's true. He was the one who encouraged Brand and me to join the war effort!" Finn made a rude gesture that had a blush jumping into their mother's cheeks. "I only thank God he expired before he discovered how injured I was, for that might have made him care. He bloody well didn't take notice of me like he had with you." Hurt and envy were stamped on his gaunt face. "The spare didn't matter as much as the heir, right?"

"Oh, no?" Drew gripped the wooden back of a sofa in a bid to remain upright instead of letting anxiety have at him. "Father fairly glowed with pride when he talked of his sons who were off fighting for their damned King and country." Paternal pride was something Drew would never have a chance to feel or bask in.

Their mother glanced between them. "Boys, please, practice decorum. The servants will hear."

Finn looked away first. "Perhaps, Drew, you should walk it off or drink yourself into oblivion. Wouldn't want you to damage that inflated ego."

"Damn you." Rage shook in his voice while his chest tightened with the force of the storm battering him inside. A button popped on his waistcoat. It bounced off one of the wheels of Finn's chair. "I'm not one of your subordinates—Major. You have no idea what I've had to endure in your absence."

He flicked his gaze to Drew's waistcoat. A hint of puzzlement crossed his face before annoyance covered it. "I'm not cowed by your damned title, so stop thinking you know what's best for my life. I scarcely know myself right now."

The truth of that statement lingered in the air a long time, for Drew felt exactly like that. Not for worlds would he admit to it though. Instead, he glared. His hold on the internal storm was slipping rapidly. "I'm the head of this bloody family now. You'd best mind that or I'll cut off your allowance."

That brought his brother's head up. Red splotches of anger mottled his cheeks. "Go to hell, Drew. Life has changed for all of us. Until you accept that, we will always be at each other's throats."

A red haze fell over Drew's eyes. The specter of anxiety squeezed his chest until he was gasping for breath. "I'll throw your arse into the street. See if I don't. I won't be disrespected in my own home."

"Our home." Finn chopped at the air with a hand. "If you do, it'll ruin your precious image. Then what will the *ton* think? God, you're like Father's shadow." He snorted. "Except you'll never be the earl Father was. You lack compassion and empathy."

Don't you think I already know that? Black spots appeared at the corners of his vision and he held onto the sofa back like a lifeline. "Bugger off." He had to leave, run, get away before he embarrassed himself with weakness.

"You first, bastard."

Their mother wept. Each tear she shed added fury to the storm battering his body. She threw out a hand to Drew and laid the other on Finn's shoulder. "I never wanted you at odds. I thought after everything you'd mend fences." The disappointment in her face nearly sent him to his knees. "For your father's memory."

I'm failing at everything, and I don't know how to fix it.

"I don't know if we can," Drew whispered. It was the only truth he could utter at the moment. "Too much has happened, too much time has passed."

His mother wiped at her cheeks. "If you'd find a woman to stand at your side and help you with the title like I did your father, you'd see things differently. You were never meant to bear the burden alone."

"Ha!" He shook his head, but that didn't alleviate the sense of being broken apart. "But I *have* been alone these past two years, haven't I?" His mother had dealt with her own grief and had been often out of pocket, while his brothers had the war to worry about. There'd been no one to counsel him; no one to turn to for comfort.

"Well, Mother, it's no wonder he hasn't married at his advanced age," Finn said, further needling him. He narrowed his eyes and stared at Drew. "You're too much of a prick for a woman to stomach."

Drew let himself free-fall into the flames licking at his soul, for he was beyond rational thought. "At least I *can* please a woman with my prick."

Their mother gasped as Finn went pale and withdrew into himself, shrinking against the chair's back. "For God's sake, Andrew."

That wasn't well done of him at all. "I apologize."

Finn's lips were white as he held Drew's gaze. "You wouldn't have said it if it wasn't true. Thank you for reminding me of what I've become and what my new place is."

The fiber of their family was rapidly deteriorating—because of him. The darkness at the edges of his vision intensified. Anxiety came at him like a beast with gaping, tooth-filled jaws. He needed the privacy of his rooms before he broke down. "Perhaps it would be best if I retire to the Derbyshire estate." If he weren't here, he couldn't do more damage.

And neither could they.

"If that's what you wish." Finn waved a hand. "Regardless, I will have made other arrangements by your return. Now, if you'll excuse me?" He wheeled himself out the door. His calls for a footman echoed back into the drawing room.

"How dare you, Andrew." His mother rounded on him. "If you

leave, be certain you come back to London a better man." Lines framed her mouth and tears glistened in her eyes. "Not for us, but for you. I won't let another of my sons become broken."

I broke the day Father died.

When he didn't answer, she said softly, "I shall write to William."

"Obviously, if you don't have faith me, then by all means, do what you must." It took the remainder of his willpower to fight off the urge to give into tears. "And so will I." Then he quit the room without a backward glance.

CHAPTER TWO

June 14, 1817
Derbyshire, England

M ISS SARAH COPELAND bit the inside of her cheek to keep from screaming out her frustration while her charges continued to do whatever they bloody well pleased. The ten-year-old boy and the eight-year-old girl hadn't been interested in reading from their primers, categorically refused to take on mathematics, and pooh-poohed the idea of entering a debate about current affairs. It seemed the only thing the two wished to spend time doing was creating havoc throughout the schoolroom and littering the floor with bits of paper. What was the purpose of being installed as a governess if the children she oversaw didn't respect her authority or that of learning?

These children are the devil's own spawn, I just know it.

Not that she was an expert on children; she had none of her own, and at this point, it wasn't likely that she'd have a chance. The only reason she had the position she did was in exchange for room and board. And it wasn't that she was opposed to children. Quite the opposite. They had the capacity to bring joy to everyone they were around as well as infuse one's day with amusement or gratitude. However... these two were a handful, and due to the situation surrounding them all, they held unspoken power over her and her tenuous position in the household. Yet, she'd been here for five years. During that time, she'd instructed the oldest child, and it had been so much easier when he'd had a desire to learn.

If I'd had the choice, I certainly wouldn't have come to Derbyshire and this vocation.

With a long-suffering sigh and a slight push of her silver-rimmed spectacles up the bridge of her nose, she looked toward the floor-to-ceiling schoolroom windows. No, this hadn't been the life she would have chosen for herself. Once upon a time, she'd expected to tour London and perhaps Europe as part of a musical ensemble, for her talents lay in playing the flute. For the longest time, it had been her only passion as well as an escape, and she'd practiced every opportunity she'd had, for the dream of the stage had glimmered brightly. She'd wanted that life—lusted after it really—for she could have been onstage, clad in sumptuous gowns and glittering jewels while listening to the applause and acclaim of people in the audience.

For years, her parents had scrimped and saved so that she could go to London and audition, but they'd died unexpectedly. That's when Sarah had discovered their pockets had been to let for years, and the coin they'd supposedly set aside had been as mythical as the dragons in storybooks, lost with the ship that had sunk and taken their lives. Her musical aspirations had been dashed.

Along with the rest of her future.

Without funds, she'd been forced to throw herself onto her great uncle's mercy and his literal doorstep, which was how she'd landed her current position. Yet, such a life of drudgery hadn't halted her secret hopes. Despite her advanced age and unwed status and the life of pseudo-servitude, Sarah hadn't given up the dream of having a family of her own. Being a spinster, as well as a poor relation, didn't lend itself well to opportunities, for her great-uncle rarely entertained. He was a skinflint and hated to part with the coin. Another reason she only drew the scantest of incomes, but she always carried a tiny kernel of hope deep down that her fortunes would somehow magically change.

That was the wonderful thing about hope: one could never have too much of it, and she refused to give up her dreams until life had shown her that they were absolutely rubbish and unattainable.

A childish grunt brought her out of her thoughts. She glanced at her charges. The girl currently stood on a chair in an attempt to retrieve her brother's tin solider collection that he'd hidden on a top shelf days before. Constantly, the two bickered about their possessions until she wanted to tear out her hair.

One of the brightly shining hopes dulled around the edges. No, with the limited coin in her possession, there wouldn't be a trip to London any time soon where she might have found word of a better position with an appropriately grateful family or even tried to audition with a musical troupe.

"Mary, come down off the chair. You are not a monkey."

"But it's not fair George hides his things from me. We're supposed to share." A whine had set up in the girl's voice that set Sarah's teeth on edge. "I want to play with them." She strained up onto her tiptoes, but she still couldn't reach her objective.

"You have plenty of your own toys," Sarah reminded her. As her spectacles slid slowly down, she looked at the child from over their tops. "But now is not the time for play. We're studying geography, remember."

The ten-year-old boy crossed the room. He tugged on the hem of Mary's dress until she came off the chair. "You only want to knock my toys about and break them seeing as how most of yours are beat up. I'm saving those soldiers for a great battle when Papa gives me a tin horse. My birthday is coming, and I've told him I want one."

Ah yes, another opportunity for the indulgent parents to spoil the children. It wouldn't harm the little dears to not possess everything they immediately wanted. "Please sit down, the both of you," Sarah asked. "We are not discussing battle tactics or the greatest generals in history. In fact, I intend to return to world geography." So help her, she would drum this information into their heads if it was the last thing she did. They needed to learn about the world around them— the world far away from the dull life found in Derbyshire. As the children took seats at the table, Sarah pointed to a place on the small globe that rested in front of her. "Now then, who can tell me how large the Holy Roman Empire is?"

"Oh, Miss Copeland." A groan followed George's outburst. "No one cares about that." The tow-headed boy shrugged. "It's not exciting, you see."

"Exciting or not, you need to learn this, so you won't be a bacon-brained idiot when you're grown and sent out into the world." Sarah prayed for patience while a sliver of jealousy wormed through her chest. Once George was grown and out of university, he'd no doubt partake on a trip to either America or the Continent. *Lucky devil.* While she whittled away at her remaining years, trying to put something intelligent between the ears of his sister. "I want you to become a scholarly adult who can think for himself."

"I'll wager Papa doesn't know this sort of thing," he said with a wave of a hand. "*And* he's well-to-do and important. No one asks him about stodgy old things found on a globe."

Yes, her great-uncle happened to be a baronet, but that didn't mean anything if he hadn't the capacity to conduct himself as a kind and compassionate person, which he was grudgingly. Annoyance twisted up her spine. She narrowed her eyes on the boy. "Don't follow blindly in his footsteps. Why not make something of yourself?"

"He's a success so I will be."

At least he had confidence. "There's more to life than that." She blew out a breath in frustration and put her spectacles back into place. "What do you wish to converse upon then?" She asked because it was easier to give into curiosity than argue. There was only so much of that she could endure before becoming mentally exhausted.

The grin curving the boy's thick lips was both awkward and horrid. "You."

"Me?" She gaped at him, the spitting image of her great uncle, with his dirty blond hair, chinless visage, and rather stout build. He looked at her as if she were a bug pinned to a board. "Whyever for?"

"Papa said you're here because you have no place else to go." Apparently, that was his opening salvo, and he lifted an eyebrow as if he dared her to deny it.

"This is true enough." She'd never made a secret of her life history, but the fact that these children knew it rankled. For that matter, how had she become the subject of familial discussion? She touched a finger to the silver locket she wore about her neck on a silver chain. It contained tiny miniature portraits of her parents shortly after they'd been married, and beside her flute was the most valuable possession she owned. "When my parents perished several years ago, I was left without recourse, so I sought out my great uncle, who is my father's only sibling—your father." If he hadn't consented to take her in—since her mother had been an orphan—Sarah would have been in dire straits indeed.

The boy watched her with his beady eyes. "Papa also said that you'll always be a governess, even though you haven't any training, for you're too old now to attract a man." He rolled his eyes heavenward. "You'll forever hang onto Papa's kindness until you die, no doubt."

"Yes, he saved me from certain ruin," she murmured with a fair amount of sarcasm. Heat slapped at Sarah's cheeks, and once more her respect for her great uncle plummeted. "I don't know that my age is necessarily a detriment to finding a match. There have been women older than me who've succeeded in that endeavor."

George snorted. "It doesn't appear as if you're having much luck."

The bald fact sent prickles of hurt into her chest. "There aren't many places in Derbyshire to meet interesting people. That is hardly my fault." Why the devil was she discussing something so personal with this small human? She didn't need his judgment or condescension. "Besides, four and thirty isn't all that old."

Mary's burst of laughter contradicted that statement. "Well, it's not exactly young, is it?" She exchanged a knowing glance with her brother. "She'll always be an old maid." Then she turned her bright-eyed gaze back to Sarah. "No doubt *I'll* be married before you." Children were often terribly, horribly honest, and this was no exception. "And I plan to marry a man with loads of coin so I can always have the best, preferably in my come out Season."

As dumbfounded as she was, Sarah kept a stranglehold on her temper. It wouldn't do to show how much their conversation perturbed her, for they'd merely run and tattle to their mother, who would then tell her husband, and Sarah's shaky foothold within the household would be forfeit. After pressing her lips together, she released a long sigh as her annoyance dissipated. "That's enough personal talk for the day. Shall we return to our lessons—"

"Not yet, Miss Copeland." Mary, with the typical unabashed confidence of an eight-year-old, interrupted. Interest sparkled in her blue eyes. "*Are* you an old maid? Mama said it's an unfortunate thing to be, for that means no one will ever take an interest in you. Only a desperate man would look twice at an old maid." She stared critically at Sarah with a slight frown. "You don't really have much in the way of looks, but your hair is pretty. It's like gold in the sunshine."

Oh, dear heavens, make it stop.

"Thank you for the compliment." However, she'd been forthright and strove to instruct the children the same. "It *is* a rather unfortunate thing, and the moniker doesn't help, but the position itself isn't so bad." She clasped her hands in her lap. "I'd rather be an unwed old maid than a woman the same age trapped in a bad marriage. Being leg-shackled to a man with a temper or a violent streak is no way to live." Of this she was certain. Never would she find herself attracted to someone like that.

"I have another question." George looked up from the paper he was folding. "Papa said no one will *ever* marry you because you're long in the tooth."

"I hardly believe that's true. Anything can happen." At least that was what she kept telling herself. "Life is full of miracles."

He snorted. "*And* you're difficult besides. Always making demands."

Both children stared at her with predatory anticipation.

Ah, so then asking for wood for her grate or food for her belly and enough of a monthly stipend for personal items was demanding, then? A flash of hot anger speared through her, but she reined it in by willpower alone. Of course, if given a choice, she wouldn't have put herself in this position where she was treated little better than a servant, but only just. The trouble was the fact that the world was dominated by males who thought they knew best, and none of those thoughts was to make life better for people who didn't directly benefit them.

But the children waited for answer, and in this, she would attempt to educate them as well. She lifted her chin a notch. "In this day and age, a woman—especially one without a man or family to look after her—needs to stand up for herself. That's quite different than being difficult. It's a matter of survival." She held up a hand when George would have interrupted. "Kindness, compassion, and empathy is needed in our world, and it's up to the men in charge to start showing it. No one should ever forget that the people who work for wages are the ones who support those who enjoy their leisure hiding behind a title."

Dear heavens, if she weren't careful, she'd say too much and then land in the soup for sure.

"What can women do?" George asked, as if the very idea appalled him. "They're not as intelligent as men, and they're a fat lot weaker."

Ah, so despite her teaching, he'd grow into a prick anyway. "They can quietly guide men into doing what's right." *And if that doesn't work, a good smack to the back of head ought to set their brains into the proper mindset.*

"But, you're *old*, Miss Copeland," the little miss continued, gazing at her with a critical eye, apparently like a dog with a bone when it came to the subject of age. "And your dresses are boring. Plus, you wear spectacles. Men don't like that."

Despite herself, Sarah blurted out, "How would you know?" She shoved the maligned eyewear back into place. They had a tendency to slip when she was annoyed or aggravated.

The girl shrugged. "Mama said so."

So then, the gospel according to the wife of a no-name baronet. "I can't afford to dress with frivolity or fashion. Besides, as you two have both pointed out, who would I see?" Though she despised that her circumstances had more than once been the subject of gossip—and in front of the children—she couldn't deny it was the pitiful truth. Before the wad of bitterness in her chest could rear its ugly head, she tamped down on it. "Regardless, I'm not certain all of these reasons are the only ones I'm not wed. It's quite a simple matter, really." When they both stared at her, she continued. "No one has asked for my hand." At least it was another truth. Even before she'd been forced to plead for her great uncle's kindness, her ability to attract a man hadn't resulted in a husband, let alone an outing or a dance. She'd been nice enough and polished enough, but men in the country didn't have need for an intelligent woman whose natural inclination fell to music.

George kept folding his paper into what would soon be a hat. He'd recently learned the trick from one of the grooms. "*I think it's because you're not a looker.*"

Sarah's eyebrows rose. "I'm hardly ugly." In fact, just that morning when she'd washed her face and had peered into the mirror, she'd noted that her skin was as clear and vibrant as that of a younger woman. Her color was good, a nice strawberries and cream complexation. Sure, her vision required correction with the spectacles, but she wasn't blind yet.

"It's telling anyway, isn't it?" He shrugged as if he didn't much care on the matter.

Oh, these children were rude and spoiled. She had no choice except to play nice with them, for being a governess here was her last chance at respectability—and if she were given a favorable recommendation, a chance to gain a position with a better family in London. Which was one more steppingstone to where she needed to go. "Whether or not my looks are an impediment to a marriage is a private matter. I am quite done discussing this matter." She tapped a geography book with her index finger. "Let's return to lessons, shall we?"

"Not right now, Miss Copeland." The boy rolled his eyes in a fair imitation of his father. "If someone *did* ask for your hand, would you marry him?"

Why wouldn't this wretched child let the matter drop? Sarah put her finger on the globe and gave it a spin. What must it be like to have the freedom to travel the world to go wherever she wished without being a hanger-on to the edge of someone's charity? "If a man asked, I suppose I would accept—if we got on well enough." Doing so would take her away from this life of drudgery and not fitting in with either class. Plus, hopefully a marriage would mean putting more than a few counties between her and these children who had no manners. If he were supporting, she might be able to chase the dream of music on a stage...

"What if a man *doesn't* ask you?" Mary asked with a pout as her brother donned his hat and wandered the schoolroom.

"Oh, good heavens, Mary, what do you think?" Sarah snapped off before she could recall the words. She swallowed a wad of unshed tears that lodged in her throat. "I'll continue on here and teach the two of you until you're old enough to go off to school."

"That's forever," the girl said with a fair amount of disgust in her voice.

"Yes. It is."

"And I shall marry while you sit here in an empty schoolroom, but don't worry, Miss Copeland," she said in a fair imitation of her mother's condescending tones, "I shall take pity and have you for a governess when I have children."

"How accommodating you are," she choked out. In desperate need of activity, Sarah left the table. She drifted to one of the windows and looked out. From her location on the third floor, she could discern the rooftops of their closest neighbor. Barely visible through the spring trees, the gray shingles beckoned. A couple of miles separated the two estates, though the earl's property was much larger. If she ran away from this house where no one spoke to her—save the children—for days on end, where she took her dinners alone most evenings, where she hadn't a friend or confidence, would those neighbors offer her sanctuary?

A hysterical laugh bubbled through her chest. She quelled the urge to let it out. Of course, they wouldn't. There was no one in residence and hadn't been for as many years as she'd been governess to these children.

I have truly exhausted every avenue that might have opened for me.

George sidled over and stood beside her. "Miss Copeland, I learned something else from Papa the other day," he said, his tone conversational, as if he were much older and leaning against a fireplace mantle in a drawing room.

"Oh? About me?" *Please say no.* After all, what else was there to tell?

"Actually, no. It's about Hadleigh Hall." He pointed at the rooftops in the distance. "The earl has come to stay in the country for a bit. Apparently, he's found London rather distasteful. Papa says it's the first time in years. He figures the old earl must have died and this is his son." The boy shrugged as if it didn't matter to him.

"Is this the truth or gossip?" She didn't know much about their neighbor, for she didn't engage in the senseless chatter of the maids.

"The other day Mary and I were playing in the field. We saw a few coaches on the drive. Footmen were unloading all sorts of trunks and boxes. *Someone* has come to Hadleigh Hall and they're planning to stay for a while."

"If he's young, there might be gay parties," Mary added with shining eyes.

How interesting. She'd never seen the old earl, but she'd heard enough talk in the village about him. From all accounts, he'd been aloof, but responsible and dutiful. What sort of a man was his son? "Was your father friends with the previous earl?" She shouldn't entertain or even invite gossip, for it didn't set a good example, but she rather doubted it could do more harm to the little buggers in her care.

"I'm not certain. Mama said something about the countess being nice and elegant."

That meant absolutely nothing. All women were deemed nice until one knew their true personality. Sarah kept her own counsel as she continued to stare at the roof tops. Never had she known, or even met, a titled peer. Did he bring a wife with him, a family? Would they invite her great uncle for dinner, and if he did, would that invitation extend to her?

Eventually, George stirred. "Papa and Mama want to have a dinner party or a rout to welcome the new earl to the area." His eyes gleamed. "That means leftovers in the kitchen that Mary and I will have the chance to nab."

Now that *was* interesting. A social event meant people and *that* meant an unexpected opportunity. "How fun. No doubt your father wishes to make a good impression." Perhaps she'd be asked to help make up numbers around a table. Imagine how exciting to spend one carefree night without worrying over her future. And if she happened to meet an eligible gentleman while there, she'd use everything in her arsenal to garner his attention and secure it.

Mary came over and stood by Sarah at her other side. For a brief, fleeting moment her little hand found Sarah's before she moved on to pull a wooden duck with a string from a nearby shelf. "I like it when Mama puts on fancy dresses. Some of them sparkle."

"I'd like that too." Though every gown she owned was plain, for she hadn't spare coin to spend on silly trims or expensive fabrics. Her own skill with a needle was laughable at best. And, as Mary had said, spectacles would make certain she remained on the sidelines. She stifled a sigh of longing. *Something* had to change. This couldn't be all that life had to offer her.

It just couldn't. Years of this would drive her to Bedlam, she was certain. Again, she looked at the faraway rooftops as she wrapped a hand around her locket. *Mama, Papa, if you're looking down upon me, help move fate along. I need but one chance...* perhaps the earl would have a hand in altering the course of her future.

CHAPTER THREE

June 16, 1817

PERHAPS RETIRING TO his country estate hadn't been the best idea he'd ever had, for now that he'd been here twelve days, the slower pace and earlier hours of life had become... uninspired, dull really.

Drew shoved a hand through his hair, much to the annoyance of Barton, his long-suffering valet. "What am I supposed to do now? The manor is big and empty, and while I appreciate the silence, the lack of..." What the devil was he trying to say?

"Life, my lord? Vitality? Interest?" Barton supplied helpfully with an elevated blond eyebrow and a slight grin. Was the man mocking him or was he simply the jovial sort? It was deuced difficult to tell.

"Quite," he finally said. Breakfast had been consumed and he wasn't due to meet with his estate foreman until later in the week. He'd gone up to his rooms to retrieve his ever-present ruby stick pin for his cravat. No matter what, he could never let himself forget why he wore it, but all the time on his hands left him at sixes and sevens about how to spend his time. "I fear I shall go out of my mind from the solitude." Yet he hadn't had enough of the bucolic peace to bring the simmering anger to a cooling point. It waited, coiled and tense, like a cobra, ready to strike. "If I were a different man, I'd be content to utilize the library, but I can't cool my heels in such a manner. I require action." He needed an outlet to help relieve that slithering beast inside.

Is there nothing in this bloody world that can help me?

Comb in hand, Barton repaired Drew's hairstyle. "Might I suggest a good ride, my lord? It would clear away the cobwebs and you'll gain some exercise as well." He flashed that annoying grin once more. "There are a couple of excellent stallions in the stables that should be put through their paces, according to the stable master. And you have enough acreage to warrant the passing of a few hours."

"That does sound intriguing." A fat lot more than visiting tenants or inspecting outbuildings, which was something he hadn't realized he'd needed to do. Apparently, his father hadn't done so in the last few years due to declining health, but in his prime, the old earl had made personal connections with every person who lived and worked on the estate. Another blanket of heavy, suffocating guilt fell over Drew.

Even here, far away from London and his family, duties pressed in on him.

There is no escape. More fool I to think there was.

"Beyond that, you could pay a visit on your nearest neighbor. Baronet Gearwell is naught but two miles to the west," the maddening valet continued as if life were but a great game.

"Bah!" Drew chopped the air with a hand. The sunlight glinted off the signet ring on his pinky, drawing his attention to the depiction of a funnel-shaped storm cloud and the two crossed swords and spear that stabbed through it—the coat-of-arms of the Storme family. "I came here for the solitude, not to do the pretty in country society. I'll gladly take the opportunity to ride."

"Very well. Shall I inform the stable master you're coming?"

"That won't be necessary." For an empty manor house, there were far too many bloody servants underfoot. Yes, they were all willing to make his stay as comfortable as possible, but they rather made it impossible for him to ruminate. "I'm more than capable of handling myself." Couldn't a man hold a title yet manage to conduct his own affairs?

At the last second, he stopped himself from shoving a hand through his hair. It wasn't the staff's fault he was naught but a growling beast. Nor was it their fault he struggled under the crushing weight of his emotions and anxiety. They merely wished to feel useful in their own ways, and his father had been gracious to everyone.

I don't have that personality nor the patience. Perhaps this is who I'm destined to be—shut away from society, snarling and alone. While William took over his position.

Barton nodded. "You'll fall into the pattern and schedule of things soon enough, my lord. Country living will be second nature to you by the end of summer." His grin widened. "Shall I press a particular waistcoat for dinner?"

Oh, for the love of all that was holy! Drew clenched his teeth. Damned decisions that meant absolutely nothing in the grand scheme, but this is what an earl did... until he died. With effort, he bit back the sharp retort sitting on the tip of his tongue. "I'll leave that to your discretion." He couldn't quit the room fast enough.

A quarter of an hour was all it took to reach the stables. The irritation was shoved aside for a moment when he mounted a gray stallion with black dappling on his hindquarters. The black mane and tail provided a sharp contrast and the equine's personality seemed to match Drew's. Perhaps even animals tired of the days of inactivity, too.

"Well now. Let's see what you're capable of, shall we?" he told the horse, whose name was Ares.

The animal tossed his head and followed Drew's every movement with his dark eyes.

"Be careful with him, my lord," the stable master warned as he pushed his slouch-style cap up on his forehead and scratched his grizzled hair. "He doesn't like many people, and if you let him, he'll lead you on a merry chase."

"I think he and I shall get on splendidly." For he wasn't all that keen on the company of people either. Drew patted the horse's neck. The scents of hay and leather filled his nostrils. Oddly enough, it brought a modicum of comfort, for riding was something he remembered from his childhood when he and his father would go out in the early morning hours to check the estate. *I should have appreciated that time more.*

He shoved away the thought. Now was not the time for introspection. "Let's fly, Ares, and put distance between us and what life has become."

With the reins clutched in his gloved hands, he spurred his booted heels into the horse's sides, and they took off as if the hounds of hell were chasing them.

For the next hour, Drew gave the stallion his head. They ran neck or nothing through the countryside, tore through the village commons and main streets before hitting the wide-open spaces once more. Each thunder of hooves echoed in his blood and soon his pulse set the same cadence. The power and life of the beast beneath him brought a semblance of order to his world that solitude or discussion never could. This was as close as he came to indulging in freedom and forgetting his responsibilities as well as the emotions plaguing him.

The things he could never control.

The feelings that would eventually consume him.

By the time he reached the main road that would lead to the lane and his manor house, his mood had improved by an increment. Though the horse heaved for breath and Drew's own muscles ached pleasantly from the run, he kept up an intense gallop while leaning low over Ares' neck. "Ah, you beautiful beast! You've done marvelously this day," he crooned into the horse's ear. Riding might tame the things that plagued him. "You've earned an extra helping of oats, I'd say." A triumphant laugh escaped him as the equine tossed his head. To be as free as this. Perhaps the country did have a few positives that

London didn't.

A flash of brown caught in the corner of his vision. "What the devil?" Drew straightened in his saddle. *Damn and blast.* A woman walked the road, parallel to the path he bore down. A straw bonnet sat on her head, but her focus was at the ground. Never once did she look up. Lost in her thoughts? He waved an arm in the hopes of gaining her attention. "Get off the bloody road!" Anxiety built in his chest, for this was yet another problem waiting to strike.

Either she didn't hear him, or she didn't care, for her course wasn't altered. Ares tossed his head and whinnied, perhaps trying in his own way to warn the pedestrian.

"Move, you stubborn female!" His bellow finally reached her ears. As he raced to her location while pulling tight on the reins, the woman dove into the slight depression that followed the road. The basket she carried went flying from her hand; the contents decorating the meadow grass, and the bonnet she wore tilted crazily off the back of her head.

"Bloody hell," he muttered as the horse slowed to a trot. Manipulating the reins, Drew turned his mount about and returned to the woman's location. His chest was still tight, and his pulse pounded in his temples. "Why the deuce wouldn't you move?" She sat, apparently stunned on the ground, the ugly brown bonnet askew, the silver-rimmed spectacles dangling off one ear, her plain brown skirting rucked up to her knees revealing sturdy brown half-boots and slender calves encased in black stockings. From the cut and style of her clothing, she wasn't a member of the *ton*.

Thank God. That would have been a disaster. Adding accidental murder by equine to the list of his various shortcomings wouldn't do at all. As it was, begging the pardon of a villager would come with its own issues, but he would manage.

Then annoyance surged to cover the relief and mix with the crushing anxiety. "It would behoove you in the future to have some intelligence and move off the road if you see a rider approaching at a fast clip." His tone was cold and short as he glared at the outraged female person in the ditch. "Otherwise, you're liable to find yourself in jeopardy." Honestly, who didn't have enough sense to put themselves out of danger?

"Is that so?" Both her blonde eyebrows rose. Ice hung from those few words. She dusted her gloved hands together, presumably to rid them of dirt.

"I wouldn't have said it if it wasn't." Would she now treat him to tears or a hysterical display? Damn, but he didn't have the patience for such. "I could have killed you."

"Oh, I'm well aware of that, you dim-witted nob." Slowly, as if cataloging possible injuries, the woman managed to stand but favored her left foot as soon as she put weight on it. Wrinkles and dust covered the brown skirting, and a sprig of meadow grass rested on the top of her equally brown spencer. She reminded him of a drab sparrow or some other dull bird. "Because you're apparently too addlepated to make use of common sense, I would caution you to mind your surroundings when you're racing like an imbecile down a public road."

What the deuce? Who did this woman think she was talking to, with insults to boot? Another spear of anger stabbed through him. Well, he wouldn't tolerate it. He drew himself up fully in the saddle as Ares danced impatiently. "If I were you, I would hold my tongue."

"And if *I* were *you*, I'd correct my behavior post haste before you do even greater damage." She huffed, and the breath ruffled an escaped tendril of blonde hair. Since the bonnet no longer covered her head, her tresses gleamed like gold in the sun. "What sort of man tears about the countryside as if all the demons of the Underworld were on his heels anyway?" With a trembling hand, she put the spectacles back into place on the bridge of her narrow nose. The lenses slightly magnified the richness of her brown eyes, turned a honey-hue in the bright morning light.

No matter that fury wove through the dulcet tones of her voice and spoke to gentle breeding, Drew couldn't let her challenge go unnoticed. "One who has the power to do what he pleases, especially in this area. A man, I might add, that you have no business addressing in such a manner."

"Ha!" She shook her head. A smudge of dirt marred her angular chin, and his gaze dipped further to along the slender column of her neck. "It's people—men rather—like you who make the world we live in unstable and completely unfair, which leaves people like me always struggling for survival."

He rolled his eyes. *Damnation.* She was one of those crusaders or rabble-rousers that believed everyone in England should stand on the same societal footing. "Spare me your lectures, madam."

The woman sailed on regardless of his warning. In fact, she popped her hands on slightly rounded hips and glared. "You men, no doubt high on the instep, think all of us mortals should dance attendance on your every whim, as if we don't matter or have our own thoughts, dreams." She paused, no doubt because she'd run out of breath. Mottled red color filled her cheeks as fire flashed in her eyes.

Bloody hell. No, she wasn't an uninspired bird at all. In fact, in the avian world, she'd be a hawk, going in for the kill regardless of the other danger around her. Drew stared at her from his perch in the saddle while attempting to calm Ares, who danced with restless energy. Never had he been given a dressing down like that from a woman. It was both unsettling and exhilarating to exchange words with her. She had spirit, and for that she had his respect. Then he cleared his throat as a sense of responsibility sank in to mix with everything else running roughshod through him. Long seconds of silence stretched between them, before he finally broke it and said, "I beg your pardon for turning you off the road."

The harsh frown pulling at her lips lessened slightly. "Actions will prove louder than words. I trust you won't do such a thing again."

"I can't promise that, for riding has been the one thing to date that has the ability to…" At the last second, he cut off his words. She didn't deserve to know more about it.

"Ah." She roved her bright, inquisitive gazed over his person, and for one insane moment, he held his breath. "It's quite obvious you rarely apologize or you don't mean the one you just gave to me."

How the devil could she know that? His jaw dropped. The nerve of this tart-mouthed woman! Anger surged through his chest in a familiar hot rush. One of the buttons popped off his jacket. It sailed between his horse's ears to fall onto the road. God, his valet wouldn't be pleased that he'd done it… again. "You have no idea who I am or what my word means." Second-guessing wormed its way into his confidence and ire. What exactly *did* his word mean in Derbyshire? He hadn't been the earl his father was, didn't know if he ever would be…

When the woman attempted to take a step forward, she winced. Pain flitted briefly over her plain face. "Then perhaps you should enlighten me. Who *are* you? I can hardly wait to discover how you explain your importance." A trace of mocking had set up in her tone as she crossed her arms at chest level.

"Who am I?" He gripped the reins so tight in his hands that Ares tossed his head and danced about. Slowly, Drew released his hold, but his anger hit the boiling point. When he caught her cool gaze, calm trickled over him for a glorious second before annoyance trampled it into oblivion. How exceedingly odd. Nothing about this woman proclaimed peace or a safe haven. "I am the Earl of Hadleigh."

"Oh, drat." The response was said beneath her breath. Red color stained her pale cheeks as she executed an awkward curtsy. "I apologize, my lord." She kept her eyes downcast.

And damn if he didn't prefer the spitfire that had berated him over the demure picture she now made. "I'll wager you don't," he said in a quiet voice. His lips twitched with amusement, and he almost smiled when she snapped her gaze to his once more, her chin tilted at a stubborn angle. "An argument like that carries some truth." When he expected a cutting response, he received silence instead. A niggle of cold disappointment bored through his chest. "Regardless, do you require assistance reaching your home?" The least he could do was not be such an arse... or needle her into displaying that high temper, for he rather enjoyed their conversation. It provided the same sort of freedom galloping did.

Indecision warred with defiance on her expressive but plain face. "While pride demands I say no, the two miles I've yet to go argue otherwise." She shrugged. "I'd rather not hobble there, and I also hope there's no permanent damage to my ankle."

"Perhaps you do harbor some intelligence after all," Drew couldn't resist saying as he dismounted. When she sputtered and searched for a reply, he flashed a grin. God, how long had it been since he'd been properly entertained and... relaxed enough to smile? "Let me help."

Her chin went up again into a stubborn set that tagged his interest. "I can manage."

"That I rather doubt, and since from your own admission I'm little better than a nodcock, I'm certain I can gather your belongings." After plunging into the depression, he recovered the willow basket and then tracked down her scattered possessions—a silk fan, two red apples, a few candles, a packet of tea, a bag of peppermints, and most surprising of all, a pair of while silk stockings embroidered with green vines, pink roses, and a few blue birds. Immediately, his imagination leapt to life and he saw her slender legs encased in the hosiery that was much different than what she currently wore. A moan echoed through the chambers of his mind as he imagined caressing those legs before he went to roll one of the stockings down a delectable limb...

Get hold of yourself, man. You aren't in the market for a woman in any capacity.

No, he wasn't, but this one had managed to intrigue the hell out of him with one meeting. And he had no bloody idea of who she was. Without a word, he handed her the basket, being careful not to brush gloved fingers with hers, but those damned stockings or that vision wouldn't leave him alone. What was her situation and why did he suddenly hope she wasn't attached?

"Thank you." She looped the handle over her arm. The nicety sounded pulled from her, and grudgingly at that. Without looking at him, she limped from the depression to stand near Ares. As she stretched out a hand, the horse put his nose to her fingers.

Interesting. She couldn't be all harridan if the horse liked her. "Shall we continue then?" Daring much, Drew put his hands on either side of her waist. He more or less tossed her onto the horse's back, and since it wasn't a lady's sidesaddle, she was forced to scramble into place and let her legs dangle over one side, her skirts hopelessly tangled.

Her squeal of surprise or outrage caught his imagination as much as the stockings had. What sort of woman was she behind the penchant for plain speaking? For that matter, who the devil was she? "I... you could have given me a warning." She fussed with the bonnet, and once it was properly on her head, he gave into a sigh of relief.

Perhaps now that she was properly covered, she wouldn't stir such naughty thoughts for something he didn't need. "Yes, I could have, but I didn't." He mounted the horse and settled behind her, obliged to slide his arms around her to reach for the dangling reins. "Pardon the trespass," he said with what he thought was indeed a cheeky grin as his chest rubbed against her shoulder.

A squawk of outrage escaped her. "This is hardly proper, my lord," she gasped out but didn't turn her head to look at him.

"Then you can hobble." She was a rather pleasing bundle. A faint hint of violets and clover teased his nose as he slapped the reins.

"Fine." When he set them into motion, her precarious position demanded she secure her seat, and when she clutched at his shoulders, the action put her more firmly into his hold. "I appreciate this." Once again, her tones had returned to their dulcet pitch, and he rather like that too.

"You're welcome. Where are you headed?"

"Baronet Gearwell's home. Two miles west of here."

His interest in her rose. How was she connected to the man? Not wishing to take her there and become embroiled in a thousand questions or be accused of compromising this woman, he guided Ares up the lane that led to Hadleigh Hall. "I'm not of a mind to meet the baronet today."

"Where are you taking me?" Fear quavered in her voice, but he couldn't see her face thanks to the brim of the damned bonnet.

Why was she afraid? Had rumors of his temperament already reached the country? Annoyance swelled his chest. "To Hadleigh Hall."

She straightened her spine, and the back of the headgear smashed into his chin. "But—"

"I won't have you talking in the village that I left you injured and without recourse on the roadside."

A snort escaped her. "I hardly gossip, in the village or otherwise." Then she glanced up into his face. "You have no right!" Righteous indignation rang in her voice, and he couldn't help his grin.

Damn, but he rather liked it when she was in a temper more than when she wasn't. "I have every right. I'm the earl, remember."

"Arrogant prick," she mumbled beneath her breath. Her body was stiff with outrage. With a huff, she turned her head to stare at the road.

Bloody hell. Tension fairly crackled between them. He felt more alive in her company than he ever had before. Why the devil was that?

The remainder of the trip was conducted in silence, but Drew didn't mind. With every movement of the horse, her hip rubbed against his length. That combined with her warm body between his arms, his right sleeve brushing her breasts had his imagination inventing countless scenarios in his mind. Would she employ such fervor in the bedroom? By the time they arrived at the hall, he was well on his way to having a raging cockstand from the unaccustomed friction and thoughts.

Of course, she protested when he assisted her from Ares' back and carried her into the house. The butler followed, aghast, behind him until he reached the drawing room.

"Jeffries, go to the kitchens and procure a cold compress and perhaps tea for the lady." He had no idea what her name was, but the butler appeared nonplussed. "There has been a bit of an accident on the road."

"Right away, my lord." With a curious glance at the willful bundle in Drew's arms, the older man departed the room.

"For God's sake, put me down," she demanded, as imperious as a queen, her brown eyes snapping with annoyance. "I'm not an invalid."

"Best we make certain, so you don't attempt to trap me or cry foul." The fact of the matter was, no matter how he felt in her presence, he didn't trust anyone, especially while he was an eligible, unmarried, and titled peer. The reality of the situation returned and brought renewed anger with it. Was she one of those women who'd angle to get at his title?

She snorted as he dumped her unceremoniously on a low sofa. "I have more integrity than that."

"We shall see." Drew kneeled on the floor at her feet and made quick work of removing his gloves. Once he'd tossed them in a negligent wad on the sofa beside her, he dared much as he took her left foot into his hands and began the task of unlacing the half-boot. "What is your name?"

"Miss Copeland." She clutched the handle of her basket so tight he feared it might snap. What was she afraid he'd do to her?

Which brought his thoughts back around to her situation. She almost acted like an untried virgin, but she was well past the first and second blooms of youth. "What are you to the baronet?" Once the boot loosened, he slipped it from her foot, where it fell to the Aubusson carpet with a muffled thud. He didn't much care about her answer, not now when her stocking-clad calf and foot were warm in his hands.

"Governess to his children." Trembles that affected her limb transferred to him. Did his touch do that or was she merely frightened and nervous from recent events? "Also, he is my great uncle."

"I see." The slender ankle wasn't swollen, so she must have merely landed wrong upon it. After a cursory examination, he couldn't stop caressing the area. Her foot, not overly large or excessively petite, was quite average, but when he gently rubbed the appendage under cover of seeking knotted muscles, a stifled moan escaped her. The sound sent awareness skittering over his skin. *Intriguing.* "How long have you lived there?"

"Several years."

"What were you doing on the road today?"

"It's my day off, so I walked into the village to pick up a few things I'd ordered."

When he traced the high arch of her instep with a fingertip, she gasped and yanked her foot from his hold. As her gaze careened into his, her pupils had dilated. "Stop that this instant. I'm not badly injured and shall be fine." There was a certain breathlessness to her words as she reached for her boot.

And that made him insanely curious. Was she a virgin or did she have experience behind her? For that matter, was she spoken for? Then he shook his head. Why did he care? Before he could ask her more questions, the butler returned along with a footman bearing a tea service. Drew rose to his feet. "Thank you, Jeffries." He took a wet, folded towel from a silver salver, and when he would have kneeled again, Miss Copeland snatched it from his hand.

"I can tend to myself." She pressed the towel to her ankle. "I'm sure after a brief rest I can return home without consequence." Her eyes remained on her task. "Thank you for the kindness, but it wasn't necessary."

Drew frowned, for she'd dismissed him without apology. Did she find him lacking? Hot anger mounted. She didn't know him enough to decide that. Jeffries directed the footman to place the tea service on a low table nearby. Meeting Miss Copeland had been the most exciting part of his stay in the countryside to date, but that didn't stop the familiar burn of rising annoyance in his chest. If she wished to ignore that spark of attraction between them, so be it.

"Obviously, since you have no more need of me, I'll leave you alone." The last thing he wanted was for her to witness the worst of what he was so early in their acquaintance. "Ring for Jeffries when you're ready to depart. He'll have a carriage brought around."

He quit the room with more questions than answers, and for the first time in years, none of them revolved around his title, his family, or him personally.

CHAPTER FOUR

June 19, 1817

"Excuse me, Miss Copeland, but you have a visitor."

Sarah's head came up from the book she'd been reading. She stared at the butler as if she'd never seen him before. "I beg your pardon. A visitor for me?" She nudged her eyeglasses farther up the bridge of her nose.

"That's what the gentleman said." The butler came forward with a calling card on a silver salver. "I've shown him into the front parlor."

"Thank you." With a shaking hand, she plucked the card from the tray, glanced at it and gasped. *Lord Hadleigh.* Oh, dear lord, the earl had come to pay her a visit. Heat slapped at her cheeks. "I'll be there presently."

"Very good, miss." The butler departed on silent feet.

What could he want with her now? Immediately, her last interaction with the earl jumped into her mind. The strong, solid feel of his arms around her as they rode through the countryside, the way pleasant tingles of *something* had assailed her when his arm had brushed her breast during the ride, or the wicked awareness that had stolen up her leg when he'd examined her ankle came rushing back to her. She swore she could still feel every delicious moment that he'd touched her, could hear the breathlessness in her voice as she'd answered his questions.

I acted like a ninny, pure and simple.

Had he been able to tell she'd never been that close to a man before she wasn't related to? Oh, it was maddening to think that she'd left such a silly impression upon him. Once more her musings ran away, and she saw him in her mind's eye.

When he'd nearly plowed her over with his horse, she'd felt nothing except annoyance and contempt for him. Clearly, he'd never given thought to anyone other than himself. Once he'd revealed that he was the Earl of Hadleigh—her neighbor to boot—her stomach had nearly rejected the breakfast she'd eaten that morning. And she'd argued with him for goodness' sake! Right there on the public road as if she'd had no class. What would her great uncle say if he discovered that little scandal? Surely, she'd be turned out onto the street without a reference.

Drat, drat, drat. I dressed down an earl.

Perhaps that's why he was here today, to call her out on her behavior and demand an apology. The heat intensified in her cheeks. She would offer it, of course, but there had been a flash of need and longing in the depths of his stormy blue gray eyes she'd seen briefly when he thought she must not have been paying attention. Who was he beneath the title, and why did he represent such a mystery that compelled her to solve it?

The book Sarah had been reading slipped off her lap to land on the floor with a soft thud. She ignored it and stared at the calling card in her hand. The stock had a hefty weight, so he'd spent good coin on it. The printing was elegant and slightly raised. When she brought it to her nose and took a sniff, faint traces of bay rum and lime drifted into her nostrils. Invigorating and as intriguing as the man himself. It spoke of exotic places and a freedom she could only wonder about. Why had she not noticed it the day she rode in front of him on that large horse? Probably because her nerves, her senses, her brain had been flooded by the situation.

With him.

Oh, bother.

As the muscles of her stomach knotted, she passed a hand over the front of her muslin day dress—a serviceable charcoal gray to hide stains and wear. It wasn't her best dress, but not her worst, either. A sigh escaped her. It would have to do, for she wasn't vain enough to change for him. Earl or not, he'd been rude and arrogant, and he didn't deserve anything more than bare civility. She'd give him that and then send him on his way.

Yet he'd also been a touch concerned for her ankle…

Only because he didn't wish to have me make a scene or demand some sort of recompense. And her injury had been his fault to begin with! She gave her head a shake to clear her thoughts. *I must stop dithering. He's here to see Uncle. Nothing more.* Then another thought occurred. Did he mean to inform her uncle of their meeting and blame the entire circumstances on her? *We'll see about that.*

After retrieving her book, she tucked the calling card into its pages and then hid the novel beneath a cushion on the sofa. Since it was in her own sitting room, no one should disturb it, but there was a chance one of the children would snoop. Then she stood and shook out her skirts, smoothed a hand along her stomach and left the room. By the time she reached the parlor on the first floor, her belly hurt from worry and a smidgeon of dread.

"Oh, drat," she whispered to herself the second she saw him. He was as stimulating as he'd been the last time.

The earl rose when she entered, his stormy blue gray eyes focused entirely on her with an intensity that stole her breath. "Good afternoon, Miss Copeland." His baritone put her in mind of shadowy corners in ballrooms and wicked assignations in a garden maze. "I trust you've been keeping well since we last met."

"Good afternoon, Lord Hadleigh." Gooseflesh popped on her skin. Perhaps she'd read too many thrilling novels and that was the reason for her silly reaction. He was an earl and her nearest neighbor. This was an ordinary social call, but Sarah didn't hesitate to set him straight. The sooner he was gone, the sooner she could think about something that had nothing to do with him. "I'm sorry to disappoint you, my lord, but my uncle and aunt have taken their children to a summer fair in the neighboring county. Perhaps you should return at a later time."

"How fortuitous, for I am here to see you, not them."

"You're here to see me," she repeated in a monotone as if she were the world's dullest parrot. "Why? I'm nobody." As her spectacles slipped down, she shoved them back up with a slight push of her finger.

The earl cocked one midnight eyebrow. "Only if you believe that." His expression didn't indicate whether he did or did not think such of her.

Annoyance twisted through her chest. "So says the man who didn't hesitate to tell me he was an earl." What was it about him that made her want to argue? "I'm quite certain you never think you're a nobody." He couldn't relate to her even if he tried.

"You'd be surprised," he said in a soft voice, almost to himself. Then he straightened his spine and shrugged. His blue superfine jacket drew her notice to the breadth of his shoulders, and the gray satin waistcoat embroidered with fruit done in blue thread had her gaze wandering to his flat belly. "The earl is who I am."

The normal pitch of his voice snapped her attention back to his face. "I'm naught but a governess or poor relation. What do you want with me?" No sense dancing around the issue. Already, her wariness of him battled with the skitters of awareness sailing over her skin.

Why was that? She'd not experienced such a thing before with a man. Of course, she'd never had cause to find herself in the company of one alone either, yet this one was different. It was almost as if he needed help but had no idea how to ask for it. That vulnerability lurked in the backs of his eyes, waiting. Why, though? He should want for nothing in life.

The earl watched her with a slight grin curving the most chiseled set of lips she'd ever seen outside of a statue. "Put away your claws, Miss Copeland. I'm not here to antagonize you." He clasped his hands behind his back. Each time he moved, threads of silver highlighting his midnight hair, arranged in a popular style, glinted in the sun. Heavier silver marked his meticulous sideburns, so he wasn't a young man any longer, even if he looked virile and powerful. "In fact, I wished to see how you've fared with your ankle." He raked his regard down her body with such a leisurely pace Sarah swore she felt as if he'd caressed her.

That wasn't proper behavior from a neighbor simply visiting. Tamping the urge to give into a shiver, she cleared her throat. "Oh, it's healed nicely. No further damage. Thank you." Her nerves were strung too tight and knots pulled in her belly merely from his proximity. Surely, he would leave soon. After that she could finally relax.

"That is good to hear." The man had wicked promise in his stormy eyes, but why? Was he amusing himself at her expense? Again, for what purpose?

"Yes, well, if that's all, my lord?" She was much like a bumpkin in his presence, for he was so elegant and well dressed. His dove-gray breeches alone probably cost more than half her yearly stipend. "I have things to attend."

"Ah, but that's a lie. You said yourself your charges were out of pocket, thus leaving you nothing but free time."

"The children don't occupy all of my time. I do practice on a flute when I'm free." In fact, she'd planned to do so later today.

"Interesting." He came forward a few steps, and the gleam in his eyes was more pronounced. A tiny tremor danced down her spine. "Since you've suffered no ill-effects, would you walk with me between this house and mine?"

Sarah stared as if she were a green girl just out of the schoolroom. "Right now?" It came out as a squeak that showed her as hopelessly inexperienced.

"Why not? You've nothing on your schedule."

This type of situation never happened to her. "But—"

"Do you have other tasks to perform around the house?"

"Well, no but—"

"Are you practicing your flute for a concert?"

"I can only wish, but sadly, no."

"Then come with me, else I'll pull rank on you again and order you to." The command in his voice was both thrilling and troubling. "Where is the harm in keeping me company?"

Ah, so he'd only asked her to help pass the time. Some of the nervousness eased. He wasn't interested in her as a woman; he was merely being his prickish self. "So I understand, you wish to walk with me for no other reason than to…?" She trailed off, perplexed, and gazed at him from over the rims of her spectacles. That didn't put things into greater clarity.

He rolled his eyes to the ceiling. "To spend time in your company."

"Oh." Her heartbeat accelerated. This was too fantastic to believe. Surely she hadn't gained his interest with that one volatile meeting three days ago. "Spend time with me." When had she resorted to repeating someone else's words? She had more intelligence than that.

"Of course." Banked power rumbled in his baritone and fairly sang in his tense body language. She'd already seen his temper, but the hint of vulnerability shadowing the back of his eyes tugged at her, begged her for help. But why and how?

The awareness of him rushed back, more insistent this time. Surely, he didn't mean anything more than a walk. They'd just met. But the underlying current of tension crackling between them compelled her to agree. Slowly, she nodded and put her eyeglasses back into place. "Very well." She'd be an idiot of the first order if she didn't at least discover what it was he didn't say.

"Good." A tiny grin flirted with his lips. "Shall we? No time like the present." He swept an arm outward to indicate the door while he stood back so she could proceed him. "Perhaps we'll indulge in another invigorating conversation."

There was all too much room for interpretation in that statement. Heat stung her cheeks, but it intrigued her to know he found their argument the other day stimulating like she had. Still, did the earl have a hidden agenda? As she passed him and moved into the corridor, she dismissed the silly thought. Of course he didn't. They were practically strangers. Perhaps he was indeed here to ask after her health and merely take her walking.

Except... *life isn't that transparent or easy.*

"I must find my bonnet and gloves."

He nodded but his eyes narrowed. "Wouldn't want to do something so scandalous as appearing on a country lane *sans* one's headgear."

"It is a bit ridiculous. However, one malicious comment from a passing villager, and my position will be in jeopardy." Did he not understand how the world viewed women and judged them twice as hard as they did men?

A quarter of an hour later and once outside, gratitude filled Sarah, for the sun was high and it warmed her skin. The birds chirped in the trees and shrubbery, and the fields were filled with wildflowers or hay and wheat, depending on the whim of the farmers. She breathed in deep lungfuls of the country air and released them. Yes, a walk on such a day as this was what she needed for a new perspective. At the last second, she couldn't quite stop the sigh of pleasure that escaped.

"Have you lived in Derbyshire all your life?"

"Only the past five years. Before then, I resided in Surrey, for my father was a merchant and needed to maintain a residence closer to the capital, but London is too expensive to live in."

"That leads me to my next question." Though he kept his hands clasped behind his back as they walked, his commanding presence beside her couldn't be ignored. He was much like a distant storm, not yet a threat but looming. "Who are your people?"

She frowned. That was rather personal. "My father worked in importing whatever goods he could find that he thought would prove interesting to the public. His business was fledgling, but he did well enough. I am an only child."

"Where is your father now?"

A sudden stab of grief went through her. It would never go fully away, of course, and neither should it, for she would miss her parents dreadfully her entire life. She raised a gloved hand and wrapped it around her locket. "He perished on a ship coming from France to England. Papa and his business partner had gone over to pick up a shipment of brandy and champagne. Since the war ended, they could legitimately import it, and there is quite a demand for the liquor here." She stared straight ahead on the path, not daring to look at him lest she catch pity in his eyes.

"What of your mother?" he asked in a soft voice.

"She went with them. I declined the trip due to my suffering a head cold at the time." She paused, forcing a swallow into her tight throat. "There was a fire onboard. They were trapped on a lower deck." Her voice broke. "The people on the upper, more expensive decks mostly survived." That was the way the world operated in all its crevices. The ones with coin and titles and prestige were often handed chances to survive where everyone else was left to flounder.

"Besides your great uncle, do you have any other relatives?"

"No." She could hardly force the word from her tight throat. "I'm afraid my lines are hideously short-lived, and those that didn't perish early either couldn't reproduce or only had one child." Not a very grand pedigree.

"I apologize for causing you discomfort. I well know how disappointing life can be." The earl looked at her the same time she turned her head. Their gazes connected. That fleeting trace of vulnerability shadowed his eyes and compelled her to keep walking beside him. "I lost my own father two years ago."

Sarah blinked away sudden tears, whether for her own story or for his she couldn't say. Needing something to do with her hands, she fiddled with her spectacles. "Grief doesn't hurt any less, does it, no matter how many years pass. It is something we must adjust to, learn to live with lest it consume and destroy us."

"I haven't experienced any sort of adverse reactions."

When she glanced at him, she caught a muscle spasm beneath his left eye. That was... odd. To say nothing of the flash of anger in his stormy blue-gray depths. Had he not made peace with his loss, or had he not let himself feel the grief? Either way was damaging. To think upon it was both fascinating and concerning, but it wasn't her place to ask. This walk was an aberration. All too soon, once his conscience stopped berating him for causing her injury, he'd go about his business and forget her.

Silence brewed between them as they walked before Sarah broke it due to curiosity. Him being here simply wasn't ordinary. "Tell me, Lord Hadleigh, why exactly did you seek me out today? I've lived long enough to know men don't suddenly show up on my doorstep and ask for an outing." She shrugged. "If you wished to take in the air, you could have done that yourself, though I trust you were more careful about your riding habits."

He huffed out a breath. "I enjoy galloping and don't intend to change it."

"That answer isn't unexpected, but you didn't answer my question." Was he deliberately being difficult, or was he simply to remain an unsolved mystery?

"No, I didn't." The earl walked in silence for a while as she attempted to puzzle out his intentions. He didn't hold himself relaxed as one would do for a mere bout of exercise. In fact, tension fairly emanated from him and he clenched his jaw so hard, the muscles in his cheek stood rigid. Finally, he said, "I do have a specific purpose for this outing."

"Oh?" Her heartbeat skipped. What could he possibly want from her?

"Please, call me Andrew or even Drew. That's what everyone has named me."

Sarah cocked an eyebrow. "You asked me out for a stroll to tell me your Christian name?" Really, the man had windmills in his head if that were the case.

"Not exactly." A hint of annoyance threaded through those two words, but why? If wasn't as if she were the one who made the conversation difficult.

She tamped a sound of frustration. "Then why? Pray enlighten me."

"It's something I've thought about since meeting you three days ago. The idea simply won't let me alone, and the more I ponder it, the more I think it might have some merit," he continued in the same low voice that would drive her made before too long.

"I'm afraid I don't understand." Had that first conversation been an aberration then? He'd seemed highly intelligent and able to debate as they'd stood arguing on the side of the road. Now, it seemed he was bedeviled with something of his own making.

"Doing the pretty doesn't come easy to me." Aggravation under-scored his reply, but for the life of her she didn't know why he was annoyed.

"Some men simply don't have the personality to be charming and unaffected in situations where their peers might judge them." *What the devil is your point, my lord?* But she said nothing further until he could give her a clue as to what he drove toward.

"That's not what I meant." There was no mistaking the growl in his tone.

She blew out a breath as frustration mounted. "Then stop hedging. What exactly are you talking about, for I'm lost at sea in the muddle of this conversation."

"Perhaps it would be better if I showed you, for the subject matter is rather abrupt and far-fetched without a hands-on aid." The earl brought them to a halt and touched her shoulder, turning her so that she faced him on the lane. As she frowned, he tugged at the ribbon beneath her chin. The bonnet tumbled from her head to land with a thud on the hard-packed earth.

"What are you—" Before she could voice the whole protest, he swept her into his arms and claimed her lips.

Sarah's world tilted sharply sideways. She fought against him, more from the shock of it than anything else, but when it became apparent that he wasn't dissuaded from his present course and those chiseled lips *were* quite wonderful against hers, she relaxed.

Seemingly of their own accord, her hands came to rest on the hard wall of his chest, and she gave herself over to experiencing the first kiss of her adult life. When her eyes shuttered closed, she had no idea, for the firm pressure of his warm lips on hers dashed away her ability to think straight. The veriest tastes of coffee and mint came away on her palate as she mimicked what he did to her. When he kissed the corner of her mouth, she did the same to him. Tiny butterfly wings brushed the inside of her belly.

He reeled her in closer with a hand at the back of her head and fit his mouth more decidedly over hers. With the tip of his tongue, he explored her bottom lip, and when she gasped from the sheer pleasure of it, he kissed her upper one, gently sucking it before he released it. Then he paused, their lips barely a hairsbreadth apart, his gaze boring into hers before he claimed her mouth once more, this time with a touch more urgency and power behind the overture.

A moan escaped Sarah's throat. Anticipation sizzled along each nerve ending and heightened her awareness of him as a man. She slid her hands up his chest to clutch at his strong shoulders. A confusing mix of deep need and abject fear twisted along her spine. Through the haze of desire that had suddenly enveloped her brain, common sense rushed in and her eyes popped open.

Dear Lord, she was being kissed in public by the Earl of Hadleigh! She wrenched away, put a step between them as she gawked, her chest heaving, her breath coming in fast pants, her spectacles slipping down her nose while she both marveled at the fact and acknowledged the horror of what had happened.

Why had he done it? To humiliate her? To put her in her place? To remind her of his mastery? Heat jumped into her cheeks. Oh, he was quite skilled in that, but such treatment was outside of enough. She wasn't a throwaway member of society nor a woman of poor morals. Sarah lifted a trembling hand and without thought, she brought her palm crashing into his cheek. The resounding sound of her kid glove slapping his skin sent a rush of satisfaction through her.

"What is the meaning of this, Lord Hadleigh? To that end, what is wrong with you?" she demanded in an effort not to chase her errant thoughts down yet another rabbit hole.

Or remember how delicious the kiss had been, and how she'd enjoyed every second of it.

CHAPTER FIVE

A NDREW STARED AT the fuming woman before him while he held a gloved hand to his stinging cheek. She'd slapped him, and with enough force to leave heat behind. No one had ever dared challenge him since he'd assumed the earl's title. "There is nothing wrong with me." Except, he'd apparently taken leave of his damned senses by kissing her after a single meeting, but he'd had to discover if the attraction that snapped between them three days ago had been his imagination.

It had not. If anything, it had strengthened.

After her initial surprise, she'd thrown herself into the embrace, and though she was acutely inexperienced, she'd been a quick learner. Her tentative exploration had left him more than a little aroused.

"Then what the devil was the meaning of…" Sarah's words trailed off as she gestured between them, her kiss-swollen lips parted, her eyes wide and reflecting a myriad of emotions he couldn't quite sort behind the lenses of her askew spectacles. "Why did you…?" The color in her cheeks and the not-quite-hidden wonder in her countenance put animation into her plain face.

Andrew gave himself a mental shake. He couldn't keep standing here like a nodcock. It was time to let her know the reason he'd asked her for a stroll. "I've confirmed something I suspected during our first meeting." He couldn't help admiring her heaving bosom or the way a few tendrils of her blonde hair had escaped their pins to frame her face. The spectacles that sat at the end of her nose only added to the look of her becoming undone.

Did passion lurk beneath her straight-laced surface? What would it take for him to unleash it, and more to the point, why did he want to?

"And what is that?" She'd collected herself enough to put a few more steps between them and set her spectacles right. Then she planted her hands on her hips and glared. "You still haven't explained yourself. I would ask that you focus on the problem at hand instead of woolgather."

Oh, that tart mouth of hers! He'd be a proper nodcock not to admire those gentle curves or how much her annoyance called to his and made him want to cross verbal swords with her again. Something about that sparring gave his seething feelings an outlet... but he owed her an explanation. "There is an attraction between us. Surely you can feel it." God, what he wouldn't give to kiss those lips again, merely to lend credence to his claim. The bottom one was slightly fuller than the top, and she'd tasted of innocence and heat.

"Are you completely daft?" She gawked and took another step backward.

"Not completely, I'll wager." Drew hadn't meant to sound flippant. Hell, he hadn't meant to kiss her or feel desire for anyone when he'd buried himself in the Derbyshire countryside, but here he was, battling exactly that for this plain spinster who would never have caught his eye had they been in a drawing room in London.

"Attraction, you claim?" Miss Copeland shook her head while amazement and consternation warred for dominance in her eyes. "We have only just met, but you've deemed it proper to kiss me?"

His nod was a tad curt. "Yes, for the enticement is there regardless of the length of our acquaintance." She hadn't denied it, so it must be true for her as well. That was something. Perhaps this next bit wouldn't become such a chore.

"Conversing with you is proving impossible. Again, I ask, what is your point, my lord?" She bent to retrieve her errant headgear, and when she straightened, her gaze fell to his mouth—briefly, but he didn't miss that tell.

She wasn't as immune to him as she wanted him to believe.

A rush of blood shot through his shaft. How long had it been since that had happened, and why with this bespectacled miss of no consequence? "Right. My point." Yes, he was fit for Bedlam with what he'd say to her. Would she slap him again? Run away screaming? Anxiety tightened his chest. Would she agree? "Marry me." There was no finesse or romance involved, how could there be? As she'd pointed out twice, they'd met once before today. The only thing between them was desire and perhaps the niggling thought that being in her presence had the ability to take the edge off his anger. He wished to explore that more readily, for it was quite a novel idea.

"I... what?" Her eyes widened behind the lenses.

"Marry me." There was more confidence behind the suggestion this time. He hadn't given her an explanation as to why, yet it felt right to ask. Actually, it was a jot more complicated than that. The last thing he needed was to add a spouse to his already mucked-up life, but... he wanted Miss Copeland, plain and simple.

Why shouldn't he have her? After all, he was an earl, and he had a duty to the damned title. And it seemed she wasn't averse to his advances...

"What gammon is this?" The bonnet dropped from her lax fingers to thud upon the ground once again. "You're having me on. This is naught but a cruel joke at my expense," she said in a soft voice, almost to herself.

The astonishment in her expression rivaled his own, but Drew grinned and hoped it was as wicked as he felt. "I am not."

"Such fustian." She shook her head. Annoyance snapped in her doe-brown eyes, bringing out fire in the depths. "How dare you presume I'll fall desperate upon your offer."

"Won't you?" He shrugged. "Not to bring light to your situation, Miss Copeland, but you're not getting any younger, and I rather doubt you've had a steady stream of offers to reject."

The red stain in her cheeks deepened. "I... I don't know what to address first, but perhaps your horrid lack of manners shall be my jumping off point." She fairly shook with ire, and damn if that energy didn't call to him. There were times when only another's storm could take the sting from his. As yet he'd never had cause to witness that, but in her the potential was there.

Save me...

"Stating a fact isn't bad manners." Drew came forward and closed the distance between them. Taking one of her hands, he said, "If we marry, the alliance will benefit us both, you see."

"You're mad." Miss Copeland shook off his touch, though a light of understanding lit her eyes. "You don't even know my Christian name but you're proposing marriage."

"Then tell me. There was plenty of opportunity while we talked, but you didn't go that far." He enjoyed her being at sixes and sevens all too much. It gave life to her plain face as well as brought him out of the dark pit his anger usually cornered him into. Would she pull him up?

"I... you..." She lifted a hand that fluttered about, and she blinked as if he'd managed to startle her. Her mouth worked as she stared. "It's Sarah."

"It suits you." Not exactly feeling jovial but not squarely in the grip of the usual angst that plagued him, Drew gave her a brief bow from the waist. "I believe I've asked you a couple of times to call me Andrew, so now we are acquainted." He couldn't help another grin when she narrowed her eyes. "Regardless of the shocking way this has come about, let me give you a few reasons why we should wed. Will you listen?"

She nodded. "Yes."

"Neither of us are growing younger. For whatever reason, we've both let life slip away and have done nothing in the way of leaving a legacy." He ticked off the items on his gloved fingers. "You've had no opportunities and even less fortune in landing a man." When she sputtered, he continued quickly to his next point. "I have little patience for entering the Marriage Mart in London. Plus, I need to do my duty to the title—"

"Stop." Sarah held up a hand. "I won't lie. The idea holds a certain merit, and I'm aghast that I'm actually considering it."

"Why? Marriage solves a myriad of problems." In this he was confident that he'd prevail. It was only a matter of convincing her.

And then what? You'll have caught a tiger by the tail. How will that help you? He had no answers, so he ignored that inner voice of reason.

"I know nothing about you, nor you of me. We're strangers who have met once before today." She shook her head. "And that first go 'round wasn't exactly civil."

"What does that matter?" He watched her. Why didn't she consider the offer as the boon that it was? "If I had to select a bride in London, it would be much the same." He shrugged. "Only this way, I do have some control over the woman who'd be my countess. Thank the Lord it won't be handed to an empty-headed debutante, for you are intelligent and possess a backbone." He shrugged. "You and I will learn of each other as we go along."

"I haven't said yes yet." Sarah crossed her arms at her chest. "Although I have long wondered if I'd ever marry, having an earl suddenly ask for my hand isn't quite the romance that I dreamed of." A frown pulled her lips down at the corners. "I would have preferred a husband to want me for me, but I suppose life doesn't present itself in that fashion, does it?" A hint of bitterness rode upon those words, and for one second Drew could fully empathize with the feeling. "Especially not for one like me."

"If you continue to think yourself as less than, then perhaps you wouldn't be the best fit for a countess like I thought." What, exactly, was she opposed to: marrying him or taking up a title? The fact she'd found fault with either had sparks of anger flaring in his chest. He was giving her the opportunity to better her standing in society, and she would throw it away with a snap of her fingers? *Bah!* Perhaps the life of a hermit would be best for him after all.

Yet the title demanded that he bring his life into order. He refused to give up his control to his cousin. Without marrying, could he do that? Familiar, crushing anxiety gripped his chest and he put a hand to his heart as he struggled to breathe property, fought against the onslaught of emotions battering his insides not to show that weakness in front of her. Would he fail in landing a wild female such as her too? Damn it all, couldn't he succeed in something?

For long moments she stared at him; he could almost see her mind working as she considered every aspect. Finally, when he thought he might expire on the spot, she spoke. "When did you think up this mad scheme?" She relaxed her arms only to clutch the silver locket that hung about her neck, the sun glinting on the silver chain. "I'm old enough to know I have neither the looks nor the figure to render a sane man mad with lust."

Then she obviously needed a better cheval glass. "Perhaps you've underestimated yourself." Since he'd already acted rashly, he dared go farther and swept his gaze up and down her person in a slow perusal. The dull colors she chose in her clothing did nothing for her, but that was easily changed. And with very little imagination, he could see her *sans* those clothes. Tiny fires licked through his veins. With his temper, her spirit, and the building attraction, they wouldn't pass the time bored. "Perhaps I'm mad indeed, but I'm not wrong. I knew as soon as I put you on my horse that we'd suit."

"Suit who? You or your title?" she asked in a quiet voice.

"Does it matter?" His chest tightened as anxiety had its way. "I mean to be faithful to both my title and to you."

Confusion clouded her eyes. For another swath of long moments, she remained silent. Then she once more retrieved her bonnet. As her gaze found his, a hint of longing filled those brandy-hued depths, gone at her next blink. "When would this wedding occur?"

Ah, she was coming around to his way of thinking. He gave into a tight grin. No, she wasn't a feathers-for-brains female, and perhaps that's what initially drew him to her. "Five weeks if you'd like the banns read. A week or so if you wish for a common license. I have no preference."

Sarah—God, the name sounded all too plain—snorted. "As long as you have your way, you mean?"

A quick spike of anger stabbed through his chest to collide with the heavy anxiety. He gasped for breath. There was nothing to hold onto as black spots chased at the edges of his vision. *Please don't let me have an episode here on the road.* "How dare you assume that."

"It's not an assumption. You've showed yourself quite arrogant on several occasions while in my company. I'm merely stating a truth."

Devil take her anyway. Every breath he took came with a shower of pain, for his body didn't wish for proper or outward calm. It wanted to let each emotion battling inside have at it even though that would destroy him. "I haven't lied. I do need a countess."

"I understand that, but why me?"

"Why not?" He gasped for breath. For the love of God, when would this terrible pressure relent? "You're long in the tooth, true, but you're more intelligent and knowledgeable than debutantes. That alone puts you well ahead of anyone else I might have chosen." An involuntary shiver went down his spine as she sputtered, and her eyes snapped fire once more. If she let herself, would the storm she'd bring cleanse his soul? A yearning for that added itself to the pile and churned through the gripping anxiety.

"Oh, well, thank you very much for your regard," she shot off, bitterness and annoyance clearly ringing in her voice.

Drew rubbed his fingers over his heart. Would it suddenly stop beating like his father's had while he'd fought the lingering failing of the same? For that matter, had his sire battled with the relentless anxiety too? "I'm certain you'll want to have children sooner rather than later, yes?"

"I don't..." Her mouth worked as if she were a caught fish. "Insults couched as compliments will not help your cause, my lord." Her fingers crushed the brim of the ugly bonnet. "Are you merely tired of bucolic country life or do you only wish to relieve other... needs?" She let her gaze drop to the front of his breeches. Another streak of desire went through his shaft, tightening it.

Oh, God, could she discern that evidence?

"Damn it all, Sarah," he said from around gritted teeth. No, there were no other feelings for her other than blatant lust, but he could do worse. Perhaps over time they'd form a friendship of sorts, and that was something he sorely needed. "I need an heir. You're smart enough to know how such things come about." And he'd bloody well enjoy taking her to bed, merely to discover if she was a virgin as he suspect-ed. If she were, he'd relish the opportunity to teach her the finer points of carnal pleasure.

A blush jumped into her cheeks that fairly proclaimed her an inno-cent at such an advanced age that he had to stifle a groan. "How fascinating, but I do know. Thank you." Her words were clipped and cold. "Also, how flattering you think to use me as a breeding service."

Her annoyance stirred his own. It rose to fight with the anxiety, made his chest so tight he feared he might cast up his accounts at her feet, but in the background, fear wormed through. Would he fail at this, be alone for the rest of his life? "That is how life goes, Miss Copeland." He couldn't resist needling her. If she continued to "my lord" him, he'd revert to using her surname. "Don't most women angle to marry a titled lord?"

She huffed. "I am not most women."

"Oh, I'm well aware of that, which is why I made my offer initially." She had the potential to sweep through his life and make everything new. Why couldn't she see that? When she stared at his hand that pressed against his chest with narrowed eyes, he immediately dropped it to his side. "I'm extending you an opportunity to do what you wish, for marrying will give you a certain freedom."

"Ha!" Both of her eyebrows lifted skyward. "If you think I'm going to forever show you gratitude for rescuing me from a life of drudgery when I didn't ask, I'll disabuse you of that notion this instant. Earl or not, I will not grovel at a man's feet."

For all her outward appearance as a meek, drab governess, Sarah possessed a sharp mind and a tart mouth, and he wanted nothing more than to tame her. But the damned woman hadn't agreed to his proposal. "It would definitely relieve the dullness of being in the country, for that I won't attempt to cover with niceties. Again, because I need to do my duty, if it's not with you, it will be with someone else." He shrugged, for that was the bald fact. "But I'd rather wed a female I find interesting and who is near my own age, who can converse on more erudite topics beyond the contents of Debrett's Peerage or the latest fashions from Paris."

Her lips twitched. She pressed them together but that didn't erase the sudden twinkle of humor in her eyes. "I'd be an idiot to consider your proposal given your arrogance and temper. I always told myself I'd never marry a man with a temper, yet here I am."

A frisson of excitement danced down his spine. The crushing anxiety and heated anger faded a smidge. She was wavering! "Quite frankly, you'd be an idiot not to, for what other choices do you have? Once those children grow, what will you do? From what little I know of the baronet, it's unlikely he'll see you off with a favorable reference."

Anger flashed in her eyes. "I could go to London anyway and find work with a well-to-do family."

"Without a letter of recommendation, it will prove an uphill battle." Matching wills with her would be quite the challenge, for she stirred that simmering rage and poked at the annoyance always brewing, but he couldn't pull his hand from the flame. He suspected he needed her more than she needed him in this moment, though he had no idea why.

Please don't let me fall. I'll never survive the crash.

She rolled her eyes. "Fine." With a slight lift of her hand, she pushed her spectacles back into place high on the bridge of her nose.

"What?" His heartbeat leaped. "Could you please expand your thinking? I want no misunderstandings."

Her nod was definitive. "I agree to marry you. Consider it a business arrangement."

"Except for bearing me an heir." On that he refused to compromise.

"Of course. How crass of me to forget or you for beating that fact over my head." Sarah's cheeks blazed, out of annoyance or the reference to begetting a child, he couldn't say. "After that, we will very much live separate lives, for this isn't a love match as you've said yourself."

"Agreed." Some of the anxiety holding him captive lessened. It was a small step, but at least he hadn't failed to take a wife. "When do you wish to wed?"

"A week from today. It will coincide with my employment anniversary."

Practical to a fault. "Providential." Drew nodded. He drew a nearly normal breath and let it ease out. "I shall apply to the parish officials for a common license soon."

"Very well." Her nod was perfunctory. "I shall inform my great uncle of my plans and resign my post." She snapped her gaze to his. "Unless you think I should keep it."

The fact she had deferred a decision to him was telling. Perhaps she was beginning to trust him. "You'll have no need to hold a position as my countess. Whatever else we are to each other from this point forward, I will take care of you."

And he suspected she desperately needed someone to care for her.

"I appreciate that." Suddenly, her guard slipped. She curled a hand over the silver locket. What did it mean to her? Naked vulnerability reflected on her face. "Stability is most welcome at this point in my life."

"As I said before, we're both benefiting from this arrangement." Though, it rankled. The title always came first. When would he ever matter to someone as the man he was? Broken or not, would he never have value in someone's eyes?

CHAPTER SIX

S ARAH'S HEAD SWAM. Her thoughts circled around like ponies on a loop, while her gut churned with both anxiety and unexpected anticipation. Merciful heavens, she had agreed to marry a man she didn't know, let alone didn't love or even like overly much.

What am I doing? Her heartbeat surged. After a few deep breaths as she stared at the man before her, her pulse resumed its normal placid course. Then she straightened her spine and pushed her spectacles back to the bridge of her nose. What was she doing? Looking after her future, for there was no one else to do it for her. No longer would she need to worry, or scrimp and save.

What was more, perhaps with the earl's power, she could more easily reach her dream of playing on a London stage. That alone was worth the price she'd need to pay.

When she met his eyes, the anger roiling there as well as depression and a tiny bit of fear stole her breath. What demons did he fight with, and why did she wish to immerse herself into that angst? Because she'd seen a silent cry for help on his face as they'd conversed, and it had tugged at her compassion. She knew those emotions well, had dealt with them herself a time or two, and this man had the look of someone who was three steps away from a complete collapse.

Finally, she nodded again as if to solidify her decision. Yes, he needed her for more than fulfilling his duty, and the reason why intrigued her enough that she'd agreed. As soon as she could, she would discover it. "Thank you. I'd like to say we'll be happy together, but the world doesn't work that way. Instead, I'll say that I hope we won't destroy each other as we enter this new phase of life." For with his temper and her backbone, the nuptial merger didn't make much sense.

"In this, you might be more correct than you know." Then he cleared his throat. "In any event, think nothing of it. We are merely two people using each other as a means to an end." He waved a hand in dismissal, but that didn't remove the bitter sting in his statement. "Who shall I speak with about the terms of our betrothal—the baronet? Another relative?"

The words made everything all too real, and what a sad state of affairs it was. Sarah forced moisture into her dry throat with a hard swallow. "As I said before, I have no other relatives." Sweat trickled down her spine, for the sun was quite warm. She might be desperate to change her fate, but she wasn't stupid. If her great uncle oversaw the contract, it would only benefit him, and he didn't deserve it. "I am quite capable of negotiating the terms as well as—if not better than—him. He's done the bare minimum for me and my well-being already. You may show me the terms instead."

"I beg your pardon?" He stared at her with annoyance and grudging admiration mixing in his blue-gray eyes. "You're a woman, and you wish to enter betrothal negotiations." It wasn't a question.

"I'm glad you're so observant, my lord." Sarah smiled, but it felt all too forced. "I meant what I said." Her fingers dug into the straw brim of her bonnet as her eyeglasses slid down her nose. "You may discuss everything with me. I am advocating for myself." She took a deep breath and let it ease out. "Never again will I allow a man control over my future."

Except, marrying an earl would bring certain complications to that statement.

"I see." He gawked at her as if he didn't know what to make of her. For the first time in Sarah's life, power licked through her veins. No wonder men fought for it. As would she. Finally, she had the opportunity for control over her own future, and it almost made her giddy.

Or perhaps too confident, for she felt compelled to continue. "If you think to cheat me merely because I'm a female, or you've decided that me bearing you children is enough, you're sadly mistaken." The thought of doing *those acts* with him to find herself in that state sent a thrill sailing down her spine. Heat burned in her cheeks. Though why she had even agreed to that without feeling anything beyond annoyance for him, she couldn't say.

You're a liar, Sarah.

Yes, yes, she was, for the attraction he'd spoken of earlier was there and it pulled at a need deep inside her. The fact that he might desire her left her at sixes and sevens, but she'd aim to enjoy the ride for as far as it took her. Why should she not? She shoved her spectacles back into place and looked at him, waiting for his rebuttal.

A trace of disappointment shadowed his face for a few brief seconds before his customary disagreeable disposition obliterated it. Why he should take refuge in that instead of the charm he could display was beyond her. "Fine." The earl chopped the air with a hand. "I am many things, but I am *not* a cheat or a swindler." Anger flashed in his eyes— so much fury inside his person all the time. But why? "Come to Hadleigh Hall tomorrow at one o'clock. The paperwork will be waiting for you."

Apparently, the battle of wills between them would begin now. "I have lessons until four." But she wouldn't back down, not with so much riding out the outcome.

"God damn it, Sarah, must you prove so stubborn in everything?" He shoved a gloved hand through his hair, leaving the mass in upended furrows.

The sound of her name in his voice had a few flutters moving through her belly, but she shook her head. "Women have few rights as it is in this world, my lord. I aim to see that my future is secure."

"Despite this inauspicious beginning, I won't leave you wanting." Drew curled a hand into a first before relaxing it when she flicked her gaze to it. "Come for tea at five." Without another word, he turned to leave, apparently forgetting that he'd ridden to her great uncle's home or that he should escort her back.

Arrogant prig. Did she truly wish to align herself with a man like him? At the moment, it was the lesser of two evils. "Is that it then?" she said to his retreating back. "You have what you want and now you're done?" Would he conduct everything else between them in such a cold, perfunctory manner?

He came to a halt. Was it her imagination or did a growl emanate from him? "What more could you possibly want? You are being give the better end of the bargain, by far." When he faced her once again, the grit of the dirt road scraping beneath his boots, the loathing on his face left her trembling with apprehension. Was it for her or himself, and why did she want to know?

Still, Sarah refused to let him treat her as a piece of rubbish on his heel. "A fat lot more than this. You're a stranger to me, an arrogant arse of a man who will take me to bed to beget an heir." As she made each point, his chest swelled, and red color mottled his neck above his cravat. A button popped from his waistcoat to land in the meadow grass at the side of the road. But she plunged on, unwilling to stop. "Perfunctory and without feeling or even companionship between us." She ignored the heat in her cheeks. No, she hadn't thought ahead at what marriage to him would encompass, for she'd only wanted out of her current situation.

As she stared, her imagination took flight. What would he look like in the nude? Already, he cut a powerful figure of broad shoulders, lean hips, and a narrow waist. Perhaps he would resemble a statue of a

Greek god she'd seen once while visiting a friend years ago. What sort of lover would he be, and would she enjoy that sort of attention? The thought sent her mind reeling once more.

Dear heavens, I've no more knowledge in that than I do of conducting myself as a countess. What would he think of her ignorance?

"What is your point, Miss Copeland?" Ice dripped from the inquiry.

A huff escaped her. "Oh, this is impossible." Sarah whirled about and jammed her bonnet upon her head. "I'm naught but a fool." Security wasn't enough to spend a lifetime with a man so obviously lost in personal problems. She took a few steps in the direction of her great uncle's house.

"You'll leave without giving me respect, like all the others." Yes, the perpetual anger he carried resonated in his voice, but there was also a hint of resignation, and that tugged at her sympathy.

Her eyebrows rose. Here was a break, a crack in his armor so to speak, that she could use to know him better. "Respect is earned, my lord. People are not for you to order about like pawns on a chessboard." But she kept walking. If he wanted this marriage, he would need to work for it or at least show her that it mattered—that she did.

"So then you're a coward." The challenge in his tone rang clear. "I expected more from you than that."

Why must he act the dastard? Slowly, Sarah turned about. "I am hardly that."

"Yet you run away." He rubbed a hand upon his chest in the region of his heart as lines of strain etched themselves over his face.

What was wrong with him? Did he suffer from poor health? That would explain his haste to marry and have children. Then she shoved the questions to the back of her mind. Until he understood that he wasn't the only person in the world who mattered, she couldn't let the numerous mysteries surrounding him suck her in. She fairly shook from the hot aggravation that coursed through her. "A coward would have given up when faced with what I've already overcome." No, she didn't care that a warning threatened in her voice; he was out of line. Titled or not, she refused to let him treat her in such a manner.

Andrew leveled those cool stormy eyes on her, pressed his lips together, but some of his color had paled and his breath came in quick pants.

Concern for his health rushed once more to the forefront. She eyed him with alarm. "Are you quite well, my lord?"

"Yes." The one-word answer seemed forced from his throat. "Why won't you stay and talk with me?"

"You are not giving me that option. Remember, you were the one who walked away first. Have you changed your mind?"

"Perhaps." Blue lightning roiled in his eyes.

"Good." She glared back at him. Exhilaration surged through her veins. Why the devil did arguing with this man feel so... wonderful? "Fine then. Let's talk. What did you mean about the others? Women? Lovers? Friends?" Somehow, she had the feeling that he didn't have many friends, let alone contemporaries who'd stuck by him.

"Family," he managed to gasp out.

Now *that* surprised her, but the opportunity to learn about his life was tantalizing. "Why do you think that is?"

"I'm rather... difficult just now." Some of the color returned to his face and he relaxed his death-grip on his jacket.

"An understatement to be sure." There had to be a reason, and drat her, she wished to know more. "Why are you so arduous?"

The chords of his throat worked with a hard swallow. "I'm left with the responsibility of the earl alone." Uncertainty flickered in his eyes—another crack in the thick armor he wore about himself.

"I'll wager that's not the whole of it, but this is a start." Despite the doubts she harbored, Sarah went toward him a few steps. She pushed her spectacles back into place. "Why did you come to Hadleigh Hall, my lord? Surely not to marry the first woman you saw so you wouldn't be alone."

"No." His lips twitched, but he didn't give into a full smile. A sliver of cold disappointment went through her, for she'd hoped for a return of the charming man she'd only met briefly once before. "Perhaps I'm a beast who isn't fit to mix with proper society any longer." He focused his gaze on a point over her left shoulder. For the first time since she'd met him, he shrank into himself as if trying to hide from scrutiny.

Or judgment and censure.

"Now we are making progress." When he allowed himself to show his vulnerability, they were on equal footing.

"We are?" Andrew snapped his attention to her face. Annoyance mixed with faint hope, and that fired more of her curiosity. "How so?"

"Trust." Sarah shrugged. "When you put your ego and your anger aside, you became approachable. When you did that, I saw the man you are beneath, the man who is trying so desperately to reach out, yet you keep him hidden." She held his gaze. Perhaps she could come to understand him after all. "I saw the man I would be glad to converse with." When she smiled, he once more gawked as if he'd never seen her before.

Long moments went by in silence. Finally, he relaxed enough to offer a tight grin. "I'll warn you that marrying me won't be an easy feat."

"I'm not one to shy away from a challenge." She didn't look away. Neither did he. Her heart beat in double time. "If you can manage to talk with me like a gentleman instead of a wounded bear, I will allow you to walk me home, my lord."

"Allow me?" Red color crept over his collar. "I am the earl here and I—"

Sarah tsked her tongue. "None of that. I wasn't joking. If you come the crab, I shall return home right now and leave your sorry arse on the road."

He blew out a breath. "I apologize for my behavior this afternoon."

"Thank you." This was one small step in building a relationship, but it was a start. She was willing to work with him if he allowed the same courtesy to her. "Andrew," he said abruptly.

"What?" She peered at him over the tops of the spectacles that had slid down her nose.

"My name is Andrew, or if you prefer, Drew." There wasn't a smile accompanying the request, but his expression had softened slightly. That little concession brought out a hint of the handsome man he could be when he wasn't trying so hard to hide himself.

"I prefer Andrew. It suits you better." When he nodded, she pushed up the spectacles. "You may call me Sarah, though you used my name earlier in the conversation. I suppose I can't remain Miss Copeland."

"It would become rather awkward." He offered her his arm. "The least I can do is escort you home."

"Indeed." As she slipped her hand into his crooked elbow, tingling heat danced up her arm. "Also, in the event you wondered, you were correct."

"Oh? In what way?" He set them into motion.

She fought off a blush. What was it about him that made her want to melt into a puddle at his feet from the unaccustomed heat she felt in his presence? "There *is* a bit of an attraction between us. I don't know why," she admitted in a quiet voice.

"Ah! I'm pleased to hear you acknowledge it." Then he lowered his voice to a whisper. "At least now I know I'm not fit for Bedlam."

That remained to be seen. "I've never experienced such a thing before. Sudden and intense attraction, that is. It shouldn't happen to a woman my age."

"How old are you, Sarah? Because, if I might say so, you're hardly elderly."

The thread of teasing in his tones caused her to miss a step. She clutched his arm in an effort to remain upright. "I turned four and thirty two weeks prior."

He snorted. "That's hardly ancient. Hell, I'm forty."

That was a surprise. "I would have thought you'd have a string of admirers vying for your attention."

"I kept myself rather aloof from functions where flirting or matchmaking could find me."

Did that mean he would resent marriage to her? She was too much a coward to ask. "Ah." What would he think of her, an old maid who'd been on the self so long the dust had settled on her, who'd never been kissed except for earlier when he'd done so? "I trust that means we won't spend all our time together fighting."

The rumble of his laughter filtered into her being before the sound burst into the air. It was genuine mirth without being marred by bitterness or anger, and it increased her awareness of him. As she glanced at him, she caught the softening of his jaw and a slight lift at the corners of his mouth. "I'm quite certain we'll argue and disagree, only there are other, more pleasurable, outlets to funnel those emotions into that marriage allows."

"I... I don't know what to say." Her cheeks heated again. Tingles of foreign need played through her insides.

"Now, that *is* a first." Another laugh escaped, as clear and true as the one he'd uttered before. "I'll need to savor the victory."

"Arse." When she attempted to extricate her hand from his arm, he secured her touch. Not that walking beside him was a hardship. He did cut a rather dashing figure when he wasn't lashing out or making himself difficult. So many thoughts danced about her mind, but she focused on a concern that wouldn't leave her be. "Does it... bother you to do... *that* with a woman you hardly know?

He shrugged and his shoulder brushed hers. Hints of his bay rum and lime cologne wafted to her nose. "It is what it is, and we'll have a week to become more fully acquainted. Tomorrow morning, I shall request the common license."

"Thank you." The answer annoyed her for some reason. The wad of it lodged in her chest. Was wedding and bedding a stranger so commonplace in his world that he didn't think it deserved a concern? "As long as you have what you want," she muttered beneath her breath. Somehow, security and protection didn't seem like a fair trade for innocence and intimacy with a man she knew nothing about, especially when the softer emotions weren't involved.

Then a sigh escaped her. *I hope I'm strong enough.* But then, nothing in her world would change if she continued doing that which she'd always done.

A challenge, indeed.

CHAPTER SEVEN

June 20, 1817

F OR THE THIRD time that afternoon, Drew crumpled the letter he'd been writing to his mother. How the deuce should he break the news to her in any event? The thought of her reaction and objection, not to mention that of his brother's snide remarks, turned his stomach and tightened his chest with anxiety. Yes, telling his family in this manner might be a touch cowardly, but it was the safest way.

For all of us.

After removing a fresh piece of stationery from the leather box on his desktop, he sighed as he stared at the blank expanse. The words wouldn't come. How could he inform his mother that he'd decided to marry, and to a woman he barely knew? Not to mention she had absolutely no connection to the *ton* nor did she have looks or youth to recommend her.

What if his mother didn't like Sarah? If she wouldn't accept his wife—if the *ton* wouldn't accept her—well, he didn't wish to think about the ramifications. That didn't stop his eternal foe, anxiety, from rising and putting the crushing weight upon his chest.

That had happened all too often these past few days. He'd suffered one such attack while conversing with Sarah on the road in his roundabout attempt to have her agree to the betrothal. It had been bad enough that she'd noticed, and she'd asked if he was well. Of course he'd had to lie, for what woman in her right mind would wish to align herself with a man who consistently had the overwhelming episodes that stole his breath?

Perhaps she'll commit me to Bedlam and sit on her heels enjoying the profits from the estate. As soon as the uncharitable thought crossed his mind, he dismissed it. Sarah wasn't that sort of person. There was a certain calm sensibility beneath her put-together exterior. Yes, she was a storm to reckon with once angered, but unlike his rage, hers cleared the air and allowed the sun to shine and usher in better things. *Can she teach me?*

When Barton knocked at the open door, Drew was more than ready for the distraction. "Come in." He waved a hand at his valet. Putting off the task wouldn't see it completed any faster though.

"I met Dalton in the hall. He'd just put a Miss Copeland into the parlor." Curiosity blazed in the valet's expression. "She's apparently here to see you."

A niggle of excitement tripped down Drew's spine. "That's right. We have an appointment." When Barton hovered, clearly wanting more information, Drew set his pen in its holder. "What do you think of her?"

Confusion creased the other man's brow. "I haven't thought of her, my lord. This is the first time I've seen her."

"No, I mean do you think she'll be a decent countess? If you look past her penchant for drab clothing and see her dressed in silks and satins with jewels about her neck, will she pass muster within the *ton*?"

"I beg your pardon?" Barton's eyes widened. "Surely, you're not—"

"I am." Needing something to occupy his hands, Drew once more took up his pen. He dipped the nub into the inkwell. "I asked her yesterday to marry me." Then he began the letter to his mother. It was really quite easy. He would set down the facts. She didn't need more information than that. Hadn't she been after him for years to settle down and set up his nursery? Now he was doing just that.

"You're marrying the woman in the parlor." It wasn't a question.

"I am. She's our neighbor to the west."

"But... why?" Barton was aghast. He darted his gaze about the room before landing it once more on Drew. "Do you think that's wise given your, ah, disposition?"

"Why not?" Doubt worked with the anxiety to tighten his chest. "I need a countess and to do my duty to the damned title. She needs a secure future."

"Yet you have recently met her." Poor Barton. He was struggling valiantly to make sense of the news, and Drew found it rather amusing.

"True enough, but that doesn't negate the facts." Once more he scratched out a line on the stationery. Would his mother have much the same reaction?

Barton softly cleared his throat. "Do you and she suit?"

"I have no idea. We spend a good portion of our time together arguing." That gave him pause. He held his pen over the page, and when a drop of ink fell, he continued to write. No, he wouldn't put much stock into the already turbulent meetings, for beneath that was the attraction which grew each time they were together. "Does it matter, really? Perhaps half of my anxieties will disappear once the deed is done." He hoped. God how he hoped, though this stunt would bring a whole new host of issues...

"Let me understand the situation." Barton arched one eyebrow. "You arrived in Derbyshire not long ago, and at some point after, you met an unattached woman who you decided, apparently on the spot, to marry and make your countess, without care to whether or not she's up to the task or even if you and she suit."

"Exactly." Drew didn't care how insane it sounded from someone else's viewpoint. The fact was that he liked Sarah—wanted her in a purely physical way—and she possessed enough mettle to battle his own horrid disposition as well as the rigors of being a countess. What more did a man need?

To quell the demons that haunt me. Would she be able to do that too?

"I see." Though the look on the valet's face said he didn't see at all. "I'm not one to gossip or speak badly of anyone. However," he lowered his voice, "are you quite certain? Marriage is a rather permanent business."

Drew jammed the pen back into its holder lest he make more of a mess on the letter than he already had. "No, I'm not positively certain. One can't be over anything these days, of course, but I might as well have it over and done with. As I told Sarah, if it weren't her, it would be someone else."

"Sarah." Barton's lower jaw dropped. "Have you spent time with her then?"

"We've had two meetings." He glanced at the nearly complete letter and nodded. It would do. "Miss Copeland aggravates me and provokes my anger, but I admire her spirit. If she's tried by fire, I have no doubt that she'll survive."

I only hope I don't manage to destroy her or turn her against me like I have everyone else.

Though doubt clouded the valet's eyes, he said, "What of your mother? Your family? Will they have a say in this?"

"Absolutely not. They will have a letter, and right now I'd rather not hear their opinions." Again, he took up his pen, dipped the nub into the inkwell, and then continued to write, the words flowing. He was the master of his own fate; this felt right.

Silence reigned in the study for the space of several heartbeats before Barton spoke.

"What prompted you to make this decision?"

"I didn't wish to have that duty hanging over my head any longer." With a strong hand, he continued the letter until the short missive had been finished. Then he rested the pen in its holder and blew upon the ink. "I should finalize that business." Urgency compelled him to move things along, but the tingle of anticipation buzzing at the base of his spine spoke of a different story. Was he truly looking forward to seeing Sarah again? He shoved the thought from his mind. "Please tell Dalton to show Miss Copeland into my study."

"I will." The valet nodded. "Should I give you congratulations or commiserations?"

"That remains to be seen." He offered a wry grin to his friend of near ten years. "But I appreciate the sentiment all the same."

Barton left the room without another word.

Drew frowned as he folded the letter and then stuffed it into an envelope. Was the betrothal careless? He melted a bit of wax from the stick. Perhaps it was. After putting a glob of the green goo onto the envelope's flap, he then pressed the official Hadleigh seal into the wax. Would his father have approved of the match? He pulled the seal away and set it back into the tray with the wax stick. Categorically, no. His mother would be hurt by the exclusion, and his brothers would never miss an opportunity to chide him about the decision.

Well, too damn bad. *This is my life.* A quick wave of hot anger rose in Drew's chest. He could handle himself but knowing he would disappoint another person—and probably Sarah too, eventually—only added to his growing ire and uncovered a yawning, deep trench of cold fear.

Ultimately, he would end up alone, and it was his own fault, but he didn't know how to stop a stone from rolling downhill once it started.

When Sarah arrived, Drew rose to his feet. Under no circumstances would he let her see his weakness... at least not until after they'd said vows. Clad in the same brown dress she'd worn the first day they'd met, she immediately met his gaze with no hint of demure attitude in her posture.

"Good afternoon, Lord Hadleigh." Her tone suggested efficiency and no nonsense.

A trace of disappointment went through him. Could she not find a modicum of joy in the upcoming arrangement? "Good afternoon, Miss Copeland." If she wished for formality, so be it. "The draft of the contract has been written. Once we agree to terms, I'll send everything to my solicitor in London. He'll then draw it up for official signatures."

"Thank you. I'm anxious to start."

When he glanced closer at her, slight shadows beneath her eyes stood as a testament to either worry or a poor night's sleep. "Very well. I don't wish to cause you undo anxiety, so this should be a straightforward process." He came around the desk to stand at her side.

"I appreciate that." She offered a slight smile. The scent of violets and clover drifted to his nose. "It's been a whirlwind week."

"Indeed." Suddenly, he didn't wish to discuss contracts, or anything related to the business side of the betrothal contracts. He wanted to take tea with her and discuss, well, her. It would behoove him to learn about her history before they wed.

She eyed him with suspicion. "Do you still wish to do this?"

"Do you?" Would she back out of their arrangement and leave him to flounder? Anxiety pulled tight through his chest, and he ignored it.

"Yes, actually. Though I tossed and turned about it last night, once this morning arrived, my decision was clear. I'll marry you, come what may." Briefly, she touched his arm. Tingling awareness climbed the limb from the point of contact. "Thank you, again. It's a rather freeing feeling to know that my future is taken care of."

What did such freedom feel like? For he labored beneath a mountain of responsibilities, and he would add another once he wed her. "You're welcome." Perhaps marriage wouldn't be the disaster he assumed. Drew spread out four sheets of handwritten paper over his desktop. "As I've stated before, by wedding me, you will have security and the ability to move about the *ton* as you please. You may take up charitable causes, volunteer with various organizations, and perhaps you'll have a child."

She nodded. "And you will have done your duty to the title." Her inquisitive gaze found his. "I would like to hope that this eases some of the stress you seem to labor under."

"Yes." He had no idea to which statement he replied, but he clenched his jaw so hard, he feared his teeth would crack. "Finally, I can have done with this portion of my responsibilities."

One of her eyebrows rose in question. "Do you think your duty is finished merely by marriage or begetting an heir?" She shook her head. "You have tenants, income to make and distribute, as well as obligations to Parliament. No doubt there is more than that involved in being an earl, so please do not pin all your hoped-for success on me. I am but one person."

How the devil did she assume he was? Anger flared, hot and swift, in his chest. This woman could irritate him like no other. "Don't presume to dictate to me what I'm doing or why. I've had enough of that in my life already." He tapped a finger to the first paper. "I will give you all the gowns, jewels, fripperies, and baubles you wish in order to outfit yourself in the manner of a countess."

"I appreciate that." The tiny catch of excitement in her voice intrigued him. Why? Clothing a spouse was what any man worth his salt would do.

Drew brought her attention to the next item on the paper. "In the matter of living arrangements. While Parliament is in session, of course we will reside in London. However, should we find we don't get on, you may have the London townhouse. Or, if you'd rather, you may live here at Hadleigh Hall, for you might find that the city doesn't suit."

"My mind is spinning." Then a frown pulled the corners of her mouth down, and he stared at her lips while his musings delved into all the wicked things she could do with them once they'd wed. "Are these the only two properties you own?"

The question yanked him from his thoughts. "Of course not. I have a townhouse in Brighton as well as a hunting box in the north of England."

"Ah, then I will take the Brighton house." Her eyes sparkled when she glanced at him. "It sounds more relaxing than London, and if I'm to change my life, I'd rather not spend my days as a neighbor to my great uncle, who has never cared genuinely for me. I imagine I'll see rather more of him than I'd like once you and I wed."

"Fine." Never had he been in the acquaintance of anyone as pushy or determined as Miss Sarah Copeland. Drew took up his pen, slashed through a line of writing, and then modified it with a heavy scribble. This new concession irritated the hell out of him, for he enjoyed the Brighton property; why should he agree to give it up? Damnation, that's where he should have gone when he'd run from London.

But had he done that, he would never have met her...

"I have many memories of being in Brighton with my father—before he became too ill to travel," he said as he finished altering the document.

"Perhaps it's time to create new ones—with *you* as the earl." Her dulcet tones shivered over his skin, tugged at a piece of his soul he wasn't ready to give up.

So, he grunted. "Do you remember your parents fondly?" She was intriguing, and he needed more from her than she'd told him.

"Yes." The word was said so softly he had to lean closer to hear. Sarah wrapped a hand around the ever-present silver locket. "However, that is a conversation for another time." She kept her focus on the second sheet of the contract.

Another stab of hot anger streaked through him. He'd made an overture and she'd rejected it. Damn it, if she wished to close herself off, so be it. Nothing of a personal nature would be shared. "Shall we proceed to the next item? If we part while still wed, all jewels belonging to the Hadleigh estate will return to the estate."

"I object." She raised her head and stared at him over the tops of her spectacles. "If you give me jewelry, I assume they're gifts. Therefore, I shall keep them."

What gammon was this? Drew gritted his teeth. "They would have been on loan. Why should I reward a woman with jewelry if she intends to leave me?"

Sarah popped a hand onto her hip. Annoyance flashed in her eyes, turning them from plain brown to a whisky hue with golden flecks. "Ah, so anything you give to me is merely a bribe to make me stay, to pretend to fall in love with you? For what purpose? To show the *ton* you've achieved the perfect life?"

To the devil with her, the annoying little baggage. To alleviate his building rage and the anxiety twisting through his insides, turning her every word into something skewed, Drew picked up an empty brandy snifter from the sideboard and then hurled it against the fireplace. The satisfying tinkle of broken glass echoed in the silence. "Fine. You may have the jewelry, but I ask that you don't sell the pieces unless you're desperate." With savage strokes that tore slits in the paper, he modified the document.

"How lovely. You've devolved into acts of tantrums such as my ten-year-old charge might." She shoved her spectacles back into place. "It is not acceptable from him, and neither is it from you." While he gawked, she took the pen from him and proceeded to add notes to the document. "The next item deals with children. Which follows nicely into what I just said. I won't tolerate your temper, and if we do have offspring as a result of this union, if we end up going our separate ways inside the marriage, the children will go with me. There is no reason for them to witness their father conducting his life as a beast."

"Absolutely not!" His roar of objection echoed through the room. Drew rounded on her, turned her to face him as rage boiled in his blood. "I'll not have you poison my children against me."

"Listen to yourself." She rolled her eyes heavenward. "I have more class and dignity than that." As he tugged on his suddenly too-tight collar, the intelligent minx searched his face with her gaze, looking for God only knew what. Did he pass muster even when in the grip of anger? His hands shook from the need to belong. "I would prefer the children to know a loving parent over the company of a bevy of servants. No doubt you will be busy enough."

Something inside him snapped. It could have been logic, but the dam that held back the bulk of his rage was no longer there. "How dare you tell me how to run my life. I need air." Shoving a hand through his hair, he left the study before he said—or did—something he would regret later.

He'd barely cleared the room when he was obliged to gasp for breath, his chest tight and squeezing. Black spots flirted with the edges of his vision and he sagged, his back against the wall. When would the terrible pressure and impossible burden of who he was lessen? He rubbed the heels of his hands on his closed eyes. With every new day, he found another reason to antagonize her, and anxiety was always a step behind him, taunting him, pointing out all the ways he'd failed— himself and his title.

Why can I not do better?

And more appalling yet, if he couldn't look after himself, what the devil would he do with Sarah? She didn't deserve the life she would consign herself to, for he wasn't fit company for anyone. Yet, he needed her. In her, he felt that she'd take him in hand and perhaps pull him from the sucking darkness if only to tell him how wrong he was. Would she remain with him once she knew how mucked up he was as a person, how close to breaking he truly was? Had she only agreed to wed him on an assumption that he would be the strong one?

Oh, God, I'm going to fail her. He shook his head. No. Whatever it took, she would be the one person that he'd impress. Somehow, some way, he would do right by her. He had to, for he suspected that he didn't deserve her at all, but he wanted to.

It took several minutes of deep breaths for his pulse to stop ratcheting and for his temper to fade to a more manageable level. Then, after straightening his spine, Drew returned to his study. "I apologize for my absence. There are times when I must step away to avoid—"

"I know," she said in a soft voice. "I've seen your battles and witnessed those attacks you have." When she touched his sleeve, her hand trembled. "Please know I never wanted to add to your concerns."

It was as if she'd punched a hole in his chest that allowed some of the hot ire out. The sudden surcease of the turbulence staggered him. "Once we wed, you will become a responsibility. That is inevitable."

"Perhaps, but I'm quite capable. If you cannot seem to interact with me unless you're yelling or storming off, then we shall live separately. All the benefits of the marriage will apply, except for the begetting of an heir. Obviously, the logistics of that won't work."

Was she so anxious to use him for the title that she'd let him go without another thought? The metaphorical hole in his chest closed, and anxiety came swooping back in like a darkened beast. "I am the earl, Miss Copeland, and as such if I tell you to do something, it will happen. There will be no separation until you have borne a son." Even to his own ears, he sounded like the biggest blowhard alive.

But how to change that without giving into anger?

Sarah glanced at him with a raised eyebrow. "You can't force respect or compliance, my lord." She held up the third page of the contract where she'd written in a paragraph. "In the matter of a divorce—"

"That will *not* happen." Dear Lord, she *was* thinking of leaving him! Drew crossed his arms at chest level and glared.

"Perhaps not, but the clause needs to be added all the same, for if you can't stand to be in the same room with me for the length of time it takes to discuss a contract, it doesn't give much hope for a lifetime, does it?" Notes of disappointment and resignation threaded through the statement.

"It's not you—"

"Hush, my lord. This is simpler." She went on as if he'd never spoken. "If you take a mistress, I refuse to look the other way. You are marrying me—no matter the circumstances at the present—and you will honor those vows until you have an heir."

"Now see here—"

"But if you don't, a divorce will be procured at your expense without fully besmirching my reputation, though the both of us won't come out of such proceedings unscathed. You will assume all responsibility and fault in those proceedings."

What the devil? "You can't be serious."

Sarah continued. "However, if we agree to merely separate and if we don't have children and you wish to take a mistress, do so discreetly. No harm or foul. Since one of the requirements of this union was for you to have a son." The delicate tendons in her throat worked with a swallow. "I'm well aware of my age, so I might not be able to bear children at all. If that's the case, I don't want you to remain tied to me."

His heart gave an unexpected tug, for he'd never thought of any of this from her perspective. "Sarah, I'm... well, I'm glad I picked you." For the first time in his life, gratitude swamped him. "We'll weather each storm as we encounter it."

"Thank you, Andrew." When she looked at him, a hint of pleasure warmed her eyes.

Hearing his name from her lips took him by surprise. Awareness of her skittered up his spine. Grudging admiration snuck in to mix with his anger and took away a portion of the sting. She wasn't a stupid woman by any stretch, and damn if she wasn't afraid to meet him toe to toe. "Is that all of your changes?"

"There is one more item." She handed him the last piece of paper. "Since my great uncle won't put a dowry on me, I want one from you."

"What?" His eyebrows rose. Was she mad?

She nodded. "If our marriage goes to hell for whatever reason, I want security in the event of a divorce." When she met his gaze, uncertainty swam in hers—the first hint of vulnerability she'd shown since marching into his study. "Ten thousand pounds in an account under my name with the Bank of England."

"Bloody hell." He gasped at the princely sum. "And if we remain married?"

"Bequeath it to our children."

Yes, she was exactly what he needed. "Fine." After taking the pen from her, he scribbled his name onto the contract next to hers. Then he threw both the contract and the pen onto the desk. The need to clear his head grew strong, and his bride-to-be would do nicely. "I'm going into the village tomorrow morning to retrieve the signed common license. Would you like to accompany me?"

"I would. I'll need time to find a dress for the ceremony, for I refuse to start a new life clothed in the rags of the old." When she spun to head for the door, he stepped into her path.

"Thank you. I appreciate your attention to detail with the contract."

Surprise jumped into her eyes. "You're certainly welcome. I want you to know that you're not alone. Not anymore." She pushed her spectacles back into place. "However, you do need to work on that temper. I refuse to live with an abusive man."

His respect for her continued to rise, as did his desire. Having her so close and enduring the rapid ebb and flow of high emotions required an outlet. "I've never hit anyone, would never lay a hand on a woman in anger. I'd sooner do harm to myself than that."

"Good. I draw the line there."

"Understandable." He dropped his gaze briefly to her mouth. Yes, a kiss would do nicely. "Let me buy you a gown for the ceremony. Something worthy of a countess. After that, you can hire a modiste to come here and outfit you."

A tentative smile curved her lips. "I would like that. Thank you, my lord."

"Andrew, damn it." Before she could speak again, he whisked her into his arms and brought his mouth crashing down on hers. She felt every bit as good in his embrace as she had the last time.

It took next to no time for her to return his kiss. Despite the intensity, she wended her hands about his neck and surrendered to his leading. She welcomed him with the same enthusiasm she'd shown in contract negotiating.

Drew walked her backward the few steps until his desk bumped against her bum and stopped the movement. He slid a hand down her back. When he encountered her hips, he pulled her flush against him. Surely she could feel how much he wanted her. Then, daring much, he ran the tip of his tongue along her lips. When she opened for him, he went exploring, sought out her tongue and asked for anything she wished to give.

With soft little sounds at the back of her throat, she fenced with him. Satin dueled with silk, and still he devoured her. This woman challenged him on every level, and she'd no doubt lead him a merry chase in the bedroom too. He groaned, his need for her ramping, and as he slipped a hand up her ribcage to cup a breast, she wrenched away.

Her breathing was as labored as his, her eyes limpid pools of the finest brandy behind slightly steamed spectacle lenses. "Wed me first. Then you can bed me." She touched the tip of her tongue to her bottom lip, and he nearly lost the last vestiges of his control. "I won't have you treat me like a fallen woman merely to alleviate your need."

Instead of letting irritation surge to the forefront, he laughed. She'd thrown down her opening salvo with the negotiations and he'd countered her with the impromptu embrace. The next move was hers, and oh how he would enjoy this little game of chess. "I shall see you tomorrow, unless you'd like tea before you go?"

Her throaty chuckle sent a shiver into his groin. "I think it's safer if I return home. The events of this afternoon have already gone straight to my head." Gingerly, she stepped around him with one last lingering glance at his mouth. "Enjoy your evening."

He would, for the mere fact that he'd think of inventive ways of routing her on their wedding night, which was approaching at a rapid pace.

Perhaps it wouldn't become the folly he anticipated.

CHAPTER EIGHT

June 21, 1817

S ARAH SAT IN the drawing room opposite her great uncle and aunt
as silence rolled heavy through the room. Earlier that day, she'd
accompanied Andrew into the village. He'd run his errand to the local
vicar while she'd gone into a shop and bought a gown—billed to the
earl—for the ceremony. It had been a wonderful moment, especially
when he'd joined her and approved of the rich green color she'd
chosen, but the joy from that outing faded in the face of doing this
current deed. She clasped her hands in her lap to prevent their shaking,
for she'd never made an announcement quite like this before. "Well?
Have you nothing to say?"

Her great uncle stared at her with disbelief stamped over his thin
face. "You're marrying the Earl of Hadleigh." It wasn't a question.

"I am. Four days from now, actually." A tiny tingle of anticipation
went down her spine. It was the first time she'd spoken the fact out
loud.

"But... why?"

It was her turn to stare like a bacon-brained idiot. "Why not? Don't
you think it's wonderful that I have a future?"

Where I'm not beholden to you and your grudging charity?

"You have a future here," her aunt interrupted. Where her great uncle was tall and thin, her Aunt Maria was short and on the matronly side. Threads of silver wove through her upswept hair, and though the pair was only ten years her senior, they weren't aging gracefully. "There are years ahead of you with us."

An unladylike snort escaped Sarah. "Perhaps, but I've had this opportunity and I'm taking it." She rubbed her hands on her charcoal gray skirting. "The only reason I'm telling you this now is I thought I owed you the courtesy." She stopped short of adding some folderol about them taking such kindness with her.

"But, what will happen to the children?" her aunt continued. Utter bewilderment clouded her eyes.

"The same things that usually happens to children. They'll grow through their lives until they're old enough to leave home for school and university." Sarah shrugged. "After that, the future is in their hands."

"True enough, but what do we *do* with them in the meantime?" her great uncle asked. Dread and confusion scudded across his face. "They still have need of a governess."

"Then you shall hire someone else to the post. If you'd like, I can write out an advertisement and have it placed in one of the papers before I go."

"I'll take care of it." He frowned. "We shall have to…" He gestured about as his words trailed away.

"Ah." Sarah huffed out a breath. "Of course, you'll need to pay them fair wages and give the next candidate all the concessions you never granted to me." That was the crux of the problem. They weren't all that sad to lose her as a person, but they were annoyed that they were losing nearly free labor.

"Yes, but, I rather thought that you would—"

"Stay here into my dotage or wait for you to turn me out once my usefulness had faded? Remain content with my lot while the children were young?" Sarah slowly rose to her feet. "I'm sorry to disappoint you, but I'm not growing younger, so it's time for me to look after myself."

Her great uncle scrambled to his feet. He shoved a hand through his thinning blond hair. "I hope you'll convey our best wishes to the earl." It would probably physically harm him to congratulate her on landing such a prize as the earl.

Despite everything, a tug of compassion halted her urge to quit the room. "I will, but please, you and Aunt Maria are most welcome to attend the ceremony. Come to Hadleigh Hall. Two o'clock four days from now." She allowed a small smile. "After all, you are my only family."

And she would gain a certain amount of satisfaction knowing that she'd become a countess and would suddenly have more stature than her baronet great uncle.

"Of course." He nodded. "Perhaps once you're married, your husband and I might entertain a friendship."

"That is completely up to him." Hopefully, Andrew would have more sense than to fall for such blatant social climbing.

"Well, it's scandalous what you're doing," her aunt said as she rocked to her feet. "You barely know the earl. People will gossip about your intentions."

Sarah bit the inside of her cheek to keep from blurting out an ugly response. "I've not cared about the tabbies' tongues all this time, and I don't guess I'll lose sleep over it now." The smile she pasted on her face felt forced. "Now, if you'll excuse me?"

"One last thing," her aunt said with a raised index finger. "Tomorrow is Sunday and your day off, so I won't begrudge you that, but the following three days are to be spent with the children in intense learning. I won't have you skimp on their education. Make the remainder of the plans on your own time." A note of annoyance had crept into her voice.

"Of course." However, learning would only occur if the children

91

were amenable to it.

"My husband and I will tell the children you're leaving... once you're gone, but not before. I don't want their routine upset. Do not say anything that will cause them sadness or distress," she continued with a hard glint to her eyes.

"If that's what you think is best." So there would be no chance for her to tell them a proper goodbye. No matter how much the two had been holy terrors, they would always think the worst of her. No doubt her "dear" relatives would perpetuate the story of Sarah's abandonment. "Then I'd best plan out my lessons. If you'll excuse me?" There was nothing she could do about the tales they'd tell or the marks on her reputation they'd make, but soon all of that would be in the past.

My future lies ahead not behind.

TWO HOURS LATER, Sarah stared at the gown that hung on one of the open doors to her wardrobe. *Merciful heavens, I'm not certain I can do this.* It was easily the most beautiful garment she'd ever seen, let alone owned. Emerald satin with a pleated, scooped bodice and short, puffed sleeves. It featured gorgeous gold embroidery around the hem and waist, and it had an overskirt that resembled two tulip petals that hung down the sides of the main skirt. By chance or fate, the alterations were minimal and the seamstress at the dress shop had finished it not an hour before. On the earl's orders, it had been delivered to her great uncle's house.

Which made the upcoming wedding all too real.

Andrew had also bought her a matching bonnet. The emerald satin ribbons decorating the straw brim were enhanced by a peacock feather. His largess had even included beautiful embroidered and beaded slippers, new gloves of the thinnest and most luxurious kid leather, plus a pelisse that complimented the whole ensemble. Not that it was cold enough for such a garment, but she couldn't take her eyes off it all the same.

I should have declined his generosity.

But it had been too much fun letting someone pamper her for the first time in her life. Yes, her parents had given her gifts and saw that she was clothed properly, but coin had always been tight and purse strings were always cinched tightly. What he had done for her was something entirely different.

Of course it was, for he wished her to look the part of a countess. It had nothing to do with any kindness he might feel toward her as a woman.

Some of the excitement brought on by the arrival of all the parcels faded. In a handful of days, she would command that same sort of power, could have a whole wardrobe made with fine fabrics and all the fripperies she could desire. Never again would she wear drab, serviceable clothing. It made her head spin, and by turns the muscles in her stomach clench.

This is folly.

It's madness!

She knew nothing about the earl, except he had a terrible temper and he struggled with attacks of some sort. Something in him called to something in her, though, over and above the inexplicable desire that boiled between them any time they were together. Wasn't that alone worth exploring?

Yet desire—lust—wasn't the same as love, devotion, or even affection, and it would soon burn out.

Then what?

Once more she glanced at the gown before transferring her attention out the window where the afternoon sun shone bright and the slight breeze blowing in through the half-opened panes beckoned. Well, it was a fat lot better than being on the street hoping to secure a new position once her great uncle's children were grown.

Oh, this is impossible to puzzle out!

Too much overthinking was... too much. Needing to escape the endless loop of musings and second-guessing, Sarah darted across her room to the trunk at the foot of her bed. She cracked open a long, slim leather case and pulled an ivory flute from the red velvet depths. The instrument was her most prized possession and she'd had it for the bulk of her life. When the mind was turbulent, the only thing that could calm the chaos was music. And since lessons had been cut short to due to the children having gone visiting with their parents, she was free for the afternoon.

With a lightness in her step and a smile on her lips, Sarah made her way outside. Soon, she'd found her favorite stand of four oak trees in the middle of a clover field. A large boulder in the shade was the spot where she often came to read, to practice her music, to remember, to dream... or sometimes to hide. Once she'd settled herself, Sarah played a few scales to warm her fingers. The coolness of the ivory and the pewter keys beneath her fingertips was familiar and exciting; the litany of the music she made easily carried her away to another time and place.

Notes swirled around her. Sarah closed her eyes, imagined herself clad in a gown made of fine fabric. Jewels glittered on her fingers as she played on a softly lit stage in front of dignitaries and titled, powerful people of England. The smooth, mellow sound floated about her head, echoed in her soul, flowed through her body, and carried her along into her musings. Her ears rang from the applause as she concluded the piece, and as she laid her flute in her lap, Sarah smiled. Satisfaction shivered over her skin, for playing made her feel much like kissing the earl did.

Interesting thought, that.

"Good afternoon, Sarah." The deep baritone greeting yanked her from the errant thoughts, and she popped open her eyes. He stood there, his strong form backlit by the sun. Then he moved close enough that she caught the look of surprise and admiration in his stormy eyes.

"I hadn't realized you had a talent for music."

Not knowing if she should talk of it or change the subject, Sarah merely nodded. "I've played the flute since a young girl. My father was so proud he'd procured it from France through one of the blockades." She caressed the instrument, gaining confidence from it. In many ways, that flute had been her most constant friend over the years. She'd seen Andrew this morning, but her silly, fickle pulse jumped now that he was here.

"You've kept up with practicing." He clasped his hands behind his back and stared at her with speculation in his gaze.

"I have."

He glanced between the flute and her face. "You enjoy it?" A tiny note of wistfulness had entered his voice. But why?

"I do. Very much so." After a quick debate with herself, she added, "I've always wanted to tour with a music company and be onstage, sharing my love of the flute with a crowd. Perhaps bring them hope." How would he react to the admission? "Or at the very least, hire my services out for coin." She shrugged. "Imagine people being enthralled by my music in a drawing room."

"You would soon woo them with whatever pieces you chose to play." A tiny frown pulled down his lips. "Why didn't you follow through with that dream?"

"Saving to travel to London so I could audition was slow. Then my parents died, and life shifted. Survival came ahead of talent."

"That's a shame. You would have made a sensation, no doubt."

She nodded, and heat went through her cheeks from the unexpected praise. "I think so too, but I won't abandon the dream. Perhaps someday I'll—"

"You'll have your duties as countess to keep you occupied." An undercurrent of surliness echoed in his tone. "Now you'll see what a burden the title is; it takes from you until there's nothing left."

"Unless you learn to work with it instead of against it," she countered in a quiet voice. Instead of expanding the conversation, Sarah fit the mouthpiece of the flute to her lips and proceeded to play one of her favorite passages from a Mozart piece. While her fingers flew and the notes filled the air, she kept her focus on Andrew.

The change was extraordinary.

He relaxed by increments, went so far as to lean a shoulder against one of the aged oak trees. The lines of strain faded from his face, making him look years younger. His stormy eyes softened. By the time she finished, the hints of a smile flirted with those impossibly chiseled lips. "I must admit, Sarah, that I could listen to this for a string of days and never find myself bored. You are quite good."

"I'm glad you've enjoyed it." Another round of heat filled her cheeks. Music was said to soothe the savage beast. Perhaps this was her purpose in life now, why she'd been destined to meet him. Once he forgot to hold onto his anger, he was rather pleasant and certainly handsome—and he could begin to heal. "Andrew?"

"Hmm?"

"Will you tell me about your family? You and I will wed in four days, and I'd like to hear about the people who are close to you." Was she daring too much by pushing him against his apparent boundaries?

"You know how I feel about them." Warning rumbled in his voice.

"I really don't, since you won't open up to me." Sarah frowned as he pushed off from the tree. Would he leave when the discussion butted into the personal?

"You are quite unrelenting," he muttered.

She snorted. "I rather think I'm inquisitive about my groom-to-be." Resettling the flute in her lap, she looked at him. "If you are allowed to order me about—"

"Without success, I might add—"

"—Then I should be given the same right." There was a certain amount of satisfaction in arguing with him, even as benign as this was.

His lips twitched but he didn't let himself smile. "Fine." Andrew raked the fingers of one had through his hair, upsetting the perfect waves. "My mother is…" He cocked his head to one side. "Well, she's the dowager countess, and she detests the moniker."

"I don't blame her. Listen to the word as you say it." She demonstrated and then shivered. "It conjures up images of an old woman."

Again, he almost smiled. "You will be the dowager someday too."

She pulled a face and stuck out her tongue.

"My mother dotes on my brothers."

"How many do you have?" Finally, she would have a modicum of information about him.

"Two. Finn and Brand."

"Odd names."

He rolled his eyes heavenward. "Their full names are Phineas and Hildebrand."

"Oh!" A giggle welled up and she couldn't stop it. "How unfortunate for them."

"Indeed." Amusement winked in his eyes.

Sarah called herself back to the discussion at hand. "I'm certain your mother loves you as well as she loves them."

"Perhaps, but she's rather out of sorts with me at the moment. Has threatened to write to my cousin and force me to sign a power of attorney to him so he can run the estate, unless I come up to the mark."

"Ah, now I understand your urgency."

"Indeed." He pressed his lips together before continuing. "When I left, I was in a terrible temper and had said some horrid things about Finn." Regret danced across his face.

"Like what?" She enjoyed the peek into his life but knew he would cut that tenuous thread between them soon. For whatever reason, he wasn't a man who liked sharing personal stories or letting anyone close.

"Finn came back from the war injured—quite severely." He

rubbed his gloved fingers over his heart as he'd done in her presence twice now. "He's in a Bath chair, paralyzed. I fear for his future, and Brand, from all accounts, will have a tough time of it as well. He lost an eye while serving." The last was said on a gasp. The color faded from his face. "I let them fight out there without putting myself into danger like I should have."

The behavior he showed was more than displaying his temper; he was genuinely upset to the point of nearly having an attack of nerves. Finally, she was beginning to understand perhaps the first layer of his angst. "Don't let the anger win, Andrew. Focus on me and keep talking."

The fleeting moment of peace broke. He looked at her with a curled lip. Rage flashed in his eyes, evident in the one hand he curled into a fist. "Don't presume to dictate how I should live my life or conduct myself." Beads of sweat formed on his forehead. "I've done well enough without you." His breath came in labored pants.

"Is that true, though?" Sarah asked softly. "Those attacks don't suddenly appear in someone's life. I'll wager you've struggled with them for some now, and with each passing day, each new responsibility you add, the weight you carry staggers you." Slowly, so as not to startle him, she stood while he eyed her with suspicion. "On some level, didn't you wish for this marriage because you want help but don't know how to ask for it?"

"I... I..." He pressed his hand to his chest, then clenched it and held the fabric of his shirt in his fist. He gulped for breath, edging backward until he put his free hand against a tree trunk. "I *shouldn't* need it. My father never grappled with being the earl, so why am I?" Confusion filled his eyes, but the pleading at the back of those stormy depths cried out for her to do something that would ease his suffering.

This was the most honest and open he'd been in her presence since they'd met. Her heart squeezed. "I suspect you didn't know the truth of the matter, and I'm sure your mother was his biggest support."

When he sputtered, hovered somewhere between anger and despair, alternately fighting for breath as the attack went on, Sarah lifted her flute to her lips. She played another favorite passage, this time from a Beethoven sonata.

By the time she finished, he'd visibly calmed and had control of himself once more. How interesting. She would need to explore the effect of music on him further. Perhaps that was how she'd reach past the walls he'd built around himself.

"Do you want to talk about your family more?"

He gave a curt shake of his head. "I do not."

That wasn't unexpected, but she would practice patience. "Have you invited them to our wedding?"

"I wrote, but the letter wasn't posted until yesterday." He didn't leave the relative safety of the tree.

"Sooner or later you will have to stop building your defenses to keep everyone out," she said, hoping for a breezy tone as if his mess didn't matter. "You don't need to do any of this by yourself." In a softer voice she added, "It doesn't make a man weak to ask for assistance or even a shoulder to heft the load for a while."

He snorted and stared as if he didn't know what to make of her. "It's to protect them—you." The chords of his neck worked with a hard swallow. "I've already hurt my family, Sarah. I pray to God I won't hurt you as well." He shook his head. "I don't want to evolve from an angry man into a monster." The waver in his voice went straight to her heart.

"Then start with trust, Andrew. Let me in." She held out her free hand.

"Where are we going?" He bounced his gaze between her fingers and her face.

"Nowhere. You can sit here with me and enjoy the fact that you're alive for a purpose."

For long moments he regarded her with narrowed eyes. Finally, he came forward and slipped his hand into hers. "I'm not certain I know how to let go long enough to trust."

It was a start and a definite opening. While she thrilled at the advance internally, she kept her own counsel as she pulled him to the boulder and then sat beside him. "We shall tackle the problem together." She squeezed his fingers in assurance. "For the moment, we'll sit here in silence with no pressure, no demands, no deadlines, for the ability to relax is also an expression of trust."

A shuddering sigh was his only answer, but he didn't release her hand.

Sarah tamped on the urge to grin. There was hope for their union, she just knew it.

CHAPTER NINE

D REW SPENT THE past two days preparing to welcome a countess to Hadleigh Hall. In his mind it felt a touch odd, for his mother had held that spot for all the years that he'd been alive, but it was time to usher in a new era—his reign as the earl. For the first time he didn't mind the need to make decisions regarding the household, for it meant Sarah would soon join him.

His for a lifetime, if only in a marriage of convenience of sorts.

Yet every minute he spent in her company revealed another facet to her personality. Yesterday when she'd played the flute for him, he'd been handed a huge surprise: the music had brought him a sense of calm. The longer she'd played, the lighter he'd felt. It was extraordinary, and he needed to explore it further.

And he would in mere days.

So he'd charged the housekeeper with creating a suite for a countess at the opposite end of the hall from his rooms. It had always been there, but his mother had never made use of it. In fact, the apartment was rarely used unless high born visitors came to the Hall. The collection of rooms contained a bedchamber, a sitting room, and a dressing lounge—the floorplan a mirror of his, but he'd personally chose the colors for the décor. The ivory and ivy-stamped striped wallpaper would remain, for it was whimsical and peaceful, so it had been only logical to fit the rooms out with shades of green.

Drew nodded at the handiwork completed so far. He hoped Sarah would enjoy the color scheme, for when they'd gone to the village yesterday and she'd selected a gown for the ceremony, she'd gravitated to one of emerald silk. The suite would give her somewhere to go when—if—she tired of his company or couldn't stomach his flaws.

Perhaps that was inevitable.

By increments, his chest tightened with familiar anxiety as he inspected the quilted brocade counterpane in swirls of green paisley shot with gold thread. How the devil did he think the upcoming union would work if he couldn't pass a day without falling victim to this horrible, weighted feeling that stole his breath and wished to see him dead? To say nothing of the anger that robbed him of the ability to think clearly.

I must try, for he suspected marrying Sarah was his last chance for salvation. If she gave up on him, he'd lose himself to emotions he couldn't control.

With a final nod, he left the countess' suite. Perhaps this gesture of goodwill would inspire her to make the best from the situation so she might accept him, befriend him, and enjoy his company.

For his own sake.

When he exited her rooms, he strode down the hall and made a quick stop in his chambers. "Barton, I don't think this cravat particularly works today." He must look his best, for he planned to surprise Sarah today. It was Sunday, her one day off from her post, and he wished to reassure himself that she wouldn't back out of their betrothal.

The valet came out of the dressing room with a pristine length of cotton in one hand. "What the devil is wrong with it? I tied it according to your preference."

"I'm not certain. Perhaps we should try again, this time with a more understated knot?" He glanced into the cheval mirror and frowned. "The stickpin isn't that visible with this one."

"I see." Barton closed the distance. In a thrice he'd removed the ruby pin, the collar, as well as the cravat and replaced the length of fabric. This time he created a more elegant knot that wasn't as fussy as the first. Once a new collar had been put into place, the stickpin was reinserted. "Remember, my lord, practicing charm can only help your cause." He arranged the folds of the cravat so the ruby winked better from its folds.

"You assume I'm surly by nature?" Perhaps he was—now. This life had been thrust upon him without waiting to see if he'd been ready.

The valet snorted. "You've grown complacent with the status quo because it's easier even if it's killing you." Barton handed him his gloves and top hat. "However, you can change."

"I'm rather old to start over, don't you think?" he asked through the squeezing of his chest. What would it even feel like to be free of everything that brought him concern?

"I think you might attempt it for your bride's sake." Barton winked. "No doubt she'll appreciate the effort and might be dazzled by your winning personality."

"Ha!" Drew scoffed. "Sarah is too practical for dazzlement. Besides, she'd see right through me if I tried such gammon on her." Drew tugged on his gloves as he strode to the door. "Regardless, I'll strive to keep my temper in check." He set his hat upon his head, but when his fingers touched the door latch, he paused and looked over his shoulder. "Why are you so interested in my wooing Miss Copeland?"

The valet shrugged. "I want to see you happy, my lord. You haven't been that for many years. Don't you think it's time you let go of old resentments and walk into your future without regret?"

"No, I haven't been happy, have I?" Those emotions crawled up to tighten his throat. "I can't blame that on taking the title, can I?"

"You cannot. And I'm..." Barton's words trailed away as concern clouded his eyes.

"Yes?" Drew cocked an eyebrow.

"I'm worried about you." The valet straightened his spine. "Those attacks of yours are growing worse and coming closer together."

"They are." His hand on the door hand shook. "I don't know how to stop them." Only when Sarah played her flute did he feel halfway normal, as if he weren't going to break apart with one more responsibility. When she'd sat with him on that boulder and held his hand in silence, he'd had a glimpse of what life could be... if only he wasn't a growling beast most of the time.

A ghost of a smile spread over Barton's face. "Then, go be charming when you see Miss Coleman. Perhaps every answer you seek starts with her."

"Perhaps." Drew fled before another attack could take hold, but he was more confused now than before.

※》》》《《《※

AN HOUR LATER, he trotted Ares along the country lanes until he spotted Sarah's familiar form, clad this time in pale blue. Leaning over the horse's neck, he whispered, "Let's see how fast we can annoy the governess, shall we?" Then he dug his heels into the animal's sides and encouraged Ares into a gallop. He didn't let up until he blew past her. She darted aside with a squeal of outrage. When he turned the horse about and came abreast of her, she stood with a hand on her hip and a scowl on her face.

Something about keeping her at sixes and sevens tickled him.

"How dare you, Andrew!" A tendril of hair had escaped its bun, and with her bonnet hanging around her neck by its ribbons, that blonde tress waved in the breeze. "I am *not* amused."

"Oh, but *I* am." He grinned down at her. How pretty she was with the splash of high color in her cheeks and her brown eyes snapping fire. "You didn't hear my approach? I thought we'd talked about that from the last time."

"I must have been woolgathering." Once more she carried a basket. When she caught him looking at its contents, she lifted her chin. "I needed a few things from the village shop."

"What sort of things?"

She dropped her gaze and the spectacles slid down her nose. "Personal things that aren't your concern."

Well, he was even more curious. "I thought I'd taken care of anything you had need of for the ceremony yesterday."

Ares stepped closer to her and snuffled her bonnet and hair, went so far as to nip at the straw brim.

Sarah snickered as she gently guided his head away. When she raised her chin, she pushed the spectacles into place. "There are some items a woman requires that a man shouldn't know about." Another wash of pink stained her cheeks, from his notice or the sun he couldn't say. "A woman only weds once, if she's lucky, and she wishes that day to feel... special, even if no one else will see such... things."

"Ah." Drew desperately wished to know what was wrapped in that brown parcel paper. Could it be that this innocent governess harbored a secret side? Awareness swept over him and went straight to his shaft. He remembered those embroidered stockings she'd had last week. What had she purchased this time? A silk robe? Fancy undergarments? He shifted in the saddle as his arousal grew.

"What are you doing out here besides bedeviling me?" The sound of her voice yanked him from his inappropriate thoughts.

"I came to take you on a picnic and had a hunch you might have gone to the village." Had it only been a week since he'd met her, argued with her, kissed her? He indicated a willow basket of his own tied to the pommel. "Are you in the mood for a light repast?"

Her eyes widened behind the lenses. "You thought to do something with me that doesn't include arguing or won't benefit you?"

A stab of annoyance went through his chest, cooling his earlier ardor, but he shoved the emotion aside. "I did." *Be charming, Drew. You want her to marry you, not denounce you.* "Is that agreeable?"

"Yes, of course." The smile she flashed was genuine, for it reflected in her eyes and the delicate skin framing them crinkled. He gawked. Had she always... glowed like that? Then she eyed his saddle. "Do you expect me to ride to your undisclosed location?"

Well, he had, and what was more, he'd anticipated holding her in front of him. "You don't enjoy riding?"

"Not particularly."

He dropped his voice and used his most wicked tone. "Not even with me behind you, holding you so disaster won't befall you?"

"I..." Her cheeks blazed with a dark pink hue.

A satisfied chuckle escaped him. She wasn't altogether in control as she wished him to see. It would be such fun to undress her on their wedding night. "Then I'll walk with you... as long as you promise to ride back with me," he added with a wink. Drew dismounted. "Besides, we're not far from the spot you chose yesterday. That's where I'd planned to picnic." When he offered his crooked arm, he asked, "Shall we?"

Her lower jaw fell slightly open, a sure sign he was doing his best at enchanting her. "Absolutely." She tucked her hand into his bent elbow and soon walked beside him along the hardpacked road. "Are you foxed this afternoon? It's the only explanation for your behavior."

"I am quite sober." He'd imbibed in a snifter of brandy last night before he'd settled into bed, but by and large, he hadn't ingested vast quantities of liquor since leaving London. "What makes you ask?"

"You're acting so... so..." She floundered.

"Charming?" he helpfully supplied.

"I would have said nonconfrontational, but charming is a better word." Sarah glanced at him with speculation in those honey-hued depths. "How did you pass the evening last night when we parted? Did the calm you found last long?"

No, that calm hadn't lasted. The moment he'd stepped foot in Hadleigh Hall, everything had come pouring back. "Suffice it to say I had a glass of brandy before I retired." She didn't need to know what a mess his life had become just now. All too soon she'd witness it for herself. Another pull of anxiety knotted his insides.

How long would she stay after that?

"Mmm, I see. How did you sleep?"

He frowned. Did she truly care or was this inane small talk? "Well enough." That wasn't fully the truth. He'd slept for six hours straight without waking with an attack. For the first time in years.

Because of her. Could she guess how frantic he was to discern if she were truly the answer he sought?

"Good." She squeezed her fingers on his arm. "Relax, Andrew. I won't hurt you, and in the event you wondered, I promised to marry you. I won't back out now."

How the devil could she have known that was uppermost in his mind? "Thank you." He managed to choke out the words despite his tight throat and the emotions that threatened to embarrass him, but damn if he didn't appreciate the slight touch of her hand on his arm.

For long moments, they walked in silence while he led Ares by the reins.

Sarah broke the quiet, and he almost regretted that. "I told my great uncle of our impending nuptials this morning."

"Ah, good. Was he pleased with how well you've done for yourself and the position you'll soon find yourself in?"

"Not exactly." She sighed. "He was more concerned with who would teach his children, and how soon he could meet *you* to give *you* his congratulations in person." A trace of annoyance threaded through her voice.

The gall of the man to belittle her! Anger flooded him in a hot surge. "I'll call on him and dress him down. He shouldn't treat a future countess with such disrespect."

"Yet it's perfectly acceptable for him—and you—to treat me that way because I *don't* command a title at the moment?"

Regret froze the anger in its tracks, for he'd done exactly the same thing as her relative. "I apologized for that incident."

"I know." Sarah bit her lush bottom lip, and he had the distinct urge to kiss her. She strengthened her hold on his arm when his muscles went taut. "Please don't confront him. What my great uncle thinks doesn't matter anymore. My future is with you, not him and his family."

That mollified him slightly. She would do well as a countess, for already she knew how to deflect a potentially disastrous situation. "Very well, but only because you asked me not to." He glanced at her and found her gaze. "He won't be given another chance to treat you as he's done. I can promise you that."

Once they arrived at the designated spot, Drew turned Ares loose to graze on the long meadow grass. Then he took a quilt from his basket and spread it on the ground.

"This is a lovely idea. Thank you," she murmured with a smile.

"You're welcome." He removed a few parcels of food and a bottle of lemonade and set them on the blanket. "Cook told me she packed several of my favorite foods as well as goodies ladies usually enjoy. You'll need to inform her of your tastes."

"I will." She nodded as she sat upon the quilt and arranged her skirts about her folded legs. "Have you, ah, informed your staff that you plan to marry?"

"I did."

"How did they react?"

"Does it matter? They work for me."

She huffed. "Of course it does. Are they happy for you? Excited to have a countess in residence again?" A hint of unease clouded her eyes. "I'd rather not come into an existing household where animosity brews belowstairs."

"I suppose that would make things more difficult." Drew poured her a glass of lemonade and handed it off. "Truth be told, my staff is thrilled. They've long wished to feel useful. It's been years since Hadleigh Hall had life under its roof, and now they'll have a new mistress to attend to."

"It's all so... overwhelming. It will be a huge change from what I'm used to." Her hand holding the glass trembled. "What if I fail in my position? Or fail you?" The tiny catch in her voice tugged at his compassion and brought down a few bricks from around the wall of his heart.

Was it possible she struggled with some of the same feelings, the same fear of inadequacy, that he did? "If you do, then I have failed you first." Wanting to reassure her, he gently eased the glass from her fingers, set it aside and then took her hand in his. "Sarah, you will make a fine countess. Of that I have no doubts." He might live most of his existence lost in a quagmire of horrid emotions, but in this he was adamant.

"I hope you're right." She nodded. "You are certain you wish to go through with all this?"

"When I make a promise, I keep it. And my duty to the title demands that I wed." Dash it all, that wasn't what he'd meant to say!

"Ah." She huffed and yanked her hand away. "A business arrangement. Thank you for recalling me to what this truly is so my head won't be turned by surface niceties such as picnics."

Anger flared, and this time he didn't try to beat it back. "That's what we agreed upon, yes?" In fact, it was she who'd first offered that terminology when he'd asked her to marry him.

"Yes." Though she agreed, she dropped her gaze to her lap where her fingers were tightly clasped. "But I'd hoped you and I could find friendship along the way, for the other... tasks ahead in fulfilling your duty require a fair amount of intimacy."

"And trust," he added in a small voice as her words from yesterday came back to him. How long had it been since he'd had complete trust in another person? Not even Barton knew all his secrets... or fears. Would she be the one to take all the battered, blackened parts of him and polish them up so the light could shine in?

Did he want her to?

"Regardless of what sort of marriage we have, there must be some level of trust there, Andrew." Finally, she looked at him, found his gaze. Uncertainly shone in her eyes. "I shall do my level best in this new role, but I need for you to do the same. It will take a joint effort, especially if we wish for this union to be a success. Isn't that a portion of what the duty entails?"

He hadn't seen the problem from that perspective before; he'd only thought of marrying and producing an heir. Yet she was right. He would need to work at the marriage and make it a success, for the years were long enough without hating one's wife, no matter how many concessions for just that were built into the contract. Now that he saw it as she did, another layer of metaphorical bricks landed upon his shoulders, and he gasped from that weight.

"Oh, God." Was he already failing now because he knew nothing about his bride-to-be? In his head he imagined Finn's mocking laughter or Brand's sarcastic comments about him wasting the title, and he choked. Black spots danced at the edges of his vision.

"Andrew, breathe." Sarah crawled over the quilt to his position, paying no mind to the spilled lemonade that dampened a spot on her skirts. She kneeled beside him and wrapped her arms about him. The scents of violets and clover teased his nose and helped bring order to the chaos bouncing through his brain. "Don't think of everything at once. Take one task at a time, pay one thing your attention, and then move on to the next once it's finished." The dulcet tones of her voice sailed across his consciousness and scrubbed at the blackness that wanted to swallow him. "Rest easy knowing I'll help you if I can, as your wife, as your countess, as your friend."

"I don't have many friends. Not anymore." He'd pushed everyone away before they could see how broken he was, before they could judge him, before they could leave.

It was easier and hurt less.

Or so he'd thought.

"Shh." She rubbed a hand up and down his arm with slow, soothing motions. "Start with one and go from there. I'll wager there are plenty of people who worry about you but don't know how to reach out or help."

He turned his head into her, following the sound of her voice, and rested his cheek on her breasts, tucked an arm around her hips. Beneath his ear, her heartbeat thrummed steady and fast. She was warm and real, in this moment, with him, and she hadn't shied away at the beginnings of this attack. That was something. For long seconds he remained like that, borrowing from her quiet strength until the terror and the darkness had been beaten back enough that he could function.

Finally, he pulled away and sought her gaze. Nothing except concern and compassion were reflected in her brown eyes. "I apologize for that moment of weakness." He looked away lest she see the demons on his face.

"Never apologize for everything you're fighting against. It means you haven't given up, and that means you're alive." She sat back with her legs folded beneath her, and putting a palm to his cheek, she turned his head until she could stare into his eyes. "In this moment, you are enough. Keep building those moments before going forward."

Somehow, for some reason, she understood at least a part of what ailed him. And the freedom therein was incredible. He nodded, but then couldn't help himself. He surged into her and claimed her lips in a brief kiss that was all too short but what he needed. "Thank you. I vow to make you proud."

"Find pride in yourself first." She patted his cheek and then sat back. "Should we do justice to your cook's basket?"

"Of course, but first, I want you to have this." Drew delved a finger into the pocket of his waistcoat and brought forth a ring. Sunlight sparkled off the round two-carat emerald surrounded by tiny diamonds. The gold setting gleamed as bright as her hair. "This belonged to my grandmother. I believe it was her engagement ring once upon a time." Taking up her left hand, he tugged on the kid glove until it slipped from the appendage. "I'd be honored if you'd accept it as yours."

"It's gorgeous," she breathed.

"The color suits you." His hand shook as he slipped the bauble onto the fourth finger. "You have my promise that I'll do my best."

"That's a step toward a solid foundation." When she smiled, a trace of moisture welled in her eyes. "You're not alone, Andrew. Remember that."

Somehow, she'd gotten past his defenses and had already made an impression. How long would it be until that foundation she talked of crumbled and he was exposed as the colossal failure that he truly was?

CHAPTER TEN

June 25, 1817

S ARAH'S NERVES FELT strung too tight while flutters tickled through her lower belly. In mere moments, she would recite vows to Andrew that would forever bind her to him, yet she hadn't seen him for three days thanks to her great uncle's dictates that she should spend all her time with his children.

Not that the spoiled young ones cared. They hadn't been any more interested in learning yesterday than they'd been during her whole term as their governess. The one piece of business that caused a sensation had been Mary blurting out a question Sarah would never forget.

"Mother told George and I that you were marrying the earl next door. Is that true?"

"It absolutely is," she had replied with a slight smile, but inside she'd been sticking out her tongue.

The girl had looked incredulous. "No one can quite figure out why the devil he—or any man—would offer for you when you're nobody," she'd uttered in exasperated tones.

Sarah had shrugged. "Everyone is worthy, regardless of other peoples' opinions. Remember that." And then she'd gone on teaching as if nothing were amiss.

Even now, the memory made her smile. Let them all wonder. She cared not. This new path beckoned before her and she couldn't wait to see where it led. It was no one's business how the engagement had come about or why. The fact was, today she would marry at the ripe old age of four and thirty, and she wouldn't need to fret over her future again.

Despite her confidence, Sarah waited in the drawing room. It was as lovely as one could imagine a room in an earl's home to be. Delicate Louis XIV furnishings, cushions of pleasing shades of blue, the walls decorated with oil paintings of pastoral or seaside landscapes all in heavy gilt frames, thick Aubusson carpeting, and heavy navy velvet drapes all spoke to wealth and high position. Both impressive and a tad intimidating.

Was she truly ready to step into this life and live it? She had no prior experience of mixing with the *ton* or how to conduct herself therein. *What if I fail?*

Then she'd merely start over the next day until she figured out how to use the new title to her advantage and put her own stamp on it. None of those thoughts soothed her racing heartbeat, though. She paced in front of the windows where bright noon day sunlight streamed in while pushing her spectacles back onto the bridge of her nose. Where was he? Surely, he wouldn't beg off at the last second and embarrass her. She smoothed her palms down the front of her gown.

The emerald satin was cool against her skin, but the ruffle at the hem and around the edges of the tulip petals of the overskirt brought strength to her confidence. Two dear little fabric rosettes on the hem ruffle made her think of a garden she'd seen once in a painting. The matching slippers pinched her toes, but they were equally as beautiful. Beneath the gown that had cost an enormous amount of coin—gifted to her with Andrew's compliments—she wore garments she'd purchased for herself: fine lawn petticoat and shift, both embroidered with green vines and leaves as well as pink rosebuds, and the embroidered stockings that had been in her basket that first day she'd met Andrew. Never had she been outfitted in such finery.

This day was much like a dream, except for the delinquent groom. A slight pang of sadness went through her chest. And the absence of her parents. She touched a fingertip to the silver locket around her neck. It would have been more special if she could have them back for one moment so they could know that she'd taken steps to secure her future.

The clearing of a masculine throat brought Sarah out of her musings. "Are you quite certain Lord Hadleigh wishes to marry you?" The question from her great uncle rankled, and she turned to look at him. He and his wife sat on a low sofa near the center of the room—the only official guests. Witnesses really. "Perhaps you misunderstood the conversation."

"That's easy to do," her aunt agreed with a sage nod that had her double chin wagging. "A woman your age with no prospects or offers can often see her mind playing tricks."

Oh, drat. Sarah huffed out a frustrated breath. Her spectacles slid down her nose. After today, she wouldn't need to pander to these two, for her obligation had ended at teatime yesterday. Andrew had sent a coach for her. Whereupon she'd taken her one trunk and a carpetbag, tucked herself into the vehicle, and proceed to leave her great uncle's home for the last time. The night before she'd slept in the most luxurious suite of rooms she'd ever seen, and now she was here...

Waiting.

Would Andrew show? Was he even now suffering through an attack? "There was nothing to misconstrue, Auntie," Sarah finally said in response. "He *will* be here." She tamped the urge to lash out with the anger brewing deep in her chest. This was not the time nor place to let her temper fly. "If you'll notice, the vicar hasn't arrived either."

Of course, that fact didn't help her cause.

Her great uncle and aunt exchanged a speaking glance. Obviously, neither expected there to be a wedding here today.

A tremble of worry moved up her spine as she pushed the eyewear back into place. Sarah faced the window once more and fought against the rise of unshed tears crowding her throat. *Please, Andrew, keep your promise.* A few fat, puffy clouds moved to block the sun, and the resulting shadows were almost mocking with their indifference. Then, a commotion and the rustle of fabric at the door had her spinning about.

He's here! Her pulse hammered behind her ribs as he came into the room, resplendent and oh so handsome in his dark formal clothes.

"I apologize for my tardiness, but I wanted to extend an invitation to my staff in the event they wished to serve as witnesses." The earl stood aside.

A few women came into the room, followed by the man she'd seen as the butler, as well as another man who nodded at Andrew as he passed. All of them glanced at her with speculation and interest in their expressions. Briefly last night she'd met the butler as well as the housekeeper, but at the moment, she couldn't recall their names. Finally, the local vicar entered. In his somber and plain back suit with the white contrasting collar, he was every bit how she'd envisioned he would look on this day.

"You would have servants at your nuptial ceremony?" Her great uncle stood as Andrew made his way to him. He made it sound as if the earl had invited vermin into the room.

Now she knew exactly where she'd stood with her relatives.

"Why not? They've been much like family to me, and quite frankly, they're a fat lot less aggravating," Andrew responded smoothly, his baritone rumbling through the room. When her aunt stood, he greeted them both. "I trust you'll forgive me for taking away someone as incomparable as Miss Copeland."

"Of course, of course," her great uncle enthused as he pumped Andrew's hand. "We hate to give her up."

"Yes," her aunt said as she dropped as shaky curtsy. "She's been ever so valuable to us. The children are sad to see her go."

At the window, Sarah rolled her eyes. She hoped the earl was intelligent enough to see through their false concern. On the other hand, she didn't wish him to fly into a temper because of them.

"Well, Miss Copeland is in my care now. She'll want for nothing and shall be treated with the respect she deserves." A warning growled in his tone. "I'm sure her time will be spoken for, so please do make an appointment should you plan to call."

"We will indeed." Her great uncle nodded as if he were a puppet on a string. "My wife and I intend to throw a rout next month to celebrate your marriage, if it pleases you."

With slightly narrowed eyes, Andrew nodded. "You'd do well to make certain it pleases my new countess, but keep me informed, Sir Gearwell." Then he turned and locked eyes with her and a grin slowly curved his sensual lips.

Oh, dear heavens. Butterflies began a ballet, causing a riot with her insides. *He is rather potent.* And he'd stood up for her against the two of them. That earned him more respect.

As the various people in the room talked in low voices, the earl came toward her, never breaking eye contact. Almost as if he were a large jungle cat stalking his prey.

Me. Another tremble went down her spine, but this one also tickled through her lower belly, for tonight she would know him far more personally...

When he reached her, his grin merely widened. An answering wicked glint lit his blue-gray eyes. "I knew you'd look lovely in emerald. You should always wear bold colors. They suit you."

"I appreciate that." Heat infused her cheeks from his unexpected praise. "And thank you once more for the gown. It's stunning."

He nodded. "Have you changed your mind? If so, I'm sure your great uncle would be thrilled to have you back to work."

A wild near-hysterical giggle erupted from her. "I think I'll take my chances with you." It didn't matter that she'd wished to tease him, for the spell of anticipation had broken.

"I'd like to hope you view me in a better light than him." A trace of annoyance flickered in his expression to chase away the good humor he'd entered the room with, but it was gone by his next breath. "I assume you have met the vicar?"

"Yes. On the few occasions I've attended church."

"Then let me introduce you to some key members of my staff—your staff now. Though I suspect you've met some already out of necessity."

"I have," she whispered. Her stomach bottomed out. This was all too real. In an hour, her life would shift, and she'd begin anew as a countess.

Before Andrew could guide her over to the butler, Vicar Baring came up to them. He was a man of indeterminate years with hair the color of mud and a rather unfortunate long nose.

"It's an honor to be here, Lord Hadleigh." His long fingers tightened over a battered copy of the *Book of Common Prayer.* "However, I've been invited to luncheon at a home in the next village over, so I'd like to have this underway and soon."

Which meant the home to which he'd been asked featured a young lady who was looking for a husband. She must be quite something if the vicar flirted with upsetting the earl, who no doubt provided said vicar's living.

"Very well. No ill-will taken." Andrew nodded as the vicar moved toward the center of the room. He fit his lips to the shell of her ear and whispered, "Introductions will need to wait." The warmth of his breath skated over her cheek.

A shiver of *something* danced down her spine. "It matters not. I'll see to them later this afternoon." Sarah looked up at him while he pulled away and gave him what she hoped was an encouraging smile.

Let something good come from this union.

"Spoken like a countess. Come. We mustn't keep the vicar waiting."

In a daze, she followed him to the middle of the room where she was instructed to stand by Andrew's side. The earl gave him a small leather purse that jangled with coins, payment, no doubt for services rendered. The vicar tucked it away and then rifled through his book.

"Shall we begin?"

"I see no reason not to." Andrew frowned. "Best have it done, don't you think?"

Sarah's stomach muscles knotted. Of course, to him this was merely another task associated with doing his duty to the title, while to her... it was life changing.

"Excellent." Vicar Baring nodded. He glanced at the handful of witnesses. "Dearly beloved, we are gathered together here in the sight of God, and in the face of this congregation, to join together this Man and this Woman in holy Matrimony; which is an honorable estate, instituted of God in the time of man's innocency, signifying unto us the mystical union that is betwixt Christ and his Church..."

Oh, my goodness. If Sarah's heart beat any faster, she'd surely expire on the spot to what the minister said as he addressed the earl. If she took Andrew's arm, would he lash out? Knowing his touch now when her mind spun with everything she would promise this day would be appreciated, but he didn't move. Instead, he kept his hands clasped behind him, staring at the vicar with a bland expression.

Vicar Baring addressed Andrew. "Wilt thou have this Woman to thy wedded Wife, to live together after God's ordinance in the holy estate of Matrimony? Wilt thou love her, comfort her, honor, and keep her in sickness and in health; and, forsaking all others, keep thee only unto her, so long as ye both shall live?"

Sarah couldn't stop the tremble that moved through her. Did he understand the severity of those words and the responsibility created therein? What sort of husband would he be?

"I will." The answer in his baritone resonated in her chest, but when she glanced at him, he'd clenched his jaw so tight the muscle stood out against his skin.

Perhaps he wished for support too. Daring much, she laid a hand upon his arm. His muscles flexed and jumped beneath her fingertips. All too soon, Vicar Baring addressed her.

"Wilt thou have this Man to thy wedded Husband, to live together after God's ordinance in the holy estate of Matrimony? Wilt thou obey him, and serve him, love, honor, and keep him in sickness and in health; and, forsaking all others, keep thee only unto him, so long as ye both shall live?"

Some of the words stuck in her mind. She would only obey and serve him as long as his temper stayed in check, and she had no guarantee that it would. But the vicar waited for an answer. She squeezed Andrew's arm. "I will." A fair amount of breathlessness accompanied the answer, for she wasn't entirely certain this wasn't the biggest folly she'd ever committed.

We don't love each other.

The vicar instructed Andrew to take her right hand in his right hand. He held so tight that she peered into his face, and only then did she see the signs of an impending attack. His lips were slightly parted. He took small, panting breaths. Sweat beaded at his temple. Sarah leaned into him and whispered, "Breathe, Andrew. You're not going to the gallows."

He grunted. "That would, at least, cause my demons to quiet."

Poor man. She feared he would break, and soon. *How can I reach him when he refuses to acknowledge that the struggle is part of living?* Absently, she pushed her spectacles back into place.

"Is there an issue?" Vicar Baring asked as he darted his gaze between them. When Sarah shook her head, he cleared his throat and continued. "Lord Hadleigh, please repeat after me." The words the vicar said blurred together while Sarah worried over Andrew's health. They didn't make an impression until the earl repeated them as he faced her.

"I, Andrew James Storme, the Eighth Earl of Hadleigh, take thee Miss Sarah Elizabeth Copeland to my wedded Wife, to have and to hold from this day forward, for better for worse, for richer for poorer, in sickness and in health, to love," he choked over that word, "and to cherish, 'till death us do part, according to God's holy ordinance." He gasped for breath as he squeezed her hand hard. "And thereto I pledge thee my troth."

Tears welled in Sarah's eyes. He both wished to wed and dreaded it, for he couldn't see a way out what he considered a morass of the title. She patted his hand, hoping to give him a modicum of comfort.

They were directed to release hands, and Sarah was told to then hold Andrew's right hand with her right hand. Vicar Baring addressed her while she stared into the earl's eyes. The anger and resentment that roiled in those stormy depths cramped her stomach. "Miss Copeland, repeat after me." He gave her the words, and she nodded.

There was no calling it off now. "I, Miss Sarah Elizabeth Copeland, take thee Andrew James Storme, the Eighth Earl of Hadleigh to my wedded Husband." Her hand shook, both in anticipation and fear. "To have and to hold from this day forward, for better for worse, for richer for poorer, in sickness and in health, to love, cherish, and to obey, 'till death us do part, according to God's holy ordinance." She didn't care that a tear fell to her cheek. Would she come to love Andrew over the course of their union? If she did, would he return the sentiment? At the vicar's prompt, she rushed onward. "And thereto I give thee my troth."

Dear God, please let this not show as a mistake.

They were instructed to again release their hands. Then Vicar Baring asked Andrew if he had a ring.

"Yes." The earl dug a finger into his waistcoat pocket and procured a thin plain gold band.

"Very good. Repeat after me while putting the ring on her hand." He said a string of words that flew right out of Sarah's head.

He slid the band onto the fourth finger of her left hand where it bumped snugly against the emerald engagement ring. "With this Ring I thee wed, with my Body I thee worship, and with all my worldly Goods I thee endow." A series of gasping breaths followed the statement. With effort, he continued in a tight voice. "In the Name of the Father, and of the Son, and of the Holy Ghost. Amen."

"Excellent. Shall we pray over this new union?" The vicar directed this question to the room at large.

Another tear fell to her cheek. Where was the joy that a wedding should have brought? She kneeled the same time that Andrew did, but she clung to his hand as hard as he clutched her. Could he not at least pretend he was pleased?

As the words of a prayer went on and Vicar Baring closed his book, Sarah leaned into the earl. In a barely there whisper, she said, "I know you aren't delighted with this arrangement, but I hope you'll see life will turn out better than it is currently."

Did she truly believe that?

The earl didn't answer, merely stared at her with an intensity that had her trembling. What did he think right at his moment?

When the prayer ended, she and Andrew stood. Vicar Baring said, "I now pronounce thee husband and wife."

No longer was she unwanted, undesired, unwed Miss Sarah Copeland. Now she was the Countess of Hadleigh—still unwanted, but desired. Perhaps. Only for him to alleviate a physical need or beget an heir. Not for herself and not because he cared. The urge to retch rose in her throat. She swallowed the hot saliva a few times to stave it off.

"Congratulations, Lady Hadleigh," he whispered. Though he drew her hand to his lips and placed a kiss upon her middle knuckle, there was no fondness in his eyes, but his lips lingered a heartbeat too long. What would they feel like when he employed them on her body later? "You're no doubt quite pleased."

"I'm sorry you aren't," she shot off before thinking. "I can only be who I am." There was absolutely no difference in how she felt now than she had before. If anything, she'd contracted more unease, but there was no time to analyze her thoughts, for the servants gathered around, offering blessings as well as introductions.

As they filed out, her great uncle and aunt signed official documents as witnesses. Then her Aunt Maria kissed her cheek and offered empty promises of visiting often. Soon after, they left the room.

Vicar Baring followed with his congratulations, and she was alone with her husband.

It had happened so quickly that her head buzzed with the events of the afternoon. She glanced at him. Desolation lay stamped on his face and he held himself as if he would flee momentarily. "What now?" Her stomach let out an unladylike growl. "Shall we attend to luncheon?" Not that it would be a splendid affair. There were no revelers, no family members, and no richly decorated cake to mark the occasion.

"I'm not feeling much for eating." His eyes held a slightly haunted edge. He clutched at his chest with one hand while tracing the ruby pin tucked within the folds of his pristine cravat. "In fact, I need some air before I proceed with obligations for this day."

A tingle of apprehension mixed with anticipation careened down her spine. "Did you wish to spend time in other pursuits abovestairs then?" She hadn't thought they'd retire so early, but then she'd never could have dreamed she would call herself a countess either.

Panic flitted over his face. "I believe I'll go riding," he blurted as he backed away. "After that, I have a meeting with my estate manager. It will probably run a few hours."

"Really?" Sarah narrowed her eyes. She shoved up the bloody

spectacles that refused to stay in place. "On our wedding day?"

"Poor timing, I know, but there's nothing for it."

Now that *was* outside of enough. Hot indignation rose in her chest. "You mean to leave me to my own devices so soon after we've wed? As if you had what you wanted and now you can abandon me like you have everything else?" Incredulity rang in her voice. This was not how she assumed the day would go. When hurt reflected in his eyes, she was immediately contrite. "I apologize. That wasn't kind."

"No, but it was spot on. I don't need the reminder of what a failure I am, for I live it every damned day." His voice was low, rumbling, full of ire.

She didn't care. His defection made her feel small, as if she weren't worth anything. "What would you have me do? After the understanding we came to four days ago? Am I to pretend none of this happened? Forget that the Earl of Hadleigh wed me but couldn't bring himself to bed me?" Dear Lord, why couldn't she stop talking?

"Do not antagonize me in this, Sarah. I don't have the patience."

"Ah, but when do you ever?" She popped her hands on her hips. Once more, their communication had devolved into arguing. "Are you so put off by me that you'll race out to avoid your promises? Your vows?"

"You... I can't..." He winced and massaged his chest as his faced paled. "I'm sorry," he gasped out. His labored breathing didn't bode well. "I'll join you later this evening." Then he did indeed flee the room without a backward glance.

"Well, drat." It had been a trying week. Tears welled again in her eyes. It seemed her married life wasn't beginning all that auspiciously. "I was foolish to think otherwise."

She hadn't been aware she'd spoken that last bit aloud until the matronly housekeeper returned to the room.

"Oh, you poor duck." Mrs. Hastings joined her. "I saw the earl ride out on that hellish mount of his." She clicked her tongue. "That man can't see a good thing even if it smacked him."

Sarah snorted with derision mixed with bitterness as a few tears fell. "Perhaps he needs a good smack to knock some sense into him."

"I don't doubt you're the woman who could do it." The housekeeper nodded. "Let me help you settle in. There wasn't time last night for me to show you how lovely your suite truly is. The earl ordered it up real nice for you, so that's something. He's not a complete arse."

An unexpected laugh escaped her, and Sarah wiped her eyes. "Not complete, no." She gave herself over into the woman's care. It was nice to have someone look after her, since Andrew apparently wouldn't, regardless of the vows he just took.

Why had she expected this portion of her life to be any different from what she'd already had? Silly dreams, nothing more.

CHAPTER ELEVEN

D REW GROANED WHEN the longcase clock in the drawing room chimed the eleventh hour. Its stentorian tones filtered down the hall to his study and reminded him of his duty. He drained his snifter of brandy—had it been two or three now?—and slammed his booted feet to the floor from where they'd rested previously on his desk.

Nearly the witching hour on his wedding night and he sat here hiding away like a damned coward. All afternoon the disappointment in Sarah's eyes had haunted him. He'd run from her, afraid to remain in her presence but equally afraid to begin his life with her, for she would leave eventually.

Everyone did.

Yet she was upstairs, waiting for him to consummate their marriage, for that had been a stipulation in their betrothal contract—the begetting of an heir. *Oh, God.* His chest tightened with another round of crushing anxiety, as it had done since he'd spoken those vows to her. Life had changed. He'd added her to his long list of responsibilities. Another person he'd let down, make angry, and ultimately fail.

It hurt to breathe. Hell, he couldn't take a full breath any longer. The title of earl was indeed attempting to kill him. Would he suffer an attack of the heart as his father had? What would happen to Sarah if he expired prematurely without issue? *Bloody hell.* Black spots danced at the corners of his vision. The title would go to Finn, but his brother couldn't handle the strain plus survive life with his injury. Drew couldn't let that happen. It would bury his brother as sure as it would kill him.

No. Everything rests on me.

As it always had.

The urge to retch grew. It filled his mouth with hot saliva and the bitterness of bile hit his palate. With a shaking hand, he poured out another small measure of brandy into his glass and downed it with one gulp. The burn of the liquor in his throat temporarily waylaid his tortured thoughts. *I'm not strong enough for any of this.*

But that didn't negate the fact that Sarah waited.

When he'd seen her in the drawing room before the ceremony, he'd wanted to spirit her away, for she'd been a vision in that emerald gown, and with her golden hair piled upon her head secured with glittering combs, he'd lost the ability to think. Oh, he wanted her, hadn't stopped since he'd first met her, but suddenly the magnitude of what he must do had slammed into him. Fear had taken hold.

She would expect an experienced lover, but he hadn't had a woman in his bed for a few years. She'd want an attentive husband, yet he'd already failed when he'd run away from her directly following their ceremony. She'd wish him to be a doting father to their children should they have them, but unless he took his arse abovestairs, that would never happen. They'd merely met a week ago and now life had shifted... forever. Instead of finding peace and calm at Hadleigh Hall, he had added an enormous amount of obligation.

Each of those things added stress to the weight on his shoulders that even now threatened to crush him. Anxiety worked to pull him under into the all-consuming darkness, and he gasped for breath. At this point, perhaps death would be the easier option.

How can I do this?

It didn't matter how. Do it he must. Scrambling to his feet as the urge to vomit rose in his throat, Drew stumbled to the door. It was his duty, and she was his wife, and by Jove, she wasn't horrid to look at either.

He only tripped once on the stairs. Perhaps he'd stop in his room to change out of his riding clothes and wash the day's grime off his person before visiting her bedchamber. She deserved that, at least. When he pressed on the door latch and pushed open the panel, the sight that greeted him in the dim light left him frozen.

A single candle burned on a bedside table, but that wasn't what held his attention. Sarah lay on his bed, her slender body dwarfed by the large four-poster piece of furniture, and she had the look of an angel with the masses of her blonde hair spilled over his pillows.

His heart skipped a beat the same time his length began to harden. She'd sought him out... hoping.

As quietly as he could, Drew closed the door, and after he'd toed off his boots—nearly falling twice in the process of removing them— he padded closer to the bed. A volume of poetry lay forgotten next to her, for she'd fallen asleep waiting for him to join her. The red linen cover indicated it contained selected pieces of Byron's work. Ah, so she was a romantic at heart.

How interesting.

Then he forgot the book in favor of looking his fill at her. She'd changed into a peignoir set of the finest lawn dyed a faint moss green. Trimmed with ribbons and delicate lace, he'd wager half his estate the clothing was what had been wrapped in parcel paper that day. The outfit coupled with her hair in a mass on his navy counterpane sent blood rushing into his shaft.

"Oh, Sarah." The whispered words sounded overly loud in the hushed silence. Who knew the straightforward governess would favor such delicate, beautiful clothing? Quickly, he shed his jacket and waistcoat, but his gaze never strayed from her body. The moment the garments hit the floor with a soft *plop*, her eyelids fluttered, and she stirred.

"Andrew?" Sarah raised up on an elbow. She blinked against the candlelight. "What time is it?"

"Quarter past eleven." God, he didn't deserve her. She was sweet yet tart-mouthed and an innocent while he was a growling beast shrouded in dark madness. This union had been a mistake, for he would hurt her like he'd done to his family.

"Oh." She sat up and swung her legs over the side of the bed. "Where have you been?" Her eyes, dark in the dim light, reflected aggravation. The silver frames winked with each movement. "I waited for you, but you never came." How she managed to infuse accusation and disappointment into her tone at the same time, he didn't know. When she stood, she was toe-to-toe with him. "You abandoned me on our wedding day."

All her points were valid. He had no cause to dispute any of them, but that didn't mean that anger didn't swell in his chest from being reminded. "I'm here now."

Her nose wrinkled. "You smell of brandy."

"I indulged before coming up."

"Is that what it takes for you to find the courage to bed me?" She planted her hands on her hips. The points of her hardening nipples were barely visible through the filmy garments she wore. "Is the thought of lying with me so distasteful that you must drink before-hand?"

"Of course not. I drink to forget." Close enough that her clover and violet scent teased his nose, desire roared into life. "I've wanted to bed you since I met you." When she sputtered, he grinned. Having her at sixes and sevens was most rewarding. "Since you're awake, shall we begin?" Lust fought with the simmering anger and crushing anxiety, winning temporarily.

If only he could keep them at bay longer.

Sarah huffed. Golden flecks swam in the dark brown depths of her irises. "After being gone for nearly twelve hours, you expect me to do... *that*... with you now?"

"I do." Awareness shivered over his skin. Pushing her to the point of annoyance left him heated and randy. "Yet you were waiting for me, in my bed I might add, to do just that." As she glared, he gripped her hips and drew her flush to his body. Damn, but she felt good. "Tell me you don't want me, Sarah, and I'll go."

"Why must you act so bothersome?" Her hands drifted up his chest. The heat of her seeped through the fine lawn of his shirt, made him crave more of her.

He stared at her lips before meeting her eyes. "As you said earlier today of yourself, I can only be who I am as well." Then he claimed her lips in a kiss that hopefully left no doubt in her mind that he wanted her. Those petal soft pieces of flesh cradled his, stoked his hunger. He wanted her naked and writhing beneath him, and soon. When he ended the kiss, she pulled away, her spectacle lenses steamed, her breathing slightly labored.

"I'm cross with you." Some of the bite had faded from her tone.

"You have a lifetime to berate me." Though the words were said in jest, he couldn't quell the rising anger, for he would always come up short in her expectations, would always disappoint her. Sooner or later she would resent him for it.

Everyone did.

"Then show me that my ire is displaced." Her eyes darkened with the same desire coursing through his veins. She pulled lightly on his cravat. "Show me that your absence wasn't because you've made a mistake in marrying me." Insecurity popped in her eyes. "Show me that we at least have a chance." The quiver in her voice slammed into him and brought a wave of guilt, but it also brought out a surge of compassion.

Was she as terrified as he?

It wouldn't do to grow too fond of her, so he shoved the thought away. A tug on the ribbons at the front of her robe had the garment gaping. As he shoved it from her shoulders and it pooled on the floor at their feet and her breath caught from a mere touch, he knew what he must do. He had to make her hate him, or at the very least keep her at arm's length, so that when she left him, gave up on him due to his brokenness and his demons, it wouldn't hurt as much as when his family had done the same. "I'll show you something and you can decide what it means."

I can't feel one more thing or I'll break. God only knew if he'd come out sane at the other side. Part of him wanted to reach out for her help, to plead for it, but his damned pride kept him silent.

Sarah laid a palm against his cheek. It took all his willpower not to nuzzle into her hand. "I don't wish to do this if you're incensed." One of her eyebrows lifted in a challenge. "Leave that anger. Stop holding onto it, for it's doing you no good. You're better than that."

"If I were, I wouldn't feel so shattered. Earls don't outwardly do anything to appear weak." Not wanting to indulge in conversation that might lead to introspection, Drew tangled his fingers in the golden curtain of her hair, lightly pulled until her head tipped back, and then he kissed her—hard. He devoured her lips, cupped her head in his hands through those tresses and held her still while he plundered her mouth as if he couldn't have enough of her. He thrust his tongue inside to bully hers with rhythmic strokes. Answering pulses rolled through his hardened length. Vaguely, he became aware of her palms pushing at his chest, and when she shoved, breaking the punishing embrace, he gasped for breath.

Even while attempting a kiss, anxiety wouldn't relent.

"What the devil is wrong with you?" Sarah narrowed her eyes. "I know you're capable of acting like a gentleman instead of a brute."

Except she hardly knew him or how much more beastly he could be.

Yet he wanted her approval, craved it, hoped that she'd like him for the man that he was. He wiped the moisture from his mouth. "I apologize." Would he forever muck things up due to the damned anger that wouldn't leave him alone?

Sarah's expression softened slightly. "It's all right. Try again." She tugged on his cravat, unwinding it until the length of fabric fell away along with his collar. "I may be your wife, but that doesn't mean you should ever stop attempting to woo me."

The logic was sound. Even if they'd signed a contract that never made allowances for love or even romance, there was no reason he couldn't charm her. "I'll try." But if he did that, then she wouldn't grow to hate him. It was a conundrum—please her or fall apart when she left.

This time, as he took her into his arms, he set out to make the kiss more tender, more pleasant. He finessed his way over her lips, exploring, asking, introducing, and when she followed his lead, his shaft pulsed with appreciation. Dear God, she was soft and silky as he caressed his hands up and down her bare arms, yet he knew from prior acquaintance she possessed a will of iron that didn't bend when confronted with his ire.

You basically paid her to marry you. The woman won't stay with you once you finally snap. His damned anxiety wouldn't shut up, and no matter how erotic the sounds of enjoyment Sarah made at the back of her throat or how sweet the touch of her hands as she explored his shoulders, he couldn't banish that destructive little voice at the back of his mind. *You aren't worthy of love. How could you be?*

Anger mounted, for himself as well as the situation. He growled and wrenched away from her. When she murmured something unintelligible, he grabbed the hem of her nearly transparent night-gown, and in the process of yanking it up and off her body, the fabric tore.

"Oh, no!" The exclamation couldn't break through the waves of anger roiling through him. "Andrew, be careful. I bought this so I'd look pretty for you tonight." She hung to the garment, clutching the ruined fabric to her breasts.

Of course, he was destructive; beasts usually were. He hated himself, and that made him feel even worse. "Would me giving you empty compliments make any of this better?"

Hurt stamped across her expression. She cried out when he tugged the nightgown from her fingers and tossed it away. "Well, it can't make it worse, can it?" Those damned narrowed eyes and her ire fed his own. "This is hardly what I expected on my wedding night."

"On that, you and I agree, but isn't this what be both agreed to, this begetting an heir?" They'd never discussed love or romance, so why should he make an effort? With his state of mind, he couldn't focus properly on the slender length of her body or how perfect her breasts were with their hardened rosy pink tips. Or how the thatch of blonde hair at her thighs was distracting as all hell.

No, the only thing he could focus on was the rampant lust that blinded him and the anger that clawed through his insides in a bit to tear him apart. The longer he stared at her body, the more visibly shy she grew. When she attempted to shield herself with her hands, he snatched at them. "No, countess, these belong to me." And cad that he was, he cupped her breasts, kneaded them, smashed them together. Perfect indeed. Not overly large or small, they filled his palms as if she were made especially for him, but he didn't pause to properly worship them. Not when his mind was plagued with doubts and his chest felt tighter with each drawn breath thanks to the bloody anxiety.

Confusion and apprehension filled Sarah's eyes, slightly magnified behind the lenses of her spectacles. "Please, be gentle. I haven't—"

"Hush. I know." He dipped his head and took a pebbled nipple into his mouth.

She whimpered but slid a hand to his nape and encouraged him to continue. "I had no idea…"

It didn't matter that she didn't finish the thought, for he was nearly gone. There was no strength to master control over the desire circling through him. "Damn, but this will go quickly, Sarah." As best he could, he modulated his voice, so he didn't sound like the beast he felt. "It's been too long." And he was out of practice, besides.

"Give me time to acclimate. These sensations are too big," she whispered as she delved her hands beneath his shirt. "Let me play, arouse you as you're doing to me. Teach me—"

"No." For that would only leave a deeper impression and greater regret on both their parts. "You don't understand..." It was Drew's turn not to finish a sentence. As she looked at him with trust and stark need in her expression, he'd give anything to be someone other than who he was. He cupped her cheek, drew her closer and kissed her again and again, drinking his fill of this woman who'd voluntarily braved his wrath and would have to weather his ire. As he did, he pulled her naked body flush to his. In his haste, he hadn't even taken his own clothing off.

Another reason she'd have to berate him. Then he was lost to the glory that was Sarah, her lips that tried to welcome him home despite his reluctance to go back, her wandering fingers that sent shuddering awareness into his blood. He roved his hands along her back, couldn't have enough of her warmth, and when he encountered her buttocks, he cupped them, his fingers glancing between her thighs to brush at the blonde curls.

A surprised moan escaped her throat. The innocent sound drove him onward as he strove to beat back the demons inside. She was the answer to his nightmare, but she was also another way his life would unravel. Over and over he kissed her in the hopes that he could forget all that he was if he buried himself in her honeyed heat. As he gripped her hips so hard, he feared he'd leave bruises, and that only added to the surging anger.

Of course he would hurt her. That's all he was capable of doing. *You're going to ruin this woman, use her as kindling for your ill-temper, and then what?* The damned anxiety mocked him, threw the question around in his head until it bounced like soap bubbles. *Take her by force like a savage?*

"Sarah..." Why couldn't he say it? Why couldn't he ask for her help? Something deep down in his soul called out to her, but the words wouldn't leave his tongue.

"Yes?" She put her palms on either side of his face and looked into his eyes.

Suddenly terrified of what she'd find, he growled and then half-carried, half-walked her toward the bed. When it connected with her backside and prevented further movement, he kissed her again. She couldn't know how far gone he was, how close to falling apart he was, not now. Fear cooled his blood. Would he lose her following this night or would she grant him one last chance?

"Please forgive me," he managed to whisper through a tight throat.

"For what?"

With shaking hands, he fumbled at his frontfalls. Barely did he give her time to glance at his hardened length before he spun her about so that she faced the bed. "I..." Hell with it. He couldn't talk, concentrate on bedding her, and keep his anger in check at the same time.

She's your wife now, so put a babe in her belly and be done with her. Then you can hide away and sulk.

In the end, rage and anxiety won. It always did. He'd never had a chance. With a knee between her thighs, he widened her stance. "Bear down. The first time will hurt." God, she'd hate him, and he didn't blame her. At least this way he wouldn't see the disgust and loathing that would be in her expressive eyes.

"Andrew?" She glanced backward. "Tell me what's wrong. Let me help, talk to you."

"It's too late." He swallowed. "Do you want me, Sarah?" He was many things, but he wouldn't rape his own wife. "Do you want me to couple with you?"

"Yes, I do, but this isn't the way I thought we'd do it."

"It'll be over soon." He fit the head of his shaft to her opening and with a flex of his hips, he penetrated her as deep as he could go, tearing through the slight resistance of her maidenhood and burying himself to the hilt.

A cry of pain issued from her, but he was too far gone to care about going slow. With every stroke, he held onto her hips and despised himself. She clutched the bedding in her fists as her body trembled in his hands. Her innocence and inexperience left her vulnerable, but she wriggled her backside against him, which only inflamed his unchecked desire. Faster and faster he moved, pounding in and out. His breathing, already compromised by the enormous strain he carried, labored even more, his lungs aching, and just as he'd said, need tingled through his stones. A tiny moan escaped her, followed by a sob. Those little noises broke him. The force of his release raced through his length and as he pulsed out his seed, he ground himself against her.

God, I'm a prick and a black hearted tyrant.

And he'd failed at bedding his wife the first time out.

Several silent moments went by as he lay collapsed against her back, and when he moved away, the quiet was punctuated by the sound of her crying. "Sarah? Are you all right?" When he went to touch her shoulder, she heaved upright and turned on him so fast, he gaped.

"You bastard." Tears fell unchecked. She lifted a hand and slapped him so hard, he was certain he wouldn't soon forget it. Angry red color mottled her chest and cheeks. Humiliation clouded her eyes behind her smudged spectacles. "How dare you." Emotion graveled her voice. "You treated me little better than you would a whore, and you have the gall to ask after my health?" She darted around him, casting about the floor for her robe. When she snagged it, she shoved her arms through the sleeves. "Have you nothing to say for yourself?"

Drew's lower jaw worked. He tried to make his lips form words, but nothing would come, for he couldn't deny her claims.

"Bloody arrogant prig. No woman should have to suffer through what I just did. Especially not on her wedding night." Sarah swept to the door and then looked over her shoulder at him. "Until you can figure out why this entire night was wrong, until you can apologize to me with some semblance of intelligence, until you're ready to become a better man, I want nothing to do with you." She opened the door. Seconds later it slammed behind her. The answering crash of her door put the final nail into the proverbial coffin of his married life.

Not even wed twenty-four hours and he'd already torn it apart.

He sank to his knees with his head in his hands. *I can't go on like this, but who will save me now that I've turned Sarah against me?*

CHAPTER TWELVE

SARAH MADE CERTAIN to lock her door before she leaned her back against the heavy oak panel, covered her face in her hands, and sobbed out her angst so hard her whole body heaved. What the hell was wrong with him? Through her tears, she glanced about the room, but thankfully, she was alone. The maid who'd been assigned to her wasn't in attendance, for she—like everyone else no doubt in the house—would have assumed she'd spend the wedding night out of this suite.

When had anything ever gone the way she wished?

It had been wicked and this side of sinful to let a man she barely knew do such... things to her, but oh, he had a certain skill. Too bad the act had gone so fast and had been so shameful. He'd humiliated her! The earl had treated her like a prostitute, hadn't bothered to take her virginity with any sort of gallantry or tenderness, never took the time to initiate her into intercourse so she wouldn't have felt like such a green girl. If that was what relations between them would be going forward, she wanted no part of it.

"You can pluck an heir out of the damn garden for all I care!" she yelled into the silence of her room. The light from a guttering candle on the nightstand sent anemic light through the darkened room. "I will *not* be disrespected by my husband again. Do you hear that, Andrew?"

She hoped that he did. Tears continued to roll down her cheeks.

Annoyed, she perched her spectacles on the top of her head and scrubbed at her cheeks. How unfortunate it was that when she was beyond incensed, she cried, for no doubt the earl thought he'd hurt her feelings when in reality she'd been enraged beyond all coherence. It had always been a flaw and something she was acutely aware of when people who hadn't the sense God gave a goose talked down to her or embarrassed her, which her husband had done in spades.

If he couldn't gain control of himself and stop bottling his emotions to the point that he was a slave to anxiety, she was done, completely done, with him.

Yet she'd married him and had pledged to help him if she could. Were his problems—demons as he'd called them—beyond his ability to conquer?

I've been foolish. She'd known better. Of course she had, but here she was, shaking with rage and humiliation because he'd bedded her in a way she hadn't considered nor been prepared for. Hot saliva filled her mouth, and she swallowed several times to stave off the urge to retch.

"This was a horrible mistake," she whispered into the quiet.

Oh, dear Lord. Sarah bolted over the floor. She fumbled about in the cupboard beneath the nightstand for the chamber pot and barely grasped it in time to catch the contents of her stomach as she cast up her accounts. Andrew had used her for his own pleasure and devices, hadn't given her the respect she deserved, and he callously took want he wanted in a way that an untried woman should never be shown, especially on her first bedding.

Sarah's sobs continued unchecked. It was obvious he didn't have the basic decency or compassion to make the night special. Did he even care, or had she been a means to an end all along? No doubt he did, for wasn't it her idea to keep everything between them a business arrangement? Another bout of retching followed. Regardless that she might want a friendship from the earl, none of that was possible right now, not when he was essentially lost and hurting.

Her stomach heaved again, and she spat into the porcelain recep-
tacle. When her insides quieted, Sarah replaced the pot into the
cabinet and then wiped her streaming eyes. Her body shook from
reaction, her muscles ached from misuse, and the glide of the pretty
wrapper she'd bought scraped against her still-sensitized nipples. She
recalled his hands on her body—too fleeting and rough for her to
properly enjoy the attention, and she shivered, both from emotion and
a need she didn't fully understand.

But he'd been a cad, acted like the beast he thought he was, and
he'd torn her delicate nightgown without uttering a compliment about
it. Damn him. She'd been so proud of that purchase, bought the finery
with the remainder of her pittance to mark the momentous night, and
he'd crushed the whole experience beneath his heel as if none of it
mattered.

As if *she* didn't.

Another round of tears fell, and Sarah let them. She deserved to
vent her disappointment and perhaps disillusionment. In a fit of pique,
she took off her robe, wadded it up, and hurled it onto the foot of the
bed. Bloody ego for wanting to rig herself out for that man. Shaking
her head, she marched to the wash table in the corner of the room.

"If he wants a countess and that's all, then that's what he'll have.
And an ice queen at that." After pouring water into the bowl, she
wetted a rag and cleaned the stickiness from between her legs. A trace
of blood came way on the rag, and she sobbed again, this time for
something she'd given that went unappreciated by the Neanderthal
down the hall.

Fumbling for her spectacles, Sarah wrenched them from the top of
her head. The curved ends of the arms tangled in her hair and she
cursed as she pulled the eyewear from her tresses. After popping them
onto the bridge of her nose, she inspected her hips where he'd gripped
her. Sure enough, bruises in the shape of his fingers were beginning to

form purple smudges. "Arse." Once she'd tossed the soiled rag into the bowl, she moved into the adjoining dressing room. When yanked open a drawer from the bottom portion of the clothes press, she snagged the old familiar and worn night shift she'd always donned for the last few years. With a sigh, she struggled into the garment, and when she blinked, another shower of tears fell to her cheeks.

"How stupid I was to think that this new life would start off with a bit of hope."

As much as Sarah would have liked to relieve hurt feelings and aggravation by throwing something, she was too smart and thrifty to break the new silver vanity set he'd left in her room, or the cheval glass that even now reflected her tear-stained face. She'd never owned such expensive things. Instead, she settled for returning to the bedchamber where she grabbed a pillow from the bed. Then she buried her face in the heavy goose down mass and screamed into the soft barrier.

A few minutes later, when her ire was spent, she tossed the pillow back onto the bed and followed it down, collapsing into the cool, soft sheets. "I meant what I said, Andrew," she whispered and then blew out the candle. As darkness accumulated in the room, she pulled the covers up to her chin. "I won't see you again until you apologize and commit to change. This is a partnership, and I can't do it alone." She removed her spectacles and rested them on the bedside table.

Devil take him anyway for making her think there might have been a chance at happiness between them when they'd talked that day in the meadow.

Lies, all lies. She sniffled. And stupidity on her part.

OH, SARAH HATED him all right. There was no doubt about that. Drew's cheek stung from that slap, and he'd deserved it. His ears were blistered from her parting words, but damn if the humiliation on her face and the fury in her eyes would haunt his every moment. The slam of her door resonated through the quiet of the manor.

What the hell is wrong with me?

What he'd done was unforgivable. Of course, it was, and he'd known it but did it anyway. He shoved a hand through his hair. Each breath he drew sent pain ricocheting through his impossibly tight chest. Had he harmed her physically? Oh, God, had that incident damaged her mentally, left her in fear of what carnal relations could be? So lost to anger and his own bloody lust as he'd been, he hadn't given consideration to what she might have been thinking or feeling.

With a growl, he stood. Why was he so terrified if anything good came into his life? Stumbling over to the nightstand, Drew picked up the water decanter and then hurled it against the door. Crystal and water exploded, rained down onto the floor. Sarah had been a damned virgin, and he'd taken that innocence without finesse or gentleness. He hadn't cared about anything except getting his rocks off, like a savage beast rutting in the woods.

Then he'd shoved her away so he couldn't begin to care for her.

Or she for him.

There'd been no respect given on his part, no affection, no time taken to bring her to arousal. Hell, he'd not even seen to her release, that's how much of a black-hearted cad he was. As much as he'd like to blame his lack of emotional control, he couldn't. This horrid episode rested firmly upon his shoulders. He was at fault, and he deserved her wrath.

I must apologize for my behavior.

While hastily stuffing his flaccid shaft into his breeches, he did up the buttons of his frontfalls as he moved to the door, sloppily dodging the broken crystal on the floor. Grasping the latch, he wrenched open the panel and then strode into the corridor beyond. Halfway down the hall, the sound of her soul-deep sobs reached his ears. Hot guilt collided with white-hot anger to twist with the mocking anxiety in his chest, tightening, squeezing, pressing until he could scarcely breathe. Approaching his fury-filled wife now would end in folly, and she'd probably throw something at his head.

With good reason.

Still, his heartbeat thudded fast. He wanted to see her, was prepared to grovel at her feet if necessary if only she'd reassure him that she hadn't made a mistake in marrying. Softly padding along the corridor, Drew paused at her door. From the other side, the sobs cut through his chest with all the accuracy of a sharp knife. He laid a hand on the wood panel, and to his mortification, moisture welled in his eyes.

I did that. I made her cry, undoubtedly hurt her, and broke her trust.

For the first time in his adult existence, he realized that what he said, what he did had consequences beyond the usual hurt he caused. What the ramifications of this action would be, he couldn't say, but terror froze his heart at the thought of her leaving Derbyshire after being wedded for less than a day.

How the deuce can I fix this without losing face?

Perhaps he couldn't, and that was the problem. Sooner or later, he'd need to set his ego, his pride aside and dirty his hands while taking a good, hard look at himself. For the moment, there was no recourse. Blinking until the tears cleared from his eyes, he turned and, gasping for breath, stumbled back down the hall to his room. Once inside, he slammed the door, his body shaking as guilt and regret joined the seething mix in his person.

"I deserve her ire and her loathing," he told his room at large. "I'm truly a prick." The admission did nothing to alleviate the churning tide within him, and he let it rage.

The candleholder followed the fate of the water decanter. Soon the acrid scent of candle smoke filled the room, but his rage wasn't spent.

Drew tore the curtains from around the bed, pulled the counterpane off and threw it about, took his pillows and ripped them open. Goose down feathers showered the bed and the floor, floated into the air. With a cry of rage and desolation, he shoved the mattress to the floor, and when he couldn't draw enough breath to remain upright any longer, he collapsed onto it and covered his face with his hands.

Too late he'd realized that he'd had the hope of Sarah in his life as well as the calm that she could bring, but now that dream dangled farther and farther away, left him floundering in the nightmare he constantly battled. The chance to woo or even win her if he were of a mind had been in his hand, but he'd tossed it away like so much rubbish. Beyond that, how could he push aside the demons that haunted him in order to become the man he needed to be?

There had to be more to life than the endless struggle, the always allowing anger to guide him, to drive him into hiding.

"Why can I not find balance and control over these feelings?" The silence of the room mocked him in the absence of an answer.

Damn this title that has cursed my life.

The chime that proclaimed the midnight hour from the longcase clock drifted to his ears, but Drew didn't stir; he couldn't. No, it wasn't the fault of the title that had torn up his life. He had done that himself, for he was broken and didn't know how to heal. Anxiety held him frozen while fear punched him repeatedly in the gut.

"I'm going to lose her before I've won her." But didn't he want that over everything?

Again, the dratted moisture welled in his eyes. At least if he were to cry, no one would see him. God, what would his father say? No doubt he'd lecture and say how disappointed that he was. *I never could please the man.* Black spots flirted with his vision... not that he could discern that darkness from the inky blackness currently filling the room. He labored to breathe, his lungs aching, his chest weighted, his throat tight and choked with unshed tears as well as emotions he dare not utter aloud. *Please, Sarah, forgive me.*

Then his pride slammed to the forefront. Why should he feel bad? He'd bedded her as he'd said, as the betrothal contract demanded.

What did it matter how he'd accomplished the task?

The sound of his wheezing, struggling breaths rasped loudly in the quiet. She deserved better and he knew it. No woman should have been treated to the display he gave tonight.

Pounding started in his head. He pressed his brow to the mattress and cursed himself into oblivion. Silently, he cried, stopped short at sobbing for everything he'd lost in his life due to his crushing emotions.

When he raised his head, his gaze landed on a hint of feminine, lace-edged fabric that peeked out from under the bedding's destruction. Drew snagged it in his fingers and pulled it toward him. Sarah's nightgown, the one he'd torn in his haste to bury himself in her heat. As he brought the fabric to his nose, her lingering clover and violet scent assailed him. Once more, his chest squeezed so hard, he nearly lost consciousness.

Sagging back into the mattress with the delicate finery clutched in his hand, he struggled to draw breath. He had to beat this; he had to remain alive, for there were some things in life that had the potential to be... more.

If he could, he would find a way to make things right between him and Sarah.

Or die trying.

CHAPTER THIRTEEN

July 3, 1817

S ARAH GLANCED AT the ormolu clock on the mantle of her sitting room. Half past eight in the evening. Dinner would be served soon, and no doubt she'd take the meal alone. She'd been a married woman for a week but hadn't seen her husband since their disastrous wedding night.

Though her anger with Andrew had long faded, she hadn't sought him out, neither had she actively avoided him. He was either out of pocket or keeping to his rooms, for she hadn't come upon him during meals or while wandering the corridors. Even walking the grounds hadn't produced him.

No doubt he assumed he wasn't in the wrong. Muscles in her stomach knotted. She pushed her spectacles onto the bridge of her nose. Or had the mysterious attacks he suffered gotten the better of him? Was he even now in need of medical attention but pride kept him from asking for help? Yes, she wanted to talk with him. If he were suffering, she wished to assist him, for she couldn't stand to see anything in pain.

Perhaps that makes me doubly foolish or stupidly hopeful. However, it wasn't in her nature to avoid confrontation or live her life in frosty silence.

No sooner had she settled into her novel than a soft knock sounded on the sitting room door. Sarah's heart skipped a beat. Had her husband finally come to his senses? She stood and laid her book on the chair. The silk of her gown whispered about her legs. During the week, she'd had a whole new wardrobe ordered, and this frock had been delivered earlier in the day. The bright coral bodice, trimmed with delicate lace, with an ivory and coral striped skirt had rapidly become a favorite. The lace on the hem made her feel deliciously decadent. At least if the earl were absent, she could look the part of a composed countess.

When she swung open the door, instead of Andrew, her gaze fell upon Barton, his valet. Cold concern coiled through her insides. "What is amiss?" For he wouldn't have come to her if the earl were well.

"You are as intelligent and forthright as he said." A faint grin touched the man's lips. "The earl is having a fit."

Sarah snorted. Her eyewear slipped down her nose. "When is he not?" Then she sobered. "Though I'm sad to hear he remains in a temper." That disappointment snagged in her chest. It meant he hadn't learned anything.

I had hoped—

"No, my lady." The valet shifted his weight from foot to foot. "He's suffering a mental break, I fear. As the week progressed, he's grown worse. Since he wed, the earl hasn't been himself." He met her gaze, speculation bright in his. "It's different from what he usually has." Concern rode heavy in his hushed tones.

Oh, dear. His anxiety was besting him. A tremor of unease pushed down her spine. She shoved her spectacles back into place. "Where is he?"

"At the moment, I'm not certain." Barton shrugged. "A half hour past, he had been in his rooms. Rarely has he left his rooms this week, but my worry hit the breaking point when he went unconscious not long before he disappeared. When he came to, I told him I intended to fetch you. The earl became agitated. He fled."

That didn't bode well. Sarah's compassion flared as well as her concern. "Did he go riding?"

"He wasn't dressed for it, so I assume not."

"Is there somewhere on the estate that might be special or meaningful to him? Somewhere he might hide himself away from others? Perhaps to think?"

Barton cocked his head to the side. Strain lined his forehead. "When the earl was a younger man and his family annoyed him, he enjoyed his mother's roses found at the center of the hedge maze. It's on the south lawn."

Though Sarah wasn't familiar with the feature, she nodded. "It'll be dark soon." She bit briefly on her bottom lip and brought up a hand to clutch her ever-present locket. "Have you been inside the maze?" In her time at Hadleigh Hall, she'd not had an opportunity to explore it, for she would dread becoming lost and needing to rely upon Andrew to rescue her.

"Vaguely. It's been a few years, but I think I remember the turns well enough to see you through." The valet cleared his throat and straightened his spine. "That is, if you wish to go after him."

Did she? It was one thing to be married to him, but quite another to summon enough patience and fortitude to stick with him for as long as it took until he healed.

If at all.

"Is he in a bad state?" No longer did she wish to argue with her husband. It simply made him more stubborn, but if his mind were truly plagued and his life would soon be forfeit, she had to try and bring him back. Not only for his sake, but for their marriage. Regardless that he had a tendency to act like an arse and his temper was horrid, she rather liked the man he was when not struggling with his problems.

Barton nodded. Fear flickered over his face. "It's worse than any of his previous attacks, my lady."

Sarah nodded. "He needs help."

"Desperately." The valet rubbed a hand along the side of his face. "I fear we might lose him if nothing is done soon." His voice wavered and he cleared his throat. "I'd rather not see my friend fall to his own thoughts."

"I feel the same." She heaved a sigh. "I shall go after him. Please write down the instructions for the maze while I find a wrap and my slippers."

Relief rolled through the man's eyes. "At once, my lady. And thank you."

"You are most welcome." Finally, she had a chance to be of use to someone. The life of leisure was grand for a day or two. After that, she'd grown bored and wished for a purpose.

Barton stepped away from the door but paused. "And, Countess?"

"Yes?"

"The earl is a good man deep down beneath his current... difficulties. He merely needs to believe it for himself." Then he strode down the hall, presumably to find paper and pen.

Oh, Andrew, what is happening to you? Sarah pondered his mental state while she slipped her feet into a pair of coral stain slippers. The golden embroidery winked in the candlelight. Afterward, she retrieved a lightweight ivory shawl. How far gone was the earl, exactly, and could anything bring him back? By the time she'd thrown the garment about her shoulders, Barton had returned.

He stood at the open door with a scrap of paper in one hand and a frothy garment of moss green in the other. As she eyed it, he offered it to her. "This belongs to you."

Wordlessly, she fingered her nightgown—the one she'd worn on her wedding night. "I feared he would have tossed it out for rubbish. Or burned it."

"The earl mended it, my lady."

By rote, she gave her spectacles a shove. "Please thank the maid who did so."

Barton shook his head. "There was no maid. The earl did it himself, my lady. Asked me for needle and thread days ago. Horrible stitching, but he wished to make the repair himself."

"Oh." She inspected the delicate gown, saw the rudimentary work, ran her fingers over the basic stiches. "I don't know what to say." Tears welled in her eyes. "Why would he do this?" He certainly had no skill in handiwork, but the fact he'd tried sent a tremble into her heart.

"Who can say, but I'll wager he wanted to try and make amends with you even if he couldn't find the words." Barton gave her the scrap of paper. "Here are the directions as best as I can recall."

"Thank you." Sarah moved into the room and placed the nightwear on the bed. "Would you like to accompany me, Barton?"

"Oh, no." He shook his head. "I suspect you're the one to retrieve him."

"If he's unconscious, I can't carry him." Or if she found him dead, if his anxiety had driven him to take his own life... well, she refused to finish that thought.

"Come and find me at that point, but I don't want to interfere in what needs repaired between the two of you." He flashed her a knowing glance. "Now is as good a time as any."

Heat jumped into her cheeks. Was it obvious to the household? "Very well. I'll see what can be done." Disinclined to linger for more probing conversation, she swept past him and moved down the corridor as her mind spun with horrible possibilities. The valet had no evidence that Andrew wished to make amends, but perhaps there was a chance regardless.

Was there anything more Gothic than moving through a hedge maze with trailing skirts and lace on one's gown? The sun had begun its descent, but soon twilight would blanket the area. Even with

Barton's instructions, she made a few false turns and was obliged to backtrack. When she gained the center, the heavy, cloying scent of roses met her nose. That coupled with the more pungent aroma of the evergreen hedges and the soft buzz of night insects coming awake gave the area the feel of a romantic tryst.

This mission was anything but.

An arc of rose bushes sheltered a black, wrought iron bench. Pink, yellow, red, and white buds dotted the dark greenery. Some had bloomed, beckoning her forward. The soles of her slippers crunched against the gravel path as she slowly approached. The earl kneeled before the bench, his body crumpled, his head resting on his crossed arms on the seat.

Her heart skipped a beat. From the state of his clothing, it was clear he hadn't cared about his appearance or personal hygiene in the week since they'd been apart. Stained buff-colored breeches, a loose-fitting lawn shirt that billowed in the slight breeze, scuffed boots made up his toilet. His hair stuck up in all directions, and when she came closer, the whiskers clinging to his chin and cheeks spoke of the fact he hadn't shaved for days. Every breath he took was accompanied by a horrible gasping sound as if he struggled to keep his lungs moving.

"Andrew? Are you quite well?"

His broad shoulders twitched. "For the love of God, Sarah, go away." He sucked in a breath. "Before I hurt you more than I already have." He never glanced at her.

Her chest ached with empathy. This was not the man she'd first encountered. Oh, no. This man was beaten and broken beyond the norm. "I think *you* are the one hurting." It was time to delve into the heart of his issues. She kept her voice soft and level as she approached. The last thing she wanted was for him to bolt.

"Yes." The one-word answer sounded forced. "Leave me and let me die in peace."

"I'd rather you find peace and live instead."

A terrible wheezing issued from him. Did he attempt a laugh? "I can't breathe."

"I don't doubt it, for you've let your feelings about everything in your life build up inside you for far too long." There was nothing for it. She'd have to take the matter into her own hands. Sarah reached the bench and perched on the edge, so near to him the heat from his body transferred to her. "The only way to purge those emotions and ease the anxiety is to allow yourself to feel them."

"I can't." His shoulders jerked and he pressed a hand to his chest.

"You must." At the last second, she stopped herself from touching him. "You need to allow yourself to grieve, to feel, to acknowledge what has happened, to talk about it. Above all, you must understand that all of it, except what you did in anger, was not your fault." The last was a guess, but knowing him, he'd tried to assume responsibility for everyone. If allowed to continue, it would indeed kill him.

A ragged scoff escaped him, but he didn't look at her. "I don't *need* to feel anything," he gasped out, yet there was enough of the arrogant earl in that statement to indicate he wouldn't soon expire. "Father always said that showing emotion made a man weak and vulnerable." His shoulders shook.

Oh, drat. There was much to do. "Your father isn't here any longer."

"Don't you think I know that?" he snapped with a growl.

Sarah inhaled and then exhaled in an effort to keep her own temper in check. "Why do you fear his censure?"

"This horrible burden started the day he left me." Finally, he lifted his head, and she gasped. In the fading light, his stormy eyes were clouded with so many emotions she couldn't discern just one. "Yet he lingers like a specter, judging."

It was worse than she could have imagined. Her gaze dropped to his throat. He didn't wear a collar or cravat. His shirt's placket gaped open. Tufts of dark hair peeked out. The strong column of his neck took all her attention, and she pressed her lips together to tamp the urge to sigh. She'd barely had a look at that same neck the other night, but he'd not bothered to unclothe himself before he'd bedded her. Shoving aside her wayward thoughts, she shook her head.

"You might as well dig deep and have it out. We are *not* leaving this maze until you make progress into being a better person."

"I can't." Faint purple smudges beneath his eyes spoke of his inability to sleep.

"No, you don't *want* to. This is no time to cling to your stubborn pride." Daring much, Sarah briefly cupped his cheek. Since she'd left the house rather quickly, she'd neglected to bring gloves, and the prickles of his stubble tickled her palm, left her with a rising rush of awareness for him. "Haven't you carried this weight for too long?"

"Yes, yet—"

"You're naught but an arse if you continue to let the worries keep you prisoner." Those words might prompt him into action.

Anger creased his features. He jerked away from her touch. "What do you know of it?"

"Enough that had you bothered to ask, I would have told you a week ago." She wrapped a hand around her locket. "I went through some of the same emotions when my parents died. I felt hopeless, helpless, frightened. I was alone."

He eyed her with suspicion. "How did you come out on the other side?" He clenched his fingers in the fabric of his shirt, his knuckles white.

"I didn't let them control me. I decided that despite the gaping hole their loss left in my life, there was more living yet to do. That I had much to give." She met his gaze. "I didn't run away or stuff everything deep down inside me to fester like an infected wound."

"But I don't—"

"You do." She sat back and stared at him. "Each time something new happens that shakes the foundations of your world, you bear the responsibility, and that anxiety is giving you these attacks. When that happens, you have no more room in your mind, your body, to hold on. Let some of it go, Andrew, else you'll soon join your father, and I..." She sighed again and pushed her spectacles back into place. "I'd rather keep you in the land of the living for a while yet."

"Why?" A terrible gasping sound followed. "You and I don't get on well."

She smiled, but it was small and tight. "Whose fault is that? Perhaps I'd like to see if any of that can change."

Silence reigned for long moments, marked by the steady thud of her heartbeat. Then a wordless cry escaped him. He shifted his weight, buried his face in her lap, one hand twisting in the skirting, and he sobbed. Great gulping things that pulled at her heart and sent tears into her own eyes.

With nothing else to do, Sarah finger-combed his hair, stroked her hand through the tangled, dirty mass in the hopes of soothing him. "Tell me about your father. What is your best memory with him?"

"I was perhaps twelve. That summer we came out to Hadleigh Hall. Finn was nine and Brand was six, hardly more than a baby, but Father decided it was time we learned how to fish." The words were muffled by her skirts and halting as he struggled to breathe properly. "There's a pond to the north on the acreage. We all marched out there. Father had a line in the water. I was impatient back then."

"You still are," she murmured and continued to stroke his hair.

"I tried and tried to get a fish, but I never did."

"What did your father do?"

"Chuckled and taught us how to skip rocks."

"I'll wager you weren't pleased."

"I didn't want to do it if the fish weren't going to cooperate, but Father said there was more to fishing than catching something on your hook." Andrew turned his head and rested his cheek on her leg. "I always wondered what he meant. Now I suspect it was his way of escaping from the stresses of the title and trying to find calm."

She caught her breath. This was an opportunity to go deeper with him. "What do you make of that, if it's true?"

"I wonder if he struggled too," he responded in a small voice.

"Of course he did." Sarah continued to stroke his head. "Don't you think all men who hold titles, who wish to make a go of it instead of being wastrels, constantly fight between duty and having time for themselves?" She brushed her fingertips along the side of his face. "Why do you think powerful men ride and hunt and fish when they come to their country homes? It's to relieve some of that tension."

He shrugged and wrapped his free arm around her lower legs. Tingles danced up her limbs from the point of contact. "I wish I could go back."

"To see your father one last time?" She often thought that might be pleasant too, but there was no sense in torturing herself.

"No, so I could be the man I was then, without knowing what life held for me." Such desolation hung in his voice that she swallowed down tears once more.

"Did you father not prepare you for this eventuality?"

Another ragged breath escaped, and he gasped as if he couldn't fill his lungs. "In some ways, yes, but in others, I feel…"

"Yes?" Her heartbeat accelerated. He was finally opening up.

"I feel as if I've been tossed to the wolves." Again, he sobbed, and the force of it shook his body as he clung to her.

Sarah pushed her spectacles into place. She blinked to clear away the moisture from her eyes. In many ways, he was a broken and lost young man missing his father, looking for direction and approval, but when he found none, he didn't know how to conduct himself. "You can never return to the man you were before your father died. That life is gone, but there's no reason you can't enjoy what this life holds."

"How can I when I'm failing on every front?" He lifted his head and stared at her. In the purple shadows of twilight, tears ravaged his cheeks and fear haunted the stormy depths of his eyes. Had he not eaten much during the last week? His face seemed a bit leaner. "I hurt everything I touch, am responsible for too much. Everyone would be better off if I weren't around, except Finn can't—" He gasped and clutched at his chest. "Oh, God."

"Breathe, Andrew. Don't listen to the lies anxiety tells you." She covered his hand that rested on her thigh with hers. "I refuse to let my husband give up the ghost before his time."

He shook his head. "I've failed you."

Yes, he had, but at least he recognized that.

"It's a natural course in anyone's life. You'll fail as the earl, as a husband, as a man. We all do, but that's part of being alive." She squeezed his fingers. "However, you'll also have the strength to push through those bad days. You'll learn how to do what you must in order to do what you want." A smile curved her lips. "You'll find your path and eventually, you'll also find joy, because that's never gone away. You've merely lost sight of it for a time."

"Bah." He pulled his hand away. "How can I find any joy?" The hand on his chest tightened. "I've been the Earl of Hadleigh for over two years, and I'm failing."

"But you've been you for forty. Isn't that cause for a good day or two?" She hadn't meant it to sound flippant, but it did, and when he scowled, she merely smiled. "It can't all have been bad."

"Perhaps not." One corner of his mouth quirked but he didn't give into a grin.

It would take baby steps with this one.

"Have you wished to succeed as the earl? Have you tried or did you give yourself over to bitterness from the outset?"

"Have you always been so domineering?"

She snorted. "Only when dealing with the stubborn ox of my husband."

"Ah." He did grin then, but only for a second. It was a start. "To answer your question, I did try a few times. When those attempts didn't yield results, I let bitterness have at it."

"And that's when anxiety came to call. Yes?" At least he was being honest.

"I'm responsible for... everything now." He rubbed his chest. "The estate, the tenants, my mother, my brothers, their lives... you." His breath quickened and he once more lapsed into gasping struggles. "I'm failing and everyone hates me for it."

"Listen to me. That is anxiety talking." Sarah leaned forward and held his head between her palms. She forced him to meet her gaze. "No one, not me, not your mother, not your brothers, wants you to make yourself sick with worry about us. We're all quite capable of living without your dictates." She lifted an eyebrow. "The one thing you can do is your best today. Then do a little better tomorrow. And continue to improve by increments with each following day. You needn't succeed in all of it at once. No one can."

"I'm afraid."

"Of what? Failing? That's how we learn."

"Not just of that." His jaw worked. He laid one hand against hers. "I'm alone with no guidance."

"You are *not* alone." She kept her voice low and even. "But if you keep pushing those who are close to you away, you will be."

"I don't want to hurt them... hurt you." In the last of the light, she caught the stark honesty shining in his eyes.

Her chest constricted. "You won't, but find an outlet for your anger and other emotions. We can only remain patient and forgiving for so long, but you *must* change."

"If they abandon me, what will happen to me?"

Ah, here was the crux of the issue. "You're afraid of being alone." How simple life was when boiled down to the truth.

"Yes." He clutched her hands, pulled them away from his head and rested them in her lap. "Please don't leave me, Sarah. I know I'm not worthy of you, but—"

"Shh." Another round of tears sprang into her eyes. "I promise I won't, only if you promise that you'll walk out of this maze determined to change. I meant what I said before I married you. I refuse to live with a violent man."

It all rested with him.

"What if I try to change but fail in that? It terrifies me to wonder what will become of my life if…"

"We're *all* afraid. The trick is to continue regardless. In that you'll find the courage you need to survive."

"I doubt that you're ever afraid."

"Oh no?" A laugh escaped before she could recall it. "Every day is new for me. I have no blessed clue how to be a countess."

"I made you do this," he whispered brokenly and bowed his head over their entwined hands. He gasped for breath.

"Breathe, Andrew. Concentrate on your surroundings. Listen to the sounds of the night, ground yourself into the world, and breathe." When he did as instructed for the space of a few heartbeats, she nodded. "I'm responsible for my own choices, like everyone is with theirs. But if you'll let me, I'll work with you and ease some of your strain."

"After everything, you'll choose to stay with me?"

Would she? When she walked into the maze, she wasn't certain. Now she was. She would fight for the soul of this Storme, even when he couldn't see his own worth. "Flaws and all, I'll remain by your side because I believe you're capable of great things."

He met her gaze. Moisture clung to his dark lashes. His hands shook. "I'm so incredibly sorry for the debacle of our wedding night. It wasn't well done of me and—"

A piece of her heart flew into his keeping. "It's in the past. We both weren't ready." With those words, his expression lightened. "Tonight, your new life starts. Don't waste the second chance."

"I won't." Andrew surged to his feet, pulled her up with him, and then took her into a loose embrace. "You have my word, if that means anything." He fit his lips to hers, kissing her so tenderly that she had tears in her eyes by its end.

"Oh, goodness," she managed to whisper as heat jumped into her cheeks. Awareness of him danced over her skin. When she caught a whiff of his pungent scent, she wrinkled her nose. "You stink."

"I've rather let myself go this week." His laugh sounded rusty, but it was there, nonetheless. "When we go back, I'll bathe. Barton's been beside himself looking after me." He took a shuddering breath, but this time he didn't struggle. "Will you play your flute for me again? It helps."

"Of course I will." She rested her palms against his chest.

"Thank God." He kissed her again with more insistence, his mouth moving over hers with an expertise and promise that made her head spin and tingles begin between her thighs. No, despite everything, the attraction hadn't faded.

Much more of this and she'd be lost. It was too early in their conversation to do that, but oh, those kisses were quite delicious and different from how he treated her a week ago! Before they could progress into something more wicked, she pulled away and smiled at his protest.

"Trust must be repaired and rebuilt before we move forward into that quarter."

"But I thought we—"

"Patience, Andrew. Court me, then we'll revisit our physical relationship. Your actions will tell more than words."

And it would give her time to decide if he truly meant to change.

CHAPTER FOURTEEN

July 10, 1817

D REW SLAPPED HIS evening gloves against his thigh as he turned this way and that in front of the cheval glass. Was the ruby pin in his cravat visible enough? Did it matter any longer? After the talk he'd had with Sarah a week ago, some of the pent-up rage had lessened, but he hadn't told her all his secrets, all his worries. Should he keep wearing the ruby regardless?

A soft clearing of a masculine throat yanked him from his musings. Barton stood behind him. "You must leave now to arrive on time, my lord."

"Almost ready." He tugged on the hem of his gold brocade waistcoat. Pearl buttons set in gold winked in the candlelight. Would Sarah like it? The garment had reposed in the back of his wardrobe for a few years, but Barton had finally convinced him to take a chance on wearing the elegant color instead of his usual black or gray.

The valet handed him a worn, flat leather box. "You have done well this week from all accounts. Only two attacks. How are you feeling this evening?"

How indeed? The past week had been nothing short of... eye opening. He and Sarah had come to an understanding the night of his mental break, but she hadn't judged him. They'd begun their introduction and relationship again, and he had taken her words to heart. Each day brought its own struggles, but he'd found if he tackled it by pieces instead of attempting to swallow it in large chunks, he was more apt to control his temper as well as his anxiety.

"I rather think the path I'm on will last."

At least, he hoped. Where it would lead, he didn't yet know, but he was slowly learning to enjoy each day of the journey.

"Good." Barton grinned, and it struck Drew that his friend had done that precious little of late. "That makes me happy to hear."

It felt… nice to know that there were more people who cared about him than despised him. "Me, too." Though he'd been solicitous and charming, and had spent copious amounts of time with Sarah, they hadn't returned to physical relations.

Hell, he hadn't tried to kiss her for fear he'd muck up the easy peace he'd suddenly found. Passing the time by taking dinner together, sharing the library for hours on end, taking long walks about the estate, or meeting with tenants and hearing about problems had gone well. No longer did it feel like an impossible task to assume the responsibilities of the earl.

But only if Sarah were with him.

Sometimes in the evening she'd play her flute for him, ask his opinion on different pieces or her playing style. He lived for those moments, for that was when he could forget all that he had to be and could work at being who he *needed* to be. There was a certain amount of freedom in that knowledge.

The few times he met with his estate foreman or dealt with correspondence from London, he suffered attacks of the crushing anxiety. But he practiced grounding himself to the moment like she'd told him, and they actually ended instead of rendering him unconscious.

Meeting and marrying Sarah had become his lifeline.

Belatedly, he held up the leather box in the same hand with his gloves. "I should collect the countess."

"Indeed." Barton nodded. "When you suffered your break, she was quite concerned about you. I would even go so far as to say she refused to give up on you."

A trace of irritation went through him, but Drew tamped the urge to give it attention. Not everything needed a reaction. That he was also beginning to learn. "As much as I'd like to say she needn't worry, I'm not certain what would have happened to me if she hadn't come that night." He'd been at the end of his patience, and if there had been something in that rose arbor that could have assisted in killing him, no doubt he would have utilized it.

Perhaps he was growing as a person now, thanks to her.

The valet met his gaze with a knowing light in his eye. "I think wedding her is providing you with more than fulfilling an obligation to the title. As it should, my lord."

Heat crept up the back of his neck. He ignored that too. "I'm coming to enjoy our friendship. It's rather pleasant to have someone who is determined to save me from myself."

Barton snorted. "If you continue to act the charming earl, she might be convinced to love you."

"Such gammon." He rolled his eyes. "That was never part of the contract."

"Life happens despite our best laid plans, my lord." The valet's eyes twinkled.

"Never say you're playing matchmaker." When his friend didn't answer, Drew grinned with genuine humor. How long had it been since he'd felt free enough to do that? "I should turn you out."

"Ah, but then I'd still come 'round, for we've been friends too long now, and I do wish to see how the story ends."

He'd met Barton ten years prior as a man of thirty during a game of faro, no less. Drew had the winning hand, was poised to take all a young lord's vowels, which would have reduced the boy to nothing with pockets to let. But Drew had suffered his first bout of anxiety by worrying about the lad's future after the ill-advised game. Before he could make a fool of himself in front of important members of the *ton*, Barton had sailed in, bought the vowels, and then challenged Drew to another game, thereby saving Andrew from public humiliation.

After that, they'd struck a fast friendship. Since Barton was the sixth child of a viscount and had no inclination to go into the church, when Drew offered him the position of valet, it was accepted with alacrity.

A grin tugged at the corners of his mouth from the remembrance. "Bastard. Will you always act as my moral compass then?"

"Until there's a more interesting development." The valet clapped Drew on the shoulder. "Have a lovely evening. Talk around the servants' hall is that my lady's gown is quite stunning."

"I'll bear that in mind and will give compliments as needed." Apparently, during their week apart when he couldn't climb out of the dark hole he'd been thrust into, Sarah had wasted no time in having a new wardrobe ordered. From what he'd seen of it thus far, she was already making herself into an elegant countess.

And he couldn't be prouder at her initiative.

Then he exited his suite and strode down the corridor to Sarah's. As he lifted a hand to knock, nerves assailed him, different than the crushing worry he usually experienced. This was the first time they would appear in public at a society event as a married couple.

Am I ready for this? Am I strong enough?

Before he could rap on the door, the panel swung inward. Sarah's eyes lit when she saw him. "I had thought to come for you, but here you are."

"Yes, I'm here." God, he sounded like a bacon-brained idiot. And for good reason.

For the first time he was struck dumb and not from crippling anxiety or other emotions as he swept his gaze up and down her person. "Bloody hell, Sarah, you're beautiful tonight."

How the devil had he ever considered her plain?

The gold silk gown she'd chosen shimmered with a sheer white overskirt of some sort shot with gold thread and clear glass beads. The bodice was low enough to show the tops of her creamy breasts, and it took every bit of effort he had not to ogle that portion of her anatomy. Her glorious hair, upswept into a topknot, allowed a few long curls to tumble from the crown to bounce about her shoulders like coils of spun gold. No, he couldn't stop staring, and as he finally met her gaze that danced with amusement behind her spectacles, he blew out a breath.

His chest tightened, but not from anxiety. He couldn't believe she was his. At least a little bit. "You're beautiful."

"You already said that." A tinkling laugh escaped her, and he stared all the more.

"Right." He stood there gawking like a green boy just out of university. It had been a long time since he'd been knocked on his proverbial arse merely by seeing a woman. *Say something intelligent, you nodcock!*

A faint stain of pink sneaked into her cheeks. "I'm glad you like the dress. It's one I had ordered and only arrived this morning." She returned to her sitting room. "Let me find my gloves and wrap."

Her happy chattering snapped him from the spell he'd fallen into. "The dress is lovely, of course, but it's truly you who has made the impression tonight." Drew followed her inside. "On that note, I have a gift for you." Belatedly, he remembered the leather case he held.

"Another one?" A finely feathered eyebrow lifted in question. "You've given me so much already. This suite, all the clothes, the engagement ring—"

"Not gifts," he rushed to assure her. "Things that befit your station as my wife. Things I wanted you to have—you should have had all along. Well, except the ring. That's a gift, but it definitely belongs to you. My grandmother would have liked your spirit."

Her serene smile sent awareness sailing over his skin. "I hope you'll tell me about her someday."

"I will." He should have done so already, but now there was no time. "Perhaps tomorrow over dinner or on our customary walk? I don't have a preference…"

"Are you babbling, Lord Hadleigh?" She continued to smile as she donned the white elbow-length gloves. "I've never seen you at sixes and sevens before."

A week ago, her use of the title, even in that teasing tone, would have sent him into the boughs. Now, it only brought him back to the task at hand. "I suppose I am." His grin felt decidedly lopsided. After tucking his gloves inside his jacket, he opened the worn leather box he'd retrieved from his safe not two hours prior. Emeralds glittered in the candlelight while the smaller diamonds winked like dew in the sun. "These pieces are also part of my grandmother's bridal jewelry. The ring came from this set." Drew forced a swallow to encourage moisture into his suddenly dry throat. "I should have given them to you on our wedding night."

Sarah peered into the box and gasped. Her spectacles slid down her nose. "Merciful heavens. They're beautiful." The awe in her whispered voice held him captive.

Round emeralds encircled with tiny diamonds and set in gold made up the necklace, each stone slightly larger in size until the middle stone, which stood at nearly six carats. The stones in the bracelets were the same size as the one in her ring.

She glanced at him and pushed her spectacles into place. "It's too much."

"I suspect it's not enough," he forced out in a barely there voice. "What you've given me, done for me… It can never be repaid."

"I don't want payment." Her eyes were limpid and so warmly inviting he wanted to lose himself in those brown depths.

"Think what you will about these, for it's a shame to leave that elegant neck unadorned this evening."

"Oh." Her eyes widened. "I didn't want to wear the locket, for it wasn't suited to the occasion."

"Shh." He plucked the pieces from the velvet-lined box, dropped the case on a table, then moved behind her. When he slipped the heavy necklace around the slender column of her neck and fastened the catch, his fingers shook. This was much more than giving her a piece of jewelry. Tonight, he'd unbent enough to extend trust to her, put a piece of his heart into her more than capable hands and hope she wouldn't hurt it. "Gorgeous." He didn't know if he meant her or the necklace. Letting his touch linger upon her warm skin a second longer than needed, he inhaled her clover and violet scent. As he came around to look at the effect, Sarah touched a finger to the central stone.

"Andrew?" She peered at him with vulnerable confusion on her face.

"It suits you." He took her free hand and fastened the bracelet about her wrist. "You should always wear emeralds." They were a brilliant contrast to her ivory skin and brought out the golden flecks in her irises. Holding her gaze, he brought her gloved hand to his lips and kissed the back. It trembled while he did so. Was she as nervous as he?

"We should go," she whispered, but she didn't move.

Neither did he. "Yes." She was so lovely with tears shimmering in her eyes behind those lenses and a trace of color in her cheeks that he wanted to kiss her, but fear held him back. He couldn't do anything that might sacrifice the work they'd already put in. For if he kissed her now, he'd want more, and when that happened, would he lose control over his other emotions if he were distracted? Not having answers, he shoved the thoughts away. "We should. I merely wished to see the effect of the jewelry on you."

"They're the most beautiful pieces I've ever worn." Sarah lifted onto her toes and bussed his cheek. "Let me grab my wrap…"

Twenty minutes later when their carriage trip began, familiar anxiety tightened Drew's chest. If he lost his temper tonight, word would filter to London. His name and Sarah's would be bandied about in whispers. What would happen then?

"Don't worry so." Sarah left her bench to sit beside him. She took his hand. "It will go smoothly." The touch warmed him through and brought a measure of calm. "Don't dwell of what might go wrong. Only put faith in your strengths and what you contribute to the area." She squeezed his fingers. "For as long as you need me, I'll stand beside you."

Does that mean in a forever kind of way? Did he want that?

Out loud, he said, "I appreciate that." More and more he was coming to rely on her. Merely having Sarah near, being able to see her, hear her voice helped alleviate the need to overthink every little problem.

The dim interior of the carriage hid her expression, but he imagined she smiled when she looked at him. "I must admit, I'm not keen on seeing my great uncle again, but we do what we must at times to keep the surrounding neighbors happy. Besides, goodwill never goes to waste."

Teach me how to be gracious after all that has happened to me.

Drew didn't voice the thought. Instead, he nodded and held onto her hand. "God willing, the evening will go quickly."

AN HOUR LATER saw him visiting throughout the drawing room, behaving with civility, and even letting himself laugh at a few jokes some of the men told. Every minute of being in the public eye was a challenge and he constantly fought against falling into the old habit of letting anxiety take control, but Sarah didn't leave his side. Her presence made all the difference. She was genial and demure, even in the face of subtle comments regarding her sudden elevation of position from a few of the more catty ladies.

He happened to witness one such conversation between Sarah, her great aunt, and a squire's wife as he listened with half an ear to her great uncle extol the virtues of different farming techniques.

"How lucky you are to find yourself a countess," the tall, thin woman with a horse face said as she sipped from a cup of punch. "There were many other women, younger ladies with more to recommend them, who the earl could have chosen. Why, my own daughter would truly cherish such a boon."

Sarah caught his eye. He cocked an eyebrow. Would she rise to the challenge? Then she snapped her attention back to the squire's wife. "I'm sure she would, but in Hadleigh's case, I believe he made the right choice."

Her aunt sniffed. "You've only been his countess for two weeks. As of yet, I haven't heard of you visiting, nor have you done any charity work. Inexperience might become a detriment to his career."

"Whether you believe it or not, my time has been spoken for with other matters," Sarah responded with a faint hint of annoyance in her voice. "The position of countess isn't something one can master in a fortnight."

Both women exchanged glances, then the squire's wife lowered her voice. "What of children, my lady? He'll want an heir, I'm sure, but I rather doubt someone so... well, someone your age might have difficulties—"

"That is quite my own business, isn't it?" Sarah interrupted with slightly reddened cheeks.

Drew quelled the urge to chuckle. He excused himself and then crossed the floor to where Sarah stood. "I couldn't help overhearing, but I couldn't have a better countess than Sarah. She's been an immense help to me already, and in time, I don't doubt she'll make a rather permanent stamp on society."

The squire's wife narrowed her beady eyes. "Well, if you are happy then we don't have room to complain."

Was he happy? In this moment, he was. "Thank you. I've found a woman with life experience is vastly more valuable than an untried debutante who'd probably be frightened of her own shadow, let alone the duties set before a countess."

Mottled color covered the woman's chest. "If you'll excuse me?"

"Of course." Drew took Sarah's hand and put it on his sleeve as he guided her across the room. "I adore it when your dander is up," he whispered into her ear.

She bit her bottom lip when a smile formed. "Do hush. People can hear you."

Watching her, witnessing how she reacted and responded to people, his own confidence grew, and with each new person he talked with, he was certain that attending to the responsibilities of the earl might not end as traumatically as he'd first thought.

Once the furniture had been pushed to the sides of the large room and the rugs rolled up, dancing began, and that hard-won confidence slipped. One of the guests played a pianoforte while another had procured a violin. The hold on his control wavered, for he was obliged to dance with various local women and their daughters. And when Sarah partnered other men, he discovered a new emotion he never encountered before—jealousy.

Under no circumstances did he like his wife being with other men. Regardless of whether the reels and country dances were purely for entertainment and exercise, no one had the right to touch her except him. As he struggled with a tight chest and piercing jealousy, she finally drifted back to his side, slightly breathless, with high color in her cheeks.

"Oh, these people and their false goodwill!" The words, couched in an urgent whisper, surprised him. That color wasn't from exertion, it was from anger. "They simply can't understand how an insignificant woman like me landed an earl. And because they don't believe me, they made their husbands or brothers question me during dancing." She shook her head. "The unmitigated gall of it! As if I'd give a completely different set of answers."

"Ah." He grinned. The spirited woman he knew was back, and he adored her more than the well-mannered, meek woman she'd attempted to portray the whole evening. "Sour milk, perhaps? Shall we further twist the knife then?"

"How?" When she frowned, her spectacles slipped down her nose.

"The impromptu musicians are preparing to perform a waltz," he said as he gently set her eyewear into their proper place. "Shall we indulge and set their tongues wagging even more?"

"Truly? I haven't waltzed for years though." A trace of insecurity clouded her eyes.

"It's something one never forgets." As a handful of couples assumed places on the cleared floor, Drew swept her into an empty spot. "Waltzing is something one feels as well as experiences. Follow my lead and you'll set jealousy burning in these unhappy women's hearts." With a wink, he took her into his arms, and when the first notes played, he set them into motion.

The candlelight twinkled off the emeralds around her neck. In the soft illumination, Sarah was ethereal, a vision in gold, a veritable angel fallen from the heavens and given into his care.

Where the devil had those thoughts come from?

She was merely the same woman he'd known for three weeks with the tart mouth and the ready smile, and the one person in this world who could keep him from falling into the pit of darkness that always lurked.

Yet, on this night, she had quietly become... more.

With each turn they took in the room, with every step, he pulled her incrementally closer to him. His thighs glanced along hers; his chest brushed her breasts, and he imagined a different sort of dancing with her, only in a bed *sans* clothing. Halfway through the waltz, a trill of laughter escaped her that was so clear and genuine, he stared in astonishment. The warmth of her in his arms, the softness of her skin that he fantasized about touching, the inviting rosy lips he was desperate to taste again all worked in tandem to weave a spell about them until only they two existed in the room.

The woman he'd taken to wife was nothing short of amazing. When he smiled and held her gaze, she did the same, and in that moment, *something* was exchanged between them, different than anything he'd experienced before. No longer did he want to tame her, take away the very spirit that made her a force. Oh, no. He wished to kindle that fire, build it into an inferno for the mere awe of watching her ride the wave without losing herself, for then she could perhaps teach him how to survive his own storms.

"If you continue to look at me like that, you'll embarrass yourself," she whispered with twinkling eyes.

"How so?" Ah, but he knew.

"As if you'd like to devour me right here in this room."

Drew quelled the groan that rose in his throat, but that didn't stop the sudden tightening of his shaft. God, he wanted her. That had never changed. "I won't deny your claim. However, I will temper my response."

Her gaze dropped to his mouth, and he missed a step. Though it took seconds to correct his posture, the spell broke. A teasing light entered her eyes, and when she grinned, he felt it all the way to his toes. "Naughty boy to think such things in my great uncle's house."

"I'm helpless against your beauty. What would you have me do?" Was he... flirting with his wife?

She snickered. "The music has ended, so perhaps we could refrain from continuing the waltz?"

Heat crept up the back of his neck. "I beg your pardon." He brought them to a halt, and when she pulled away, he mourned the loss of her touch. "Let me bring you a glass of punch."

"I'd like that." Those brown depths with the golden flecks beckoned him closer, but he didn't dare to lead her from the room to seek out a shadowy corner. Not here, not now, but perhaps when they arrived home…

Two hours later, while tucked into the carriage with the dark night pressing around them, he leaned back against the squabbed bench. "I thought that went rather well, all things considered."

"You were marvelous, and I appreciate your brilliant work in keeping your anger in check." Sarah nestled against his side with her legs tucked on the bench. She rested her head on his chest. "I'm proud of you."

His chest warmed from her praise as well as her proximity. "I'm learning." Thanks to her help. "If you're willing, we could…" The words trailed away when he realized she'd fallen asleep. The light arcs of her lashes against her cheeks and her even breathing testified to that observation. Drew smiled into the darkness and wrapped an arm about her, holding her steady when the carriage bumped along a rough patch in the road.

In some ways, this sort of intimacy was greater than carnal affection, and he was content to wait, for Sarah was worth it. He would do nothing to rush his fences or frighten her away.

As shock roiled through his body, he acknowledged a truth: he was coming to care for his wife. *What the devil do I do now?*

In many ways, it was more terrifying than letting anxiety have at him, for the stakes were suddenly infinitely higher.

CHAPTER FIFTEEN

July 11, 1817

R AIN DRUMMED SOFTLY against the window glass as Sarah hummed a few stanzas from the waltz she'd shared with her husband the night before. Oh, but that had been a glorious evening! With her head in the clouds, she pulled her flute from its case and then went to stand by one of the drawing room windows. It was where she set up the wooden stand that held her precious sheet music—one of the last gifts her father had given her.

Last night had been nothing short of magical. Never in her life had she felt as close to a man—or Andrew for that matter—than she had during that waltz. Her feet had scarcely touched the floor. He'd been attentive and charming, witty and dare she say protective, but beyond that, they had shared something intimate, something unexplainable during that dance, perhaps exchanged a tiny sliver of each other's souls.

That exquisite change lingered with her even now.

Had they been alone instead in her great uncle's drawing room, she might have lost herself in him, given him everything, but since they'd been mingling with the local gentry, she'd had to remain content with drifting in the strong circle of his arms. No, she wouldn't soon forget that waltz or the benchmark it had made in their relationship.

And perhaps she'd fallen in love with him a tiny bit. She caught her breath. Was that true? In the span of a week, could things between them have changed so drastically? Perhaps it had only been the magic of that one moment. He'd certainly made an effort to control his emotions as well as his responses since his mental break, but would it last?

Could a man make such deep inroads in a mere seven days?

I suppose it depends on his motivation.

Time would tell.

After Sarah warmed her fingers and lips with a few scales and arpeggios, she practiced a particularly difficult piece that she hadn't quite committed to memory yet. She'd planned to audition with it in London—if she could master it. Well, that was before she'd married. Over and over, her fingers flew through the notes as her eyes skipped along the sheet music. The lilting melodies that swooped and flew sent her soaring, and each time she arrived at the three-quarter mark, her fingers fumbled on a complicated run of notes making for discordant tones.

"Well, drat." She heaved out a breath of frustration. "That stretch always baffles me. My fingers don't move as quickly as they should." Would she have been able to tackle the piece if she were ten years younger?

What a depressing thought that was.

"Don't give up." The baritone of his voice shattered her concentration.

"Andrew." She started and glanced up from her music. He had come into the room, apparently on silent feet, and had seated himself on a low sofa, which had been his wont this past week whenever she spent time practicing. It was both endearing and nerve-wracking. "I won't, of course. This is *Paris Symphonies* from Haydn, and it's currently vexing me."

"You're determined enough that you'll master it in no time." He rested an ankle on a knee with an indulgent smile. "Why did you select that piece over another?"

Had his voice always sent gooseflesh popping along her arms? "It's a favorite and..." Should she tell him of the dream she couldn't forget?

"Yes?" The silver threads in his hair glimmered in the candlelight, and today his stormy eyes were more gray than blue.

"I had thought to audition before a few groups in London if I ever had the opportunity." As nonchalantly as she could, Sarah placed the flute in its case. "But now I'm a countess."

"What difference does that make? Have you suddenly lost the ability to play simply because you hold a title?"

"I suppose it doesn't." She peered at him, alert for any sign of brewing temper, but his body language was relaxed and his grin this side of wicked. "I didn't wish to do so in the event it would fracture my focus on new responsibilities."

"If that is something you wish to do, I don't want to stand in your way." He shrugged, but there was a guarded light in his eyes. "I can accompany you to London, say the word."

Flutters flitted through her lower belly at the concession. "I'm not quite ready for all that. Let me practice for a few more weeks."

He nodded. "Have you ever performed in front of an audience?"

"Aside from you?" She couldn't help smiling, for he was the most appreciative audience she could ever hope for. "I have not."

"Perhaps it's something you should think about." He shrugged. "What if, when you play before a crowd, you decide it's not for you? No matter how well an audition might go, and regardless of how wonderful I think you play, it's much different than standing before a room full of people, all looking at you."

Was he trying to dissuade her from a goal? "That's true." Or perhaps he was merely being logical. Sarah drifted away from the windows toward the sofa. "Once I conquer this piece, then I'll think about performing."

"You have memorized several other equally beautiful pieces," he said in a soft voice. "If you truly wish to go to London for this, you can."

Now that was a grand concession from him, and her heart trembled. "I... thank you." Why did the thought of doing this suddenly make her fearful?

He gazed at her with speculation. "Did either of your parents have a proclivity to music?"

Sarah shook her head. "No, but Papa dearly loved to listen to it. Every time he came back from his travels, he'd bring me an instrument of some kind until I came to love the flute. He sold the rest, and from then on, he would bring me sheet music." She smiled in remembrance. "It's horribly expensive, but I'm so grateful to him."

"He supported your endeavors?"

"Papa always said, 'Sarah, you're stubborn enough to teach the men of this world a trick or two, and I won't discourage that.' But when he died..." She bit her lip as a stab of grief suddenly came to life. "I didn't play for a year. Perhaps that's why I can't move past this bloody passage. It reminds me too much of him."

"You *are* quite stubborn." His chiseled lips curved with a slow grin. "We never know how much influence our fathers have on us until they're gone. Good or bad, they remain as either a guide or a warning."

"Yes." Sarah stared at him in amazement. It was a rather insightful statement for him. And there was no sign of the usual anger that accompanied any mention of his family. Oh, it was so encouraging to see such growth!

"If music is the one thing that brings you happiness, pursue it with all the passion you have in you. I won't hold you back, for I wish I'd had that too." He flicked a glance to one of the windows. A hint of sadness tinged his expression, but why? "Unless you'd like to walk in the rain, we'll need to postpone our daily constitutional."

"I don't mind. We'll spend the time here." Unbidden, she perched on the sofa with a cushion between them. When she caught a whiff of his bay rum shaving soap, a tremble moved down her spine. "Thank you for last night. I appreciated your support as well as your expertise while dancing."

"I enjoyed the evening, too, which surprised the hell out of me." He didn't change his lounging posture, but his eyes darkened slightly as he looked at her. "I'm merely sorry I had to wake you prematurely. You looked so peaceful in the carriage, but that was hardly a fitting bed for a countess."

"No, I suppose not." She ducked her head while pushing her spectacles into place. "It's been a while since I passed such a lively evening." A touch of heat infused her cheeks. "I'll not do so again, for it isn't flattering for a countess to claim fatigue and fall asleep on the ride home." No doubt the strain of being thrust into the public eye had taken a toll on her.

"I found it endearing. Also, you snore."

"I do not! I've never snored in my life." A hint of indignation echoed in her voice before she caught the amusement in his eyes. It was so out of place that her lower jaw dropped slightly. "You're teasing me."

"Yes." He straightened, planting both booted feet on the floor, and then turned toward her. "Thank you for extending such trust to me that you would fall asleep on my shoulder. I don't take that lightly."

"You were charming last night, I'll give you that." He'd been so solid and warm that she'd felt protected with him. Sarah ran her fingers over the fabric of her morning dress of yellow sprigged muslin. "And you handled my great uncle splendidly." No matter how many times her relative tried to ingratiate himself to the earl, Andrew always saw through the obviously flattering remarks and deflected the conversation.

"I dislike when anyone disparages my wife." A muscle in his jaw ticked. "You command a certain respect in England now. I won't have that overlooked by petty jealousy."

She'd never heard him directly refer to her as that before, and it caused another hoard of butterflies to take flight in her belly. "Then it's a good thing you and I don't have another society event on our social calendar any time soon." Why was her voice so breathless?

"Oh? Did you not enjoy yourself?"

"I did, though it was tiring. However, I merely meant... that is to say..." *Drat*. How had she fallen into this muddle? Never did she have issue with saying exactly what was on her mind. Why now? "I'd like to spend more time with you, alone," she finally concluded as her cheeks heated even more.

One of his eyebrows rose. "If you're of a mind, I could teach you to play whist or faro. If you have a favorite book of poetry, I could read to you."

She pressed a hand to a flaming cheek. "That sounds lovely, but perhaps we could indulge in that later." Why was it so difficult to tell him what she wanted?

Because something had shifted between them. It both frightened and exhilarated her. Truly, they had started their relationship anew, and now... well, she wanted more.

"I might be a cad, but I do so wish to hear you say it, Sarah." Andrew scooted onto the cushion beside her. A certain intensity lit his eyes. "*How* should we spend our time?" he asked, his voice a thrilling whisper that sent tingles down her spine.

Heat swept over her in a wave. "Oh, must you continue to be aggravating?"

"I will, for it keeps a nice spark between us." When he winked, she couldn't help her grin. "And a spark is the first step to building a fire."

"Fine." She leaned toward him. He smelled so delicious, and those shoulders! Oh, but she wanted to touch him, hold him. "Kiss me. I thought you might have done so last night but—"

He moved so quickly, pressed his lips to hers so fast she didn't have time to finish her sentence. The kiss was gentle, fleeting, naught but the chaste kiss of a man early in courtship, yet it left her needing so much more. When he pulled away, humor danced in his eyes with desire darkening those depths. "I *did* want to but feared of doing anything that might weaken my control over other emotions."

Sarah pushed her spectacles back into place. "How do you feel now?" Would they always need to be concerned about his state of mind before doing anything intimate?

"Like I should really go close the door."

"Truly?" Excitement accelerated her heartbeat. Was she making yet another mistake when it came to him?

"Oh, yes." He rose smoothly to his feet, and Sarah stood as well. "After last night, this next bit is inevitable to mark a new direction, don't you think?" he asked as he strode across the room, closed the door, and then turned the lock. The mechanism *clicked* into place.

"Yes." The word sailed out from her suddenly tight throat on a whisper. Tingles played up and down her spine while the earl moved to the side door that connected into the next room. He locked that one as well.

When he returned to her and took her hands, his own shook. Did he experience the same nervousness as she? It was quite different than his usual anxiety, and it was endearing. "Are you quite certain, Sarah? After the last time…"

"I suspect this time will be different." *Please let that be so.*

Andrew tugged her into his arms and claimed her lips with gentle insistence, and she eagerly surrendered to his mastery.

They connected without words, for there was no need for talking. While he nibbled at the corners of her mouth, she twined her hands around his neck, furrowed the fingers of one hand through his hair. This kiss was so much more than she'd hoped; so far removed from her wedding night it brought tears to her eyes. He drew her closer to him, so that they were essentially locked together, pressed into each other, fitting completely and seamless as if always meant to nest together like bookends.

The solid manliness of him beneath her hands, the warmth of him that seeped into her, the insistent bulge of his arousal that lay against her belly all worked to accentuate her need, and she fell beneath the wave of awareness sweeping over her. She pulled away long enough to whisper, "This is nice."

"It's merely the beginning." He trailed his lips along the underside of her jaw. At a particularly sensitive spot near her ear, a moan escaped her. How had she never known about that before? He took the hint and teased the area with his tongue, went so far as to take her earlobe and give it a nip, then he resumed exploring the column of her throat. "I want—need—so much more, but only if you're willing."

"I am." Her lips were so close to his that with each word, she brushed them. She didn't move; neither did he, and for the space of a few heartbeats, when he exhaled, she inhaled. They exchanged air, breathing in tandem. Then her eyes shuttered closed. "Kiss me again."

"Gladly." He settled her more comfortably in his arms and followed her instructions most splendidly. The kiss was more intense than the first, but not violent or forceful like his showing on their wedding night. This time, he chased her tongue, fenced with her as she sought his, and there was a slight hesitation to his embrace, almost as if he sought her permission, asked for her invitation, and finally he claimed her mouth as she clung to him until they panted with mutual need.

"You're quite... potent," Sarah gasped out, her words soft and breathless. She lifted her chin as he dragged his lips down the side of her throat. Cheeky man, he slid his hands to her hips and held her tight against him.

"Not as much as you." Andrew traced the bodice of her gown with his lips. He licked and nipped at the skin there and pulled another moan from her. With an arm supporting her back, he lowered her to the sofa and quickly followed her down, covering her body with his. A searing kiss muddled her thoughts, and the sensation of flying came over her. He kissed her so deeply she wondered if he wished to touch her soul, but then she responded in kind.

A guttural groan rumbled from him. Her eyes fluttered open. He watched her, desire glinting in those stormy blue-gray depths, the same want that thrummed through her veins. With a half-growl that conveyed his feelings, he kissed her again, more insistent. Sarah fairly drowned in the sensations racing over her.

She fisted a hand in his cravat while her hand at his nape encouraged him closer. "Touch me, Andrew." With a tug, she unknotted the crisp fabric and then moved on to the buttons of his jacket.

He treated her to a string of baby-fine kisses. All the while he pulled at her bodice until her breasts popped free of the fabric layers. She shivered at the sudden exposure to cooler air, but then he was there, reverently kissing the quivering globes, circling around the hardening nipples until she couldn't stand the teasing. She guided his head to one tip, and when he closed his lips around it, sucked it into the warm cavern of his mouth, she uttered a half-cry, half-moan. Wicked sensation streaked from the breast to between her thighs.

And it was the most glorious thing she'd ever known.

"God, you're so beautiful, so soft," he murmured against her skin as he licked, nibbled, and sucked his way between her breasts. "I should have told you that night..." His hold on her tightened.

"Shh." She didn't want him sidetracked. "But you said it now, and that's all that matters." One by one, she had his buttons undone, and once his waistcoat gaped, she tugged his fine lawn shirt from his breeches. "Let me see you. All's fair, you know."

"Minx." He lifted off her long enough to shed the clothing from his torso.

"Oh." The word was uttered on a breath as she drank in the look of him. Those wide shoulders hadn't been exaggerated by padding. A dark mat of black hair shot with gray decorated his chest. When she slid her gaze lower to his nearly flat abdomen, the hair collected into a thin ribbon that disappeared beneath his breeches. Her pulse hastened its cadence, and she desperately wished to see where that trail led.

"Can I trust from your expression you approve of this old man?" The insecurity in his eyes was adorable.

"You're hardly that. Perhaps seasoned or experienced." She swallowed to encourage moisture into her throat. "But you *are* quite handsome and…"

"And?" he asked softly as he covered her body with his once more.

"You make my mouth water to taste you," she finished with heat in her cheeks. Goodness, what had possessed her to say that?

"There's nothing stopping you." With care, Andrew removed her spectacles and set them on the small table near her head. Then he claimed her lips again with a kiss so gentle and moving that tears accumulated in her eyes.

Sarah smoothed her hands over his shoulders and down his back. Muscles tensed and flexed beneath her touch, and that strength called out to her. The coarse hair on his chest tickled her breasts to increase the desire swirling through her body. There was no use denying what she felt. "I need you," she whispered with a look into his face. "Please."

Slowly, he nodded. "I need you too." In that moment, understanding passed between them. Honestly shone in his eyes, unclouded with anything else. As if he couldn't bear another moment from her, he kissed her, made love to her mouth, sought out her tongue over and over, and in doing so, hinted at what was to come. Slowly, almost reverently, he drew her skirts upward, bunching the fabric at her waist. Then he settled between her partially splayed legs.

"You're certain?"

"Oh, yes." She'd never wanted anything as badly as she wanted him now. Running a hand down his chest, she combed her fingers through the hair there. So much power banked within him. Would that translate to carnal attentions?

"I hope to God this goes better than the other night." He fumbled with the buttons at the front of his trousers, shoved the panel out of the way and then he gripped her hips, fitting his tip to her ready opening.

"It already has." Sarah trembled, for it was much like the first time with him. She didn't consider her wedding night as proper intercourse. Due to the limited space on the sofa, she couldn't maneuver as much as she would like, so she wrapped her legs about his waist.

A groan escaped him, and he held himself above her, one forearm resting on the bolster pillow near her head. Andrew thrust into her, penetrated her as deep as he could go, and then he paused, presumably to give her time to acclimate. "Bloody hell, Sarah. You're so tight, feel so wonderful."

She could hardly breathe, so different was this experience from her first with him. His thick length filled her; the heat of him was intoxicating. She squirmed beneath him as he adjusted his angle over her body, and when he began to move, leaning over her, she gasped from the feelings. With every easy, teasing stroke, hot, tingling sensations assailed her. There wasn't anywhere on her body that didn't feel him, for he was in her, a part of her, and she of him.

When he grinned, the gesture held such innocence and cocksure confidence, that she lost a tiny piece of her heart to him.

It was all new and oh-so-amazing. Sarah looped her arms around his shoulders, held him close to her by tightening her crossed ankles at the small of his back, and closed her eyes to fully immerse herself in the wonder of him. He thrust into her body, slowly at first, rocking them both in a rhythm as old as time. As he drove deeper, his strokes grew faster, more frantic, and her breath caught. Need coiled tight in her lower belly. Desire hummed through her blood, heated her skin until she writhed, chasing something that eluded her.

Why wouldn't this terrible, exquisite pressure break?

"I can't... I don't know how..."

"Shh." He kissed her forehead and slowed the movement of his hips. As he delved a hand between their bodies and he found that swollen, all-important bud at the center of her pleasure, a cry of surprise escaped her throat.

"What are you...?" He'd not touched her there on their wedding night, but oh, it was such bliss! The faster he worried his finger over that button, the more she tumbled into a dizzying spiral of colorful bliss. How did one survive this? He added more friction; her hold on control fractured, then finally split wide open, and she fell... down, down, down into heated pleasure that caught her up in its storm. "Andrew!"

"That, my girl, is but one release I'll give you." He chuckled, his eyes dark with desire and glowing with masculine smugness, then he dug his fingers into her hips, grunting, and he drove into her as her channel spasmed, his hips moving so fast, his shaft going so deep into her core she was sure he attempted to touch her soul. His eyes bored into hers, a need buried in the backs she felt more than understood.

Something spiritual passed between them, a warmth of sorts that spun a web and connected them from that moment onward. And she sighed with the precious loveliness of it.

No, one didn't survive this feeling that made her soar. One merely rode the tide and let it consume them. Sarah's moans blended with his. She held onto him, kissing whatever part of him she could reach, touching and teasing his body the best she knew how while lifting her hips and matching his rhythm. He was powerful and strong, much like he was in other aspects of his life, but with her, in this intimate dance, he was also tender and caring, seeing to her needs. It was enough to send tears prickling her closed eyelids.

All too soon she shattered. Perhaps that wasn't the correct term for what happened to her. She fractured, broke apart, was sent flying on the wings of overwhelming pleasure and heat. It was all she could do to remain sane and hold onto him. His name left her tongue, over and over like a litany. The hysterical sound of it keened through the room until he kissed her hard and long, taking it into himself.

With another powerful thrust, he grunted against her lips, ground his hips into hers. The hot expulsion of his seed filled her passage, and he stroked once more then collapsed on top of her. Strong contractions pulsed through her core, around his shaft, her heartbeat racing. The release was so grand and different that she burst into tears.

When she buried her face into the crook of his shoulder, she sobbed; her body shook from reaction and the exquisite act they'd just shared.

"You're crying." His breathing was ragged in her ears. "Are you all right? Did I hurt you?" The concern in his baritone tugged at her heart, and another piece of it went into his keeping.

"No. These are happy tears. I think." Her laugh was a touch unstable, but she kept her face hidden, for he smelled wonderful, of limes and spices and man. "That was so... I can't explain how I feel."

"Then I did it right." Andrew wrapped his arms around her and held her close. "You were amazing," he whispered and pressed his lips to her temple. Every tiny movement he made sent a host of tingles dancing down her spine.

"I quite agree with that sentiment." Her heartbeat raced wildly, matching his that thudded beneath her ear. Eventually, she came back to Earth and was quite content to remain tucked in his arms. After two weeks of married life, she finally had a real husband.

Tears filled her eyes again, this time of gratitude. Dear God, but she hoped this newfound closeness lasted.

CHAPTER SIXTEEN

F OR THE FIRST time in his adult existence, Drew felt content. The session with Sarah had ended a half hour ago. Now, after dressing himself and putting his clothes to rights, as well as assisting her with her gown, he sat in a comfortable wing backed chair with his wife on his lap, her knees hooked over an armrest, a crocheted blanket covering them both, for the rain-cooled air wafting in from the windows had brought a slight chill to the room.

A pleasant lethargy weighted his limbs. Sarah rested her head on his chest, the candlelight winking off her spectacle lenses as well as the silver locket about her neck. She was warm and right in his arms, and she'd been exceedingly wonderful as they'd shared the greatest intimacy. Every sound she'd made, each movement of her body, the delight she'd shown when he'd sent her over the edge of pleasure, all the smiles and touches she'd bestowed upon him had driven him closer to something he'd never experienced—peace. When they'd made love together, the storms within him had calmed for a time, and during that respite, the walls around his heart had crumbled. He'd lost a piece of that organ to her, willfully let her peer into his soul and take up housekeeping if she wished it.

And still there was an overwhelming sense of peace long after the initial euphoria of the joining had ended.

How remarkable.

As he sat there in the quiet, listening to the sound of Sarah's soft breathing as she dozed in and out of consciousness, his chest tightened, but not from anxiety or anger. Of course, the worry about the future lingered, for he was responsible for her care, but it didn't attempt to crush him as before. No, what he felt was... shock. Surely, he couldn't be falling for his wife. But what else could such profound serenity mean? Especially when he'd not had that before in his life. It wasn't until the arrival of this one remarkable woman that he'd begun to... change.

It had only been one week, but he hadn't had cause to let anger rage uncontrolled. And with a few of her suggestions, his anxiety had been kept at bay. Would he be able to continue down that path for the rest of his life? He hoped so, for this halcyon time with Sarah was infinitely valuable, and he'd be the biggest nodcock to let it slip through his fingers.

Daring much, he pressed his lips to her hair and glanced across the room to where her flute rested. The sheet music resting on the stand flapped anemically in the slight breeze. If it were within his power, he would help her meet those dreams she had of playing in London in whatever capacity she was comfortable with. She was a natural with music, and he shouldn't act selfish and keep her gift all to himself. The world would benefit from her talent.

As the rain continued to drum against the windows, Sarah stirred. She glanced up into his face. The soft smile she bestowed tugged at his heart. What would it take for him to see that every damned day from this moment on? "I'm surprised you didn't leave me on the sofa and let me rest." Sleep made her voice smoky and sensual. Renewed awareness shivered down his shaft.

"And miss this chance?" Drew adjusted his hold on her. "It's no difficulty." He touched a finger to her locket. "Will you tell me about your family? Above and beyond your great uncle?" The woman in his arms had never failed to astound him, and he wanted to know everything about her.

Her eyes widened behind her spectacle lenses. "Do you truly wish that?"

"I wouldn't have asked if I didn't." Had her eyes always been as deep and unfathomable as drinking chocolate? The tiny golden flecks made him want to explore further. "What do you keep inside the locket?"

"My parents." With trembling hands, she opened the oval piece of jewelry and then turned it so he could see the miniature paintings, each an inch high. "I have Mama's looks. As a young girl, I was envious of her golden hair and used to imagine myself with tresses like that in a storybook."

"But your hair is equally as wonderful," he protested with a laugh.

"Ah, but Mama had strands of strawberry and the faintest platinum threads." She touched her mother's portrait with a fingertip. "While my father was brilliant at business and striking a bargain, Mama's gift was making connections. She had a magnetic personality that made people want to gravitate around her." A soft smile curved her lips. "Many of my father's business deals came about because Mama had laid that groundwork ahead of time."

"Who were her people?"

"She was the daughter of a merchant who made and sold ladies' fans. Some of his ivory work was masterful. That's how she met my father. He'd come into the shop with a delivery for my grandfather. I think they fell in love at first sight."

Drew glanced at the tiny portrait of her father. A rather handsome man with dark brown hair and a pair of small, round spectacles in silver frames. "You inherited your poor eyesight from him?"

"Oh, yes." Sarah chuckled as she closed the locket with a soft *click*. "Without them, I can't see past the end of my nose. The world looks mostly like large blobs of color." She talked of her parents with such fondness in her voice, a touch of jealousy stabbed through him.

"Were you devastated when you lost them?" Somehow, he

couldn't imagine his plain-speaking, optimistic Sarah as floundering in grief.

For long moments she remained silent as emotions flitted through her eyes. Finally, she nodded. "I was inconsolable for days after I received the news. And with no other family readily available, let alone close friends, I had no one to turn to, no one to console me." Her chin trembled, and he held her a little closer. "I was lost and alone."

"As you've told me on a previous occasion, you are no longer that." He suddenly wanted to be her anchor when chaos swirled around her.

"There is a certain comfort in that." She rested a hand on his chest. "You have no idea how frightening it was when I realized I had no one in my life, and beyond that, nowhere to go. Papa didn't leave a fortune or anything like that. I sold much of our possessions to pay for the rents and other obligations." She drew abstract designs on his jacket lapel. "I had no idea what to do or where to turn, but I had no time to grieve as I'd wished."

"You needed to survive." A woman alone in the world wasn't afforded many options, and all too many of them ended up as prostitutes to see themselves fed. "How did you discover your great uncle?"

"My father had spoken of him a few times over the years. Once, we visited him in Derbyshire at Christmastide." She shrugged and her wandering fingers traced the ruby stickpin in the folds of his cravat. "I took the remaining coin that I had, packed my clothes and a few personal items, and booked a spot on the mail coach, intending to throw myself upon his goodwill and doorstep. If he refused me entry, I can't imagine what would have become of me."

There were too many unscrupulous men prowling about that she might have found herself confronted with one of them. He gave into a shiver. A thread of gratitude went through him that he'd discovered her when he had, else she'd face a similar decision in another ten years. "You're here now and never need worry over your future." Warmth surged into his being, for it gave him immense pleasure to say that.

"You're a good man." She tapped the ruby with a fingernail. "Tell me the significance of this. Not a day goes by that you don't wear it."

Dread coiled, cool and dark, in his gut.

Never had he shared the reasoning behind the pin with anyone, not even Barton. Instinct told him to retreat, recoil from potentially opening himself up to pain and censure, but Sarah put a palm to his cheek, turned his head until their gazes connected, and it helped him to find balance.

"Don't go backward. Your path doesn't point there." Affection reflected in her eyes, and he reeled from the discovery. Was she coming to care for him despite the obstacles they'd already passed? "Share with me. It's what a married couple does."

As if the old feelings had been shot from a cannon and into his chest, they all came hurtling back, stacking upon each other, twisting his insides, reaching out bony fingers in the hopes of strangling him. Drew took a few deep breaths. He briefly closed his eyes to quiet the storm brewing in his chest. When the rapid beat of his heart reminded him that he was alive and with her, he opened his eyes, touched the stickpin.

"I chose the ruby to represent the blood shed on those faraway battlefields that damaged my brothers." He stared into her eyes, wished he could dive into those welcoming pools and escape the hurt and anger that lurked, waiting for him to lose control. "It was my fault they went away, my fault their lives have been upended and ruined."

"Oh, Andrew, you didn't send them into battle." Sarah took his left hand and held it. "Why would you think that?"

"My temper made them flee. My arrogance sent them away." The admission felt yanked from his very soul. "I maintained that they were cowards for not staying in London when they knew Father's health was fragile, but they went anyway, with Father's blessing."

"Which did nothing to soothe your hurts." She raised his hand to her lips and kissed his forefinger while long-stoppered emotions roiled in his chest. "Tell me about your brothers. What were they like before they went to war?"

That wasn't such a bad request. He concentrated on keeping his anger and anxiety in the background, but he clung to her hand all the same. "Finn is my middle brother. He's smart and had a great sense of humor before..." As hot saliva rose in his throat, Drew forced a hard swallow. "I think if he'd had his druthers, he would have made a career in the military. Attained the rank of major by the time he came home. He's very organized and scheduled and would have made a brilliant estate foreman. His ideas to modernize Father's holdings—my holdings now I suppose—are full of potential, but now that he's confined to a Bath chair..."

His words trailed off, for what else was there to say?

"Do you assume the spirit of the man he was has suddenly left him due to his injury?" She lifted an eyebrow and pushed her spectacles into place with her free hand. "Don't count your brother out merely because you perceive him as weak and helpless. Everyone has hidden strength that will show itself when needed."

"I know a fat lot more about it than you, I'll wager," he snapped, then was immediately contrite when her eyes widened. "I apologize. Old habits."

"It's a constant battle. Only you can decide which emotion you'd like to win and portray to the world." She threaded their fingers together. "Rise above what happened to you." A firm note of the governess she used to be rang in her voice.

"I'm trying," he admitted in a whisper. It would take more than promises, and he'd need to remain vigilant. The slip had brought the reality of his situation rushing home that despite this last pleasant week, he was in danger of losing her if he couldn't curb his anger.

"What of your other brother?" Sarah hadn't moved, nor had she dropped his hand, for which he was thankful. It meant he hadn't yet crossed a line.

"Brand." He chuckled. "The baby of the family, the boy my parents had no expectations of." His chest tightened as jealousy reared its ugly head, but he refused to acknowledge it. "Before he went into the Navy, he made a career of spending Father's coin and making a reputation as a rake within the *ton*."

An amused smile curved her lips, and for a few minutes, he distracted himself by indulging in a series of slow kisses he hoped had her well on her way to being lost. Once he pulled away, she laughed but it was decidedly shaky. "Is your brother still a rake?" She pushed her spectacles back into place.

Ah, she was smart and wouldn't let a few kisses remove her from the conversation at hand. Drew settled her more comfortably on his lap. "When his exploits became too much for Father, there was an ultimatum issued: bring himself to respectability or join the Navy. I made rather an arse of myself backing up the claim. Brand went away, and gladly, and apparently, he found his place in the world while there. Rose up the ranks as quickly as Finn did."

"But he was injured as well?"

"Yes." Familiar anxiety squeezed his chest. He spent a few seconds concentrating on his breathing, watching Sarah as she studied him, and he hoped to God keeping himself in check would last. When the discomfort eased, he let out a shuddering sigh. "Lost his left eye in hand-to-hand combat aboard his ship. He's due to arrive home in London soon, but knowing Brand, he'll return to his rakish ways." And it would be Drew's responsibility to make him respectable.

No doubt it was much like trying to bag the wind.

Pressure on his fingers recalled him to the moment. Sarah shook her head. "Your brothers have their own paths to walk. You may give them advice, but their futures are not yours."

"It is so difficult for me." He met her gaze and took strength from her. "They'll make mistakes that I could circumvent by—"

"Everyone learns by making mistakes. Those choices are theirs, like every decision you make is yours." She sighed. "There isn't a primer on how to conduct oneself through life and its pitfalls. We learn as we go, and if we're lucky, we have someone by our side who will support us through those endeavors."

Her use of "we're" instead of "you're" brought a sense of calm once more. If he weren't careful, he'd come to adore her all too much, and then where would he be?

Sarah's attention fell to his signet ring. She twisted his hand so she could study the design. What would she think about the two swords and a spear that were stabbing through the storm cloud? "Do the weapons represent you and your brothers?"

"Not likely, since the coat-of-arms was fashioned for the title four earls ago, but I assume it must have represented something similar." He remained silent for a time, content to listen to the rain. Perhaps throughout his family line the men destined to become title holders struggled with the same issues he did. "However, a good portion of men in my family have expired early in their lives. It doesn't bode well for my future." And suddenly, he dearly wished that weren't true. He hadn't spent enough time with Sarah…

Oh, dear God, can it be that I'm falling for my wife? How was that possible after such a short marriage, when one of those weeks was spent apart from her?

"That is an interesting tidbit." Amusement danced in her eyes. "Perhaps you've inherited a generational sense of duty and responsibility that causes too much strain on your heart." Then concern wrinkled her brow. "For your sake, I implore you to keep up the good fight against your temper and anxiety."

"As I said, I'm trying." When his jaw clenched, he forced himself to relax. If his heart attacked him and he died prematurely, the title would go to Finn, for he and Sarah hadn't been wed long enough to have children. What would become of his brothers and his wife? Strain moved through his shoulders, a warning sign that anxiety threatened. "I need more time to practice."

"I know." She lifted his hand and kissed the back of it. "Regarding your brothers…"

A huff of exasperation escaped him. "Must we continue to revisit the subject?" He glided his free hand up and down her ribcage, being sure to brush his fingers along the slope of her breast. "There are other, more fulfilling ways to pass a rainy day."

"Oh, hush." A pretty stain of pink filled her cheeks. It was adorable, for they'd already come together twice, but suggestive talk embarrassed her. Her expression sobered. "I'm doing this for you. Healing needs to begin, and that can only happen if you talk about the hurt you're clinging to."

"Fine." He couldn't help the growl that had formed in his voice. After shaking his hand free of hers, he wrapped his arms tighter about her body, for this conversation would no doubt stir the demons within. "Ask me what you will."

When she rested a hand on his chest, the warmth of her seared into him. "Are you angry your brothers fought in the war and you didn't, or that they don't bear the responsibility of the title?"

Was it one or the other? He must have winced or otherwise shown his discomfort, for she moved her hand to his cheek and turned his head until their eyes locked. "Look at me. Don't give that anxiety any room to bully you."

For the first time in his life, Drew didn't shove down the emotions that churned inside him. He let them bubble to the surface, stared at them in an effort to analyze what would break him if he didn't address it. "I *am* angry that I wasn't allowed to join in the fight against Napoleon." He clenched his jaw so tight his teeth hurt. When she patted his cheek, he forced himself to relax with a sigh. "I'm angry that

I couldn't protect them. I'm angry they can do whatever they want with their lives while I'm stuck, buried under the duty to the title."

Speaking it aloud took away a portion of its sting. It was there and he could confront it.

"Good." She nodded. "Has becoming angry changed the past?"

"No."

"Has letting anger consume you fixed or healed your brothers?"

"No."

"Does being angry help you learn how to be a better earl?"

He sighed. "It has not."

Sarah nodded. "Then it is a waste of your time to let it rule you." When she smiled, he savored the sense of calm she imparted. "The war is over, Andrew. What happened to your brothers, though tragic, did happen, and nothing you do now, nothing you think now, none of those regrets or anger will change the past. The measure of a man is when he moves forward and meets the present challenges."

A wad of unshed tears lodged in his throat. "I'm afraid that all my efforts will be for naught and I'll never free myself from the years of hiding emotions." Essentially, he would lose her due to that failure.

She rose in his lap and brushed her lips against his. "It doesn't make a man weak to show emotions or to let yourself cry."

"My father taught us differently." His chest ached. "I don't want you to view me as less," he managed to gasp out.

"Flaws, emotions, reacting to things don't make you less than an ideal gentleman. In fact, allowing yourself to show them makes you more approachable, more trustworthy." A trace of moisture filled her eyes. "None of that will change how I feel about you."

It was all too much, and he wasn't experienced enough to feel everything assailing him and then releasing it. "Oh, Sarah. I can't continue like this." The urge to cry, to yell, to let out some of the things that felt stuck within him grew strong. Instead of shoving her off his lap as he might have done at the beginning of their marriage, he buried his face in the crook of her neck and gave into the tears he'd denied himself over the course of his life.

"I'm so proud of you," she whispered into his ear while stroking her fingers through his hair. "Once you're through purging all that doesn't serve you any longer, you'll have room to fill your life with better things."

He suspected she was part of that. *Please, God, don't let me fail at this.*

An urgent rapping at the drawing room door broke the spell he'd fallen into. "My lord, I have a missive for you."

Drew lifted his head and frowned. "I'd forgotten I'd locked the door."

Sarah wiped at the tears on her cheeks, and the smile she flashed him was a watery affair. "Poor Dalton sounds frantic." She wriggled off his lap, and immediately he missed that connection. "Take pity on him."

He scrubbed at his own cheeks on the way across the room. No sooner had he turned the lock and pulled open one of the double doors than the butler thrust an envelope into his hand.

"This arrived for you not five minutes past by special courier direct from London. He is currently belowstairs with refreshments should you wish to send a reply."

"What now?" Drew's hands shook as he tore open the envelope and pulled a single sheet of paper out. His mother's flowery script only covered one half of the paper. The date on the top indicated the missive was two days old.

Dearest Andrew,

Come home immediately. Phineas nearly committed suicide. He was thwarted in his quest by hitting his head on a piece of furniture when he fell from his chair. Thank God. As of this writing, he is unconscious. I am fearful we'll still lose him. You need to set things right.

Fondest love,

Mother

"Devil take it!" He crushed the note in his fist and then tossed it toward Sarah as she slowly approached.

The butler cleared his throat. "Is there a reply, my lord?"

"No. I'll go myself." He shoved a hand through his hair. "Will I never be free of responsibility?"

"Andrew, what is happening?" Concern wove through Sarah's voice.

"Reality." Without bothering to explain his intentions to his wife, he strode from the room, and inevitably, anxiety roared to life in his chest, bringing with it the crushing weight of duty.

Why could he not rise above the damned emotion?

Because anger was familiar and easy; peace was not.

Once more he'd failed. Cold disappointment circled through his gut. It had been folly to expect anything more of himself.

Chapter Seventeen

DREW STORMED ALONG the corridor and then took the stairs two at a time. How could this happen? Why did his brother think life was so horrid that he needed to kill himself? *I should have been there. I should never have come to Derbyshire.*

"Andrew, wait."

His body jerked at the sound of Sarah's voice as if he'd been shot. "Leave me alone. This doesn't concern you."

"Like hell it doesn't." Gone were the dulcet tones, the soft way she'd spoken to him during their time in the drawing room. Annoyance and disappointment roiled in her voice, and the *tap tap* of her heels on the stairs behind him a testament that she followed. "You are my husband, so what affects you bothers me as well." She caught up to him on the next level, and when she took his arm, she jerked him around to face her. The crumpled note was in her free hand. "Are you going to London?"

"Don't you think I need to?"

"This note is already two days old. By the time you reach the capital, another two days will have passed. Finn is alive." She pushed her spectacles into place. "What do you expect you can do for him?"

Why did she think to challenge him at every turn? "He is family." Turning on his heel, Drew proceeded along the corridor, and at his suite, he shoved open the door. "If I had been there in the first place, none of this would have happened."

"Do you really believe that?" She marched in after him and stood, her hands planted on her hips, glaring at him.

Too bad there was no time to fully appreciate the brewing storm she was. "Yes, damn it, I do. I would have seen he was in peril and prevented this attempt."

She snorted. "This from the man who can't see to his own trauma and healing." With a flick of her hand, she flung the note onto a nearby table. "Men with Finn's mindset are in a lost place, somewhere that a man with a blazing temper and demanding attitude will never be able to reach. If they can't find their way out, they'll attempt their death again."

"Are you so selfish that you would prevent me from attending to my family?" *Oh, God.* That wasn't what he'd wished to say at all, but the anger rising in a hot tide to fill his chest prevented him from making quick amends.

"Of course not. I'm merely asking you to think this through." She took a step toward him, but he routed her and moved into his sitting room. "If Finn is farther gone than we suspect, he needs the care of someone who can control his own emotions. He needs a doctor. If you go in there barking orders and tramping through delicate issues like a bull in a china shop, you run the risk of forever ruining your chances of repairing a relationship with him."

"You wish to consign my brother to death." A growl sounded in his voice.

"Absolutely not, but neither do I wish you to make his situation worse. I'm merely stating you're not the one he needs right now."

He rounded on her. "You can't possibly know about anything concerning family since you have none. Don't you dare to dictate to me how I should act or speak." The moment he said the words, hurt jumped into her eyes, and they welled with tears. *Bloody hell.* "I apologize." Then in a more modulated voice, he added, "I couldn't protect Finn on the battlefield, but I can damn well try in this."

Surprise rounded her eyes. "That is one of the greatest truths I've heard you utter." A tentative smile curved her lips.

Her surprise and delight despite him being horrid to her only deepened his guilt, but beneath that, a thread of calm spun through his insides, further confusing him. "I *am* capable of truth and trust, you know." The words came out on a snarl. "Just now I'm not inclined to work on personal growth."

"When your anger cools and you can talk to me with a rational mind, I'll be more than happy to discuss this further." She blinked quickly as tears filled her eyes. "But remember what we talked about this afternoon. You were doing so well, and now..." A tiny sob escaped. "Don't leave without saying goodbye. I never had the chance to do that with my parents, and if something happens to you while on this trip, in the rain..."

Damn and blast. She would worry about him while he was away? A piece of his heart flew into her keeping. He rather liked that. "Sarah, wait."

But she'd already cleared the door. The rapid tap of her heels on the hardwood faded, quickly followed by the slam of her door down the hall. No, she wasn't in a receptive mood, and quite frankly, he didn't have the time or inclination to grovel.

Drew cursed himself to the devil. It was one thing to close himself off from his family, but to potentially lose Sarah because he couldn't balance the two halves of his life?

I need to think.

July 12, 1817

SARAH WAITED IN the morning room for Andrew even though her stomach protested the early morning as well as the scent of the eggs and other savories on the sideboard. No doubt something she'd eaten at breakfast yesterday didn't agree with her, for she'd skipped dinner last night after her husband had completely undone all the progress he'd made.

Finally, he arrived, his tread heavy, his bootheels ringing on the floor, the spicy lime smell of him announcing his presence in the small room. His expression was haggard as if he hadn't slept well; neither had she.

"Sarah, I..." He looked at her then darted his glance away.

"I'd hoped to catch you." She wrapped her fingers around her cup of tea, craving its warmth. "Are you riding to London?"

"Yes, with Barton. We'll return with a coach, for speed on the back side of the trip is not imperative."

"Of course." She stared at the broad width of his shoulders as he filled his plate. Why should he worry about rushing back to his wife? Also, this way, he wouldn't ask her to accompany him. There was so much she wished to say, but from his taut posture and clenched jaw, he wouldn't receive it well.

When he'd brought his plate to the table and took a seat opposite her, she sighed. They wouldn't return to the intimacy they'd had yesterday, and she mourned that closeness. "I expect to remain in London for several days." Then he tucked into his food as if nothing had occurred to drive a wedge between them.

"And upon your return? What then?"

"What do you mean?" He glanced at her from over the rim of his coffee cup.

She put her own cup down. "Will you run away whenever you begin to feel good about your life, when peace is in your grasp?" For that was exactly what was happening. He was floundering in a morass of emotion, and she suspected he didn't want the lighter ones to win.

"I don't run." He followed the statement by shoving a forkful of scrambled eggs into his mouth.

"You do, and you're doing it now." She despised the waver in her voice. "Your brother is a grown man, and your mother is there too. Until he makes peace with his own demons, there's nothing you can do."

The earl narrowed his eyes. "Are you an expert on human nature or the mind?" He threw his fork onto his plate, scattering food onto the highly shined tabletop. "You were a damned governess. I doubt you have the education needed here."

"Why am I not surprised you've resorted to belittling me?" A shaft of hot ire stabbed through her chest. None of it was fair, but with this attitude, he wouldn't listen anyway. "I don't deserve that, and I won't stand for it."

"And neither will I sit here and let you dictate to me how much better adjusted to life you are than the Storme brothers." He stood so abruptly, his chair slid over the floor and crashed against the wall. "It's becoming quite off-putting."

"Fair point." Sarah nodded. "However, I *do* speak from some experience, because I almost lost myself to grief and anger after my parents died. That's the root problem here you're struggling with." For long moments she stared at her empty plate. His anger was palpable in the air, and that caused her own mood to sink. Then she said, "Why are you really taking this trip?"

He huffed. "We've been over this."

"Are you afraid Finn will die knowing how much of an arse you are, or do you wish to order him about, shame him into doing what you want as your father did to you?"

"How can you know that?" He gawked. When she merely lifted an eyebrow, he continued. "How can I not? He's my responsibility. My father's last words were to look after my brothers."

"I understand that, but you can't live their lives, and you certainly won't convince anyone to change their path unless you're walking a new one."

His ire lessened and a trace of fear scudded through his eyes. "I *have* to be there… so they will love and respect me, so my family will know I care, even though I haven't been able to say it…"

The poor man was nearing another breaking point. She wanted to hold him, to tell him it would hurt to set the feelings free, but it would prove worth it, yet she didn't move. "They *do* love you, but you'll never see that until you love yourself."

"Gah." He waved a hand in dismissal. "What gammon."

"Is it? You and I won't have a true relationship unless to accept yourself, flaws and all, and then forgive not only you but your brothers, your father." She blinked back the tears in her eyes. "It breaks my heart to see you struggle…"

A muscle in his cheek ticked, but he said nothing.

"You needn't if you'd stop carrying it all." Sarah shrugged and rose to her feet. "When will you realize that you're worthy of love regardless of what's happened, Andrew? That you're as entitled as anyone else to a good life, a life where you let someone care for you, where you need only worry about yourself?"

For long moments, he glared at her. Then his expression softened briefly before he worked his jaw and shoved a hand through his hair. "Because… I don't love myself. You were right in that regard. How can I when I'm a veritable powder keg in human form?" His eyes implored her for help, but she didn't know how, for she was numb from his reversion. She'd given him all the tools; she couldn't do the work for him. "Like you said, acceptance starts with me, and even in this I've failed: me, you—us."

Tears prickled the backs of her eyelids. She could only imagine the struggle he battled with. "But that's the glory of it all. You can always start again with more determination and experience." She came around the table toward him with a hand extended. "Love yourself as you are, knowing you can eventually conquer your demons, else your relationships with everyone else will fail as well."

Confusion roiled in his stormy eyes. For one second, she thought he might take her hand, but then he shook his head. "Damn you, Sarah. Ever since I've met you, you've distracted me, from... everything."

Another truth, but this one warmed her heart. "That's not necessarily a bad thing." She allowed herself a tiny smile. If he would only let himself have that breakthrough.

"I... you." Anger mixed with confusion on his face. "I'm sorry." The whisper sounded torn from a tight throat. With his fingers clutching at his chest, he fled the morning room.

"Oh, Andrew. Let go and see how wonderful life can be if you'd just open your eyes to what's standing in front of you," she said to the empty space where he'd previously stood. A few tears fell to her cheeks. She'd become a watering pot in the last few days, which was odd, for she'd never been given over to wandering emotions until she'd met him.

July 15, 1817

DREW RUBBED A hand over his face and glowered into his loaded breakfast plate. Even at half past ten, his stomach still churned though his appetite had fled. Had it only been four days since he'd eaten much the same fare with Sarah?

Three days since I left her in a snit. Three days since he'd almost admitted how much he'd come to rely on her, come to... *care for her.*

When he'd arrived in London yesterday evening, he'd gone straight to Finn's room. His brother had been sitting up in bed and alert, though he sported a rather large bandage about his head and his temper had nearly rivaled Drew's. They hadn't spent time chatting, for he'd been wet from the rain and tired besides, and damn it, he'd second-guessed his decision to leave Sarah.

Devil take it!

He shoved his plate away after only two bites and stood as quickly. His mind wouldn't quiet, and he knew why. Until he attempted to make peace with his brother, he'd not accomplish anything else.

On his way abovestairs, he passed the butler. "Have you seen Major Storme this morning, Peters?"

"I came from his room just now, my lord. A package was delivered for him." The ancient butler shrugged. "He was most secretive about it."

Drew's stomach bottomed out. Had he ordered something that would aid him in attempting suicide again? "Thank you." Then he took the remainder of the stairs two at a time. At Finn's door, he pressed the latch and shoved open the wooden panel. His brother sat up in his bed with a smallish box in his lap. The expression of delight and consternation on his face wasn't what one would think if the man had ordered a knife or other implement of killing. When Finn looked at him with a scowl, Drew cleared his throat. "Ah, good morning."

"What are you doing here?"

"What's in the box?" Drew countered. When he craned his neck to see, Finn threw the bedclothes over it.

"Nothing that concerns you." His brother frowned. "What are you doing in London? I thought you'd recently married. Don't you have a wife to keep you busy, or can she not stomach who you are like the rest of us?"

As a swath of hot anger slashed through his chest, Drew counted to ten slowly in his head to help alleviate the response that sat on the tip of his tongue. "I came because you nearly killed yourself."

Finn snorted. His dark hair stuck up around the bandage, making him look like an escapee from a hospital. "I was never near death. I simply fell out of my chair and hit my head."

"But the note you left?"

"Written prematurely in a fit of pique." He shrugged. "However, that crisis point has passed."

"How?" Drew had no idea what his brother struggled with, but suddenly he wished to. "How the devil can you flip between such an intense emotion like depression and then act completely different not four days later?"

"I suppose I've found something that distracts me or makes those other emotions less important. Perhaps I've found... hope." Finn cocked his head to one side as he regarded Drew. "Don't misunderstand me. When my depression comes to call, there's every chance I won't be able to pull myself out of that dark place, especially not alone."

"That settles it. I'm staying here." At least then he could fulfil his father's last wish.

"No." Finn held up a hand. "That's not the answer. Hell, you seethe with anger even now. Your anger feeds mine, and I don't want that beast to grow within me."

"But—"

"Stop." He grew silent for the space of a few heartbeats. "No one outside of myself can remove what I'm feeling, and no one's advice can help how I navigate my way through." As he rubbed his fingers along his whisker-covered chin, he nodded. "Neither can I pretend the things that happened to me while on those battlefields didn't. It is life."

The words both confused Drew and gave him a tiny glimmer of hope. It was much like what Sarah had told him, but from a different perspective. "How do you conquer those emotions without them consuming you?" It hurt his pride to ask, but Finn, though his life had been turned upside down and confined him to a Bath chair, seemed more well-adjusted to it.

"It's a constant battle. On the days when I'm feeling weaker, then the darkness wins, and my thoughts follow suit." He shrugged, and for the first time Drew realized how fit and lean his brother was. "Having people about with sunny dispositions and determination of their own helps." A low chuckle escaped him. "Of course, my favorite people to spend time with are those who have their own struggles but have come out the victor, for that gives me hope."

"I see." Drew gawked at him. It seemed so easy, so why did he constantly fail at it?

"There is one caveat."

"Oh?"

"For myself, *I* must want that change, I need to keep moving toward being a better man despite what happened to me. Going to war showed me that life is short, and I did things merely to survive, but coming home has shown me that life has the potential to be long, and..." He swallowed audibly. "I'd like to be around for some of it, to enjoy the time I have left. Only *I* can make certain of that."

There was nothing to say. Both Finn and Sarah held the same beliefs, and unless he—Drew—made the decision to change, it would never happen. He nodded. "Well then, if you don't require my assistance..."

"I do not."

"You're well? Promise me you won't attempt this again." This was an opportunity for him to make his peace with his brother, but the words wouldn't leave his lips. Perhaps he hadn't matured enough for that.

Yet.

"I am well, but I can make you no promises. Depression is a formidable opponent."

Here was the chance to tell his brother how he felt, that he cared about him, that he was sorry, but the words only sat on the tip of his tongue without mutating into speech.

Speculation lit Finn's eyes. "My turn to ask questions. Why the devil did you marry so quickly, and to a woman you didn't know?"

Why indeed? "To fulfil my duty to the title."

"Ah." His brother frowned. "Will you tell me about her? She must have an incredibly strong will if she married you, and..." He held up a forefinger when Drew's chest swelled with anger, straining the buttons on his waistcoat. "And you're standing here, not berating me for a shortcoming, but asking me how you might overcome yours."

"Such gammon. And no, I will not." Talking about Sarah to another man smacked of gossip, but heat rose up the back of his neck and his chest ached in a different way than usual.

"Still the arse," Finn said with a shake of his head.

"You would know." He needed to leave before his brother struck upon the truth. "I won't take more of your time, but mind you remain in bed to rest. I don't want any more frantic letters from Mother."

"Oh, I intend to stay in bed, at least for some of the time." Remarkably, a flush covered Finn's face.

Not understanding what the statement or the reaction meant, Drew left and moments later returned to the morning room. When he glanced at his mother who sat in her customary chair, his shoulders slumped. He'd hoped he would have been alone to finish his meal and mull over what Finn had said.

"Good morning, Mother." He took the chair he'd vacated. His plate was gone, but Peters brought him another, filled with all the same foods as he'd had before.

"Hello, Andrew." She glanced at him with bright eyes. "I overheard part of your conversation with Phineas. I'm glad you were civil."

"Of course I was," he snapped, and then sighed. "I apologize."

When his mother's eyebrows soared, he took refuge in the fresh cup of tea the butler poured for him. "How is wedded life?" She added cream and a tiny lump of sugar to her tea.

There was no blessed way to answer that question without giving away the huge rifts between him and Sarah. "As well as can be expected."

"Hmm." As his mother stirred her tea with a delicate spoon, she rested her gaze on him. "I won't deny that your news came as a shock to me. Not to mention I was hurt I hadn't been invited or even consulted."

"Please, Mother, I refuse to sit through a lecture. What's done is done."

"Agreed. Such things never broke through to you."

Drew poked at the food on his plate with the tines of his fork. "Marrying Sarah was the right choice for me at the time." Was it still? An image of her appeared in his mind's eye: her smile when she'd been pleased with him, the amusement dancing in her brown eyes, the damned spectacles that always slipped down, the soft sounds of pleasure she'd made when they were intimate in the drawing room, the way he bossed him into seeing life in a different way.

"Oh, I don't doubt it. Regardless of your impetuous nature and your horrid temper, your head for responsibility is sound."

He barely heard her, so deep had he slipped into his thoughts. God, it seemed like an eternity since he'd seen Sarah, and what was more, he... missed her. As unobtrusively as he could, he rubbed a hand over his heart. The organ ached as if it had been ripped away from a vital part of itself.

Was it possible? Could he have only seen it with distance?

"When your father and I first married, there was a long period of adjustment." She spread a thin layer of marmalade on a triangle of toast. "He was much like you: dutiful but stubborn, and I was a bit headstrong. We fought in those days, but it only made the times we came together that much sweeter."

"For pity's sake, Mother, please don't tell me about your intimate life with Father." Drew hastily gulped his tea, which hadn't had a chance to cool. Tears stung his eyes as the liquid burned his throat.

"I simply meant that two personalities can oftentimes clash, but eventually they learn how to work together and make something truly amazing." She pressed her lips together when a smile formed. "Sarah must have made quite the impression on you."

"She has indeed." What was she doing right now? When he'd left, she had tears in her eyes. Had she recovered from the hurt, or his defection? Unease circled through his gut. Worse, had his inability to conquer his emotions sounded the death knell of his short marriage? To distract himself from his thoughts, he told his mother a brief history of his wife, but he left out anything having to do with the difficulties they'd encountered since wedding.

"Why didn't you bring her with you? I would have enjoyed meeting her."

"Because I'm a prick." And he hadn't been able to see past his own damn nose, past his own bloody offended feelings—from everyone. He might have hurt his family at any given time with his temper and arrogance, but they'd always forgiven him. What if Sarah didn't? The ache in his heart intensified.

I don't want to lose her.

This time his mother couldn't quell her smile. She tapped a fingernail against an ivory envelope next to her plate he noticed for the first time. Drew's name was scrawled on the top in his father's heavy hand. "I won't ask any more questions, for it's obvious you're confused enough already. However, your father left this letter for you, intended to give it to you on your wedding day. Since he's not here and since I missed it, I'm giving it to you now." She slid the envelope toward him.

"What is this?" Drew gave up the pretense of eating. As soon as he laid down his fork, he retrieved the envelope.

"Advice from a father to his son, things he only realized after the fact. Perhaps it will help you now." With all the dignity she'd always possessed, his mother rose. "I'll leave you alone to read it."

"No, please stay." He broke the seal—the exact crest on his signet ring—and then extracted the piece of paper within. When he unfolded the missive, a wave of grief assailed him the second he saw his father's writing. "I miss him so damn much," Drew whispered.

"So do I." His mother slipped into a chair beside him. With a slight inclination of her chin, she dismissed the butler.

"Shall I read it aloud?" The hand holding the letter shook.

"I think this first time you should keep it to yourself."

"Very well." He nodded.

To my son Andrew on the day of your wedding.

I'm not good with words, nor with showing emotion, but know I'm exceedingly proud of you this day. The best advice I can give you now is simple, and what I've discovered along my path in life.

No one knows what they're doing, though some of us might hide that confusion and fear better than others. I certainly felt as if I were lost in a morass at times, not only with the title but also in marriage. Both are huge responsibilities, and they will overwhelm you if you let them. There is no right way to handle both; you must figure it out for yourself.

When I took up the Earl of Hadleigh mantle, I was exceedingly fortunate in that I married your mother soon after. She has been a tremendous helpmate, and I honestly don't know what I would have become without her.

I hope on this day that you've chosen well a strong woman who will do the same for you. Once you take up the title—which will be soon after I've finished this letter—a calming influence in your countess will make all the difference. Be sure the two of you work together, not only in the marriage but also in everything. Discover life together, for there will be both highs and lows. The only way to weather those storms is with a good woman by your side.

His hand shook. Sarah was that. Ever since the day he'd married her, she'd been trying to make him see he could be so much more if only he'd look past all the injury he'd carried around.

You will become an admirable earl when it's your time, and I know you'll do the title proud, but you must let your brothers find their own paths. Yes, I asked you to look after them—after your mother—but I meant in a supportive way, perhaps give them guid-

ance to chase their dreams, but don't bully them into decisions. That is not for you. Only your life is in your purview. You must attend to it else you'll always be at odds. With everything.

"Oh, God." The whispered words sounded overly loud in the silence. His father essentially said what both Sarah and Flynn had in their own words.

Make your existence—your marriage and any children should you have—as fulfilling as you can. Above everything, find happiness, court peace, before it's too late. I spent too much time dwelling on regrets and holding onto grudges, anger, resentment, even fear. They festered, ate away at my soul, Andrew, compromised my relationship with my brother. No, I won't waste time now telling you the reason for the rift between us. Don't let this happen to you. If you fail at everything else in life, at least you'll still have that calm, that sense that everything will come out right in the end.

And that will take you far.

In closing, please know that I've always been proud of you. If I could have done it all over again, I would have told you how wrong I was in most everything. A man's duty is to be strong for his family, his title, of course, but that doesn't mean portray yourself as cold or unmoving. Let yourself feel everything, but only keep those emotions that serve you. Release the rest, else you'll have shot yourself in the foot before you start. Your mother tried to teach me that, but I didn't learn until I lay dying.

Hot tears prickled the backs of his eyelids, but he was beyond caring. Drew let them fall to his cheeks, and as the remaining words blurred on the page, he kept reading.

All this is a long-winded way of saying, don't model your life after mine. Put your own signature to being earl and love the hell out of your wife while you can. The time allotted to us is so fleeting...

Much love,

Father

In that moment, the storms inside him quieted and a sense of peace fell over him. His thoughts became as clear as crystal. He lifted his eyes to his mother, didn't care if she saw his wet cheeks or the tears that fell. "I have to go home to Sarah. I need to fix our union before I do anything else."

I love her.

When it had happened, he couldn't say, but there it was. He needed her in his life, for better or for worse, and he couldn't tackle being the earl without her.

Moisture welled in his mother's eyes. She laid a hand on his arm. "You've had an epiphany?"

"I believe that I have. I need to go home." Quickly, he folded the letter, jammed it into the envelope and then crammed it into the interior pocket of his jacket. Drew scrambled awkwardly to his feet. "Thank you, for everything. And know that I'm so incredibly sorry for the last handful of years." He engulfed her in a hug. "Once I'm settled, after I give Sarah a proper wedding trip, we'll come up to London when Parliament opens. Perhaps, if you'd like, we can host a rout as celebration."

When he pulled away, his mother stared at him with bemusement. "I'd like that." She waved a hand. "Go, go and win your wife. I can't wait to meet the woman who started this change in you."

Drew nodded. As soon as he left the room, he yelled for both Peters and Barton. If he were lucky, Sarah would receive him with open arms and a forgiving heart.

And he could begin his life anew.

CHAPTER EIGHTEEN

July 19, 1817

SARAH'S NERVES FELT strung too tight. Her heart was being pulled in two directions. She glanced at her maid, but Tilly was busy packing one of the two trunks they would take with them. With nothing else to do, she moved to glance out of a window of her bedroom. Gray, overcast skies, clouds swollen with even more rain than they'd already received didn't bode well for the upcoming trip to Brighton, but it couldn't be helped.

She touched a fingertip to the window glass, traced the path of a raindrop as it raced to the bottom. It was critical that she remove from Derbyshire now, for she'd missed her menses last week and that had never happened before. A trace of excitement buzzed down her spine, but she refused to let herself hope for what it might mean. However, it *was* entirely possible that she'd become with child the first time she'd had relations with a man. No wonder she'd been an incessant watering pot of late.

And if was true, even if it were too early to be certain or have a midwife examine her, it was best to make a clean break from her husband and settle in Brighton so she could start her life anew—again.

Without him.

A wad of tears lodged in her throat. No amount of swallowing would disburse the blockage. Before he'd left for London, the week they'd spent together, the wonderful afternoon in the drawing room, had been some of the best days she'd ever experienced. He had made such progress, and even when he'd been in the midst of a temper when the missive from his mother arrived, he'd almost had a breakthrough.

Too bad he'd let anger get the better of him. He'd had a choice, and he'd taken it. Never would he gain control of his emotions, which meant he wouldn't change. Not really. Perhaps the charming gentleman he'd been during his week of courting her had been false, and she'd been a woman desperate for love, so she'd believed the act.

No more. I am not foolish nor am I stupid. I won't live with a violent, emotionally cold man.

Neither would the babe she possibly carried. How horrible for a child to grow up in a world where its father was a snarling beast most of the time. She had to protect it, insulate it from that, and instead show it love, for everyone deserved that.

Unfortunately, she would never know that from her husband.

"My lady, I've finished with the unmentionables and shoes. Which gowns and dresses would you like to take?"

The sound of Tilly's voice brought Sarah out of her tortuous thoughts. She turned about to face the young woman. Perhaps eighteen, the girl had come highly recommended by a neighbor, and Sarah had been all too willing to give her a chance. She showed promise and could be trained into a vital member of the staff.

"Let's bring a few dresses and only two evening gowns. I plan to live simply and quietly, but if fancier gowns are needed, I'll hire a modiste." Of course they would be regardless of whether or not she planned to entertain, for if she were increasing, she'd need roomier clothing.

"As you wish, my lady." Excitement wove through the maid's voice. "I've never been to Brighton nor have I seen the sea."

A ghost of a smile curved Sarah's lip. "Neither have I, so we'll experience it together. Perhaps we'll embark on charity work." She glanced at the case that her flute reposed in. Or perhaps she might find a local orchestra in the holiday town that might wish to hire a flutist of some talent.

"My lady, if I may have a word?"

Sarah glanced at the open door where Mrs. Hastings stood, her expression filled with distress. "Of course." She crossed the room and joined the housekeeper in the corridor. "What is it, Mrs. Hastings? Is something wrong?"

"Everything is wrong!" The older woman spoke in hushed tones while she wrung her work-roughened hands together. "It's not right you're going. We were excited when His Lordship announced he'd marry, and we've all adored having you here at Hadleigh Hall. You've brought life to this old house again." A frown pulled at her lips and creased her round face. "If it's the earl that's the problem, tell him to stay in London. The staff here has really enjoyed having a lady about again. Perhaps you can roust him from this manor."

A bit of hysterical laughter rose in her throat, but she tamped the urge to release it. Instead, she pushed her spectacles into place. "It's a lovely property and I have grown fond of you all." She hesitated. Was she making a mistake in leaving? Then she shook her head. No, this was for the best. Andrew would come back soon. She couldn't bear to see him as the same man she'd first met, as if their time together hadn't happened, for being with his family again would cause his regression.

The housekeeper frowned. "For a time, we thought..."

"So did I, Mrs. Hastings." Sarah laid a hand on the older woman's arm. "However, I suppose it simply wasn't meant to be." Another wave of silly tears filled her eyes. She looked away, hoping they'd fade. "Perhaps had he not gone to London..." If that letter had never come, they might have made a go of it.

"If it makes a difference, the earl didn't want to leave you."

"What?" Sarah snapped her gaze to the housekeeper's face as her heartbeat accelerated. "Why would you say that?"

A tinge of a blush stained the older woman's cheeks. "I overheard him speaking with Barton in the hall upstairs. He was anxious, but it was different than usual. He worried about what would happen to you, said that perhaps he should let Major Storme—his brother—do without him."

"Did his valet convince him otherwise?"

"Oh, no, my lady. Barton said Derbyshire was the best place for him. That his time here had made a difference in his temperament."

Sarah snorted. "But he *did* leave, didn't he?" At least it wasn't just her advice he didn't listen to. "The earl hasn't learned anything during our marriage." The last was said on a sob. "He'd showed such promise a few times, but never could he let go enough to walk into that new life with me." She shouldn't tell a servant such things, but she considered some of them family, related to them better than she might with snobbish lords and ladies of the *ton* since she'd been more or less one of them, and Mrs. Hastings had been so kind to her on her wedding night...

"Oh, but he *has* changed, my lady." The housekeeper nodded so vigorously, her double chin wobbled. "He also wants his family happy."

Sarah huffed. "He wants their approval of his being an arse." Then her eyes widened, and she gasped. "I shouldn't have said that."

The housekeeper chuckled. "Oh, you're such a duck, my lady. I'm sad to see you go." She sighed. "His Lordship won't ever have happiness, for he's not that himself."

"I know." She took a shuddering breath. "Which is why I must go. It's exhausting to wonder and worry and hope. He'll never love me until he accepts himself." *And at this point, I rather doubt that will happen.* If she didn't get away, she'd burst into tears. "I've left a letter for him on his bureau. Please be certain he sees it."

"I will." The housekeeper stepped closer. She worried her pinafore apron with her fingers. "My lady, if I may ask a bold question?"

"Of course." Would that the staff here could come with her to Brighton. Wouldn't that serve Andrew right if he came home to a barren house?

A knowing gleam entered Mrs. Hastings' eyes. "Do you love His Lordship?"

Did she? After everything, she'd thought there might have been *something*, affection at the very least, between them. "It's difficult to say, but I have come to care for the earl." She rested a hand on her belly. If he knew they'd created a child together, would that usher in a permanent change? Would it make a difference if she told him?

Probably not.

"It wouldn't matter if I did, would it? He doesn't love anyone except himself."

The housekeeper clucked like a distressed hen. "Men like him don't show it."

"They should, for the people in their lives need to hear it, see that love."

Eventually, the housekeeper nodded. "He's naught but a lost little boy at times, my lady. Lord knows we've all experienced that at one time or another." With a mighty sniff, she threw her arms around Sarah. "We'll miss you, and that's a fact."

It had been so long since she'd felt such security from another person that she gave into tears and hugged Mrs. Hastings back, propriety be damned. People should feel safe enough to share and show emotions regardless of class, rank, or social setting. "Thank you for everything, Mrs. Hastings. Please tell the staff goodbye for me." When she pulled away, she wiped at the tears on her cheeks. "I adored the suite you had readied for me. I might miss that most of all."

The older woman ducked her head. "I won't give up hope he can win you back."

"That would take a miracle, I'm afraid."

Mrs. Hastings' smile held a mysterious edge. "Love is like that, isn't it?"

Then the maid called out to Sarah with a question regarding a gown, and she parted from the older woman with a wave.

Yes, it was better to leave when it was easier, and her heart hadn't been fully engaged. It was bad enough that organ felt as if it would break in half already.

THREE HOURS LATER, the traveling coach had been loaded with luggage, the horses hitched and ready, Sarah had been settled inside with her maid, and they'd been underway for nearly one of those hours. Though the gentle rain from earlier had turned heavier and the skies had darkened further, she couldn't remain for one moment longer in the house where memories haunted her at every turn.

"How long will the journey take, my lady?" Tilly asked with a fearful glance out the window. Up until this point she had been silent.

"One of the drivers told me seven days. We'll overnight at coaching inns along the way, but they'll be comfortable, I'm sure." Yet they wouldn't have Andrew and that devastating grin he flashed when something had particularly amused him. Nor would any of those places have the sound of his rumbling voice or the warmth of his laughter when he let himself enjoy life.

The maid looked more closely out the window. "It's a horrible storm."

"Indeed." Perhaps this was the biggest folly to insist on traveling in such conditions, but she had no other recourse. The coach wheels bumped over seemingly every rock and rut in the road. Over the sound of the rain, the ghastly slurping, sucking noise of the water and mud pulling at the wheels rang in her ears.

With each mile that slowly went by, Sarah's unease grew. She restlessly shifted positions—again—and tossed aside the volume of poetry she'd been trying to read for the last half hour. "I'm afraid this was a terrible decision." Perhaps it would be more prudent to ask the drivers to turn back. She could always begin the trip anew when the weather had improved.

"Don't worry so, my lady." The soothing tones of Tilly's voice gave her a modicum of calm. "Think what adventures await you in Brighton. Do you ever wonder what sand feels like on bare toes?"

"I'm afraid I never have." She hadn't given the Brighton town-house much thought except to post a letter to the butler a few days ago with plans of her arrival.

"I'll wager it feels weird at first." The maid shivered. A cheerful grin curved her mouth as she clasped her much-darned glove-covered hands in her lap. "The sunshine will be worth all the hardships of this trip, though."

While Sarah appreciated the girl's bright attitude, at the moment she wished she were alone, for she needed to grieve the death of her brief marriage—to mourn the separation from Andrew. Why couldn't he have seen his future was so much brighter than what he clung to in the past? Tamping down a sob, she drew the folds of her forest green cloak about her, for the rain had turned the summer afternoon chilly.

Another few miles went by before Tilly spoke again. "My lady, are you sure this trip is wise? I'm frightened."

So am I. "Perhaps the weather will clear soon."

"No, that's not what I meant." The girl shook her head. A tendril of her mousy brown hair slipped from its knot at the back of her head.

"What did you mean then?" She truly didn't wish to talk.

"You're in love with the earl, so is leaving him now a good decision? He'll worry so once he returns and finds you gone."

"How silly." Sarah shook her head. "Why would you think such a thing?" She certainly didn't *feel* in love with him. And wouldn't she know beyond a doubt if she were?

"When you speak of him, you have a look in your eye I saw once in a dog who really adored the stable master where I used to work." There was no guile in her expression, just honesty. "If you look at him like that, why would you want to leave? I'd think you'd wish to wait until he returns and have a nice reunion."

When she would have protested the validity of the statement, she sighed instead. "I'm afraid it's too complicated to explain." It didn't matter how she felt, for there could be no future with him if he were reluctant to change.

Tilly shrugged. "I believe you, my lady, but does it need to be? You either love him or you don't." Her eyes took on a faraway, dreamy quality. "I think I might have waited for him to return, and if my heart didn't leap when I saw him, *then* I would leave."

Sarah frowned. "What difference would that make?"

"Well, if a heart leaps, that's a sure sign, isn't it? And it's something to hang onto." She shrugged. "At least that's what my Gram says."

"She sounds like a wise woman." When Sarah turned her face to the window glass, she stifled a sigh. Was she doing him a grave disservice by abandoning him? She sucked in a quick breath. Running from him when she'd spoken out against him for doing the same? Perhaps she should accept him as he was and learn to work around his flaws, for every person had them. Yet... when she recalled their wedding night and the temper he'd been in at that time, she shivered. No, she refused to let him treat her like an afterthought or a doormat. He'd either tame his temper or he'd lose her, but he couldn't have both.

I deserve to feel safe and loved, and to have my husband show me such.

SARAH CAME AWAKE from a light doze by the feeling that something wasn't quite right. She checked the timepiece pinned to her cloak. Two hours had passed. Since they'd left well after teatime, twilight had now fallen, plunging the interior of the coach into purpling shadows. Otherwise, nothing had changed. A quick glance about the coach confirmed the assumption. Tilly dozed on the opposite bench. Rain thrummed against the roof and windows.

Then what had woken her?

Frantic shouting from the drivers reached her ears, and immediately cold fingers of fear played her spine. Before she could raise her voice in an inquiry, a large crack resounded through the coach. She gasped and scrambled for purchase on her bench, but then the vehicle lurched violently to the left, throwing both Sarah and her maid across the interior. They crashed against the wall. The drivers shouted. Words that sounded suspiciously like "bridge out" echoed in her head. Wild whinnies from the horses blended with the human shouts.

Tilly came awake with a cry. "What's going on, my lady?"

There was no time to answer. Seconds later, the equipage dropped. When it came to a rough stop, presumably against the ground, both she and Tilly cried out. Water seeped into the tilted coach, confirming the assumption.

"Dear God, we've gone off a bridge." Had it washed away in the deluge? All the rain over the last few days would have made the creeks and streams rise. Sarah struggled to stand. Her feet slipped in the murky water as she half-crouched on what was the window glass. Cool water saturated the lower portion of her gown and cloak, chilling her lower limbs. "Tilly, are you all right?" They needed to exit the coach, for if the water came up too high, they'd surely drown. It was seeping inside way too fast.

"I think so, my lady. Hit my head, though." The maid clung to the door handle above her head. A deep gash at her temple glittered wet with blood.

"At least you're alive, and so am I." Which meant they could still survive.

A pounding of fists on the door above caught her attention. "How do you fare, my lady?" It was one of the drivers.

"Well. My maid is injured." The water had risen to her waist.

"I'll have you out in a jiffy."

"Where's the other driver?"

"Unconscious. Knocked his head when we went off the bridge. Didn't see it was out in the gloom, but I got him to the bank." A string of swearing followed. Then the door wrenched open and the man extended an arm. "Come, my lady, give me your hand."

"No. Take Tilly first." She grasped the confused girl about the waist and gave her a slight boost. "Grab onto him and he'll pull you out." The poor maid shivered against her.

"I'll try." She extended both hands. Sure enough, once the driver took hold, he grunted and then he slowly hauled her up and through the gaping door.

"As soon as I get her to safety, I'll come back for you, my lady," the driver assured her.

"I understand." Yet her heartbeat raced as fear chilled the blood in her veins.

How long would that be? At the rate water filled the coach's interior, they'd have perhaps minutes before the current swept it downstream. Not wanting to wait, Sarah grabbed onto the bench above and stood on the edge of hers. She felt for the edge of the doorway, and when she was sure she'd found good enough purchase with her gloved fingers, she jumped upward, braced herself on her arms while her legs dangled in the opening. Then she hooked a leg on the doorframe and hauled her body up and out of the coach's interior.

Heavy rain battered her, plastering her clothing to her body. The water-soaked skirts weighed her down, the cloak was unwieldy, but she struggled to her feet on the side of the coach. Not far away on the bank, one of the drivers lay in the muddy grass. The second driver had reached his side, where he bid Tilly to sit. Both horses were attached to their harnesses, but alive as they stood in the rushing torrent.

When the driver saw her, he hastened down the bank and waded out into the coursing creek, using the coach wheels and under equipage to remain upright. "Let me help you down," he called up to her. "It's treacherous, so don't let go until your feet are firmly planted on the creek bottom."

"All right." She dropped to all fours on the side of the coach and slowly crawled to the edge near him. Then she dangled her legs over. The driver lifted an arm. "Should I slide down?"

"Real quick like. I'll grab onto you."

With her stomach in knots, Sarah slid off the side of the coach. When she went to grasp the driver's hand, her frivolous shoes slipped on the rocks and mud, and with a scream, she was torn from his fingers. The current caught at her clothes and shoved her against the underside of the vehicle. She clung to the far wheel as water gushed into her face.

"Hang on, my lady!"

"As if I could do anything else." *I was so terribly wrong!* She should have stayed home, should have been grateful for all that she had, regardless that she didn't have Andrew's love, and most of all, she should have told him how she felt. Then, her stomach pitched. "My flute. I need to retrieve my flute." Despite the driver's warnings, she placed a foot on one of the wheel's spokes and began to climb.

CHAPTER NINETEEN

D REW LEFT LONDON a little over three days ago. The weather had been fair in the capital and for most of his journey, but they'd headed into heavy rain with just under three hours until they would reach Derbyshire. With nothing else to do except be alone with his thoughts, he'd willed himself to relax as he reclined on one of the benches, while Barton lounged on the other.

Sleep wouldn't come, for despite the need to arrive home, a sense of renewal and peace coursed through him. After reading that letter from his father, everything in his life had turned on its head. The whole of his thoughts had changed direction. Knowing that his father had struggled with the same issues that Drew did took his anxiety by a stranglehold. No longer did he think these problems he dealt with were unique to his situation.

Every peer went through the same.

The clarification that he needn't be solely responsible for the lives of his brothers had taken considerable pressure off his shoulders. Why couldn't he see it earlier when Sarah had spoken to him? It didn't matter, for it was there now, and he couldn't stop thinking about how much of a difference those written words had made.

Father was proud of me the whole time, but because he'd never been taught to show his emotions, he couldn't tell me.

He continued to marvel at the knowledge. Even more stunning was the fact that Finn would come out all right—without his help or his orders. Somehow, his brother had found the secret to living a somewhat balanced life—he hoped—which meant Drew needn't feel anxious regarding the future.

No doubt Brand would discover the same, for at the heart of the matter, they three were Stormes, and like their namesakes, they didn't back down in the face of adversity. Both his brothers would find their way without his inept interference. And if fate were kind, all three of them would stumble upon happiness and peace.

After everything.

Another piece of anxiety's shell fell away from around his heart and chest. And if he were to follow in his father's footsteps, he would risk ruining the best thing that had ever happened to him. His pulse thrummed faster at the thought of his wife. She'd been there all along, waiting for him to make the realization for himself, supporting him as he'd struggled, guiding him away from everything he'd designed to hold him back. She'd stared into his soul, past all the ugliness, and found him worthy all the same.

And he couldn't wait to tell her—show her—how much she meant, how he was changing even now, bit by bit.

The shadows of the waterlogged twilight were beginning to give way to the inky darkness of the night. He nearly pitched to the floor when his traveling coach came to an abrupt halt. Would the rain never end?

"What the devil is going on?"

Barton picked himself off the floor and resettled onto his bench. "I'm not certain."

The faint rumble of his drivers' voices reached his ears, but he couldn't discern the gist of the conversation. After throwing open a door, he turned up the collar of his greatcoat and vaulted out of the equipage. "Haines, what the deuce is the issue?" He made his way toward the driver's box and the horses with Barton following. The rain pelted him, and he realized he'd left his hat inside the coach. Well, it wouldn't do to retrieve it now.

"Looks like the bridge is washed out and the road ahead flooded." The man came down from the driver's perch. "Not unusual for this area. I've seen it happen a few years ago."

A shout from the second driver caught Drew's attention. "There's a coach on its side in the creek up the way! I can see it through the trees when I stand." He pointed off into the distance.

Drew looked into the direction but couldn't see anything form his vantage point. "Damn this delay," he grumbled into the rain. "How many miles to the next bridge?"

The grizzled Haines shrugged. "Might be four if the other bridge is washed out too."

"That's too much time." Drew shoved a gloved hand through his dripping hair. He wanted to reach Hadleigh Hall as soon as possible, had to beg Sarah's forgiveness, needed to tell her—

A faint feminine scream broke through his thoughts.

Bloody hell. "That doesn't sound good."

His valet nodded. "Almost is reminiscent of the countess' voice."

"Surely not, Mr. Barton," the driver said. "She's safe at home."

I'll wager she's not. Guilt plowed into the worry building in Drew's chest. No doubt she'd got it into her head that he was too much of an arse to change, and she'd decided to leave him. *After she promised not to.* He wanted to summon anger, but for the first time in a handful of years, that emotion wasn't available to tap into. Only cold depression slithered through his insides, for if it were true, he'd done it to himself. *I deserve her retreat.*

"The one way to know for certain is to investigate. Haines, Barton, you're with me. William, take our coach to where the other is disabled. Even if it's not my wife, the occupants in that vehicle will need aide."

Barton snorted. "When have you become so benevolent?"

I've stumbled upon a new perspective. "It's something new I'm trying."

Not waiting to see if they both agreed to the plan, Drew bolted forward off the road. His boot soles slipped and slid over the muddy ground as he followed the swollen creek through the trees. With every footfall, his heart beat in double time. Had she truly left him? Did she not believe in him? He huffed and wiped at the rain on his face. Hell, for years he hadn't believed in himself. She'd only known him for a month, and for that, he couldn't blame her.

But he wanted the chance to show her he was a different man. Or trying to be.

When the dark body of the tipped coach appeared, half submerged in the flood waters, his stomach dropped. A glance through the rain revealed one of Hadleigh Hall's drivers lying on the opposite bank while Sarah's young maid stood nearby, her arms wrapped around herself, the picture of a bedraggled rat. The other driver had waded into the water to unharness the horses.

Where the devil was his wife?

"Sarah!" He approached the bank and then hollered at the driver. "Archie, where's the countess?"

The man jerked his head up, squinted in the rain. "Thank God you're here, my lord." He wiped at the water on his face. "Her Lordship went back inside the coach to retrieve a flute, she said." The rain almost drowned out his explanation. "I tried to talk her out of it, but she was near hysterical about finding it."

"And she stubbornly argued against common sense, all for the flute." Which represented her dreams and was the last item she had that her father had given her. *Oh, Sarah.* Drew held up a hand. "I understand." When he ran his gaze over the waterlogged coach, a flash of movement caught his attention. As he stared, dumbfounded, his wife slowly appeared, pulling herself up through the door until she perched on the side, her stocking-clad legs fully on display, the leather handle of her flute case clenched firmly between her teeth. "Sarah!"

She wrenched her head around at his call. After removing the case's handle from her mouth, she stared. "Andrew!"

Was it his imagination or did the driving rain play tricks on him, for he thought he saw a wide grin split her lips? Surely a woman in a snit with him wouldn't do such a thing if she unexpectedly came upon her absent husband. "What the deuce are you doing? Come down from there." He glanced at his valet, who shrugged.

"I had to find my flute." She glanced between him and the bank where her maid waited. "I can't climb down with it, though."

Foolish, adorable thing. Didn't she realize that she was more valuable than anything else? "Toss it to me then."

"You'll catch it, right?" Sarah clutched the instrument case to her chest as if it were a child. If they came out of this thing alive with their marriage intact, he would move heaven and earth to make her dreams of being a professional musician come true.

"Yes, of course, but Archie, Barton, and I can't attempt to rescue you unless you have full use of both your hands." He looked to the driver. Both horses were freed, and as soon as Drew's coach pulled into view far down the road, the horses splashed and struggled out of the creek to greet them.

"Very well." Her hair lay plastered to her skull, and her drenched skirts clung to her person. "Here it comes!"

As far as throws went, it wasn't the best, but as the case tumbled tip over tail in a low arc toward him, Drew launched himself and caught it like he used to do with balls his brothers threw in their childhood. When Archie climbed out of the creek and moved to his location, Drew thrust the case into his hands. "Look after this with your life, for if it's lost, I'll direct the countess' wrath to you."

"I'll be careful." Archie walked toward the oncoming coach.

"I'm coming down." The sound of Sarah's voice had him jerking around to face the tipped coach once more.

"Wait!" But when had she ever followed instructions he'd issued? As he watched with horrified fascination, she flipped onto her belly while her legs dangled over the side of the vehicle. Then she slid down, hanging onto the edge of the coach with her gloved hands. In an attempt to find purchase on the rear wheel, her hand slipped.

A scream was ripped from her while Drew's heart lodged in his throat. She fell into the water, going under briefly, but her head surfaced, and she clung to the wheel. "Andrew!"

"Bloody hell." Icy fear rooted his feet to the spot for the span of a few heartbeats.

"I'll go, my lord," Barton said, already moving toward the bank.

"No. If you must help, take one of the horses and ride of Hadleigh Hall, alert them to the situation so they'll be ready when the rest of us arrive."

"You're sure?" Barton narrowed his eyes.

"Yes. I must do this." He waved a hand.

"Very well. Best of luck." Then the man was off.

Drew turned his attention back to his wife. "I can't lose you, Sarah," he whispered. They hadn't had enough time together; he'd only just realized how much she meant to him. The current rushed against her as she held onto the wheel, and the gathering darkness coupled with the rain made it deuced difficult to analyze the scene clearly.

"If I could gain a foothold," she shouted, and broke the horrid spell he'd fallen under.

"Don't move." Willing himself into motion, Drew approached the edge of the creekbank, conscious of the muddy conditions. "I'm coming in for you."

"Be careful. It's dangerous." Water droplets obscured the lenses of her spectacles, and he doubted that she could see him all that well.

His heart squeezed. In the midst of her own peril, she worried about his safety. "Hold on." Testing the integrity of the bank, Drew gingerly climbed down but was soon in the rapidly moving swollen creek. *Christ, that's cold.* Then he shoved the thought away and concentrated on grabbing the wheel nearest to him. He sank further into the water, and it rushed hard at the center of his chest. Five feet of churning, moving, muddy creek separated him from her, but at the moment it might have been five miles. This operation required delicacy and patience—both of which he didn't have. Cold fear kept him company as he moved his hand, inch by slow inch, over the wheel, clinging to the wooden spokes. He extended an arm, merely to see if he could touch her.

Almost, but not quite.

"Give me your hand, slowly." The drum of the steady rain filled his ears, and he was deuced tired of the constant moisture in his eyes, but there was nothing for it.

She clutched the front wheel with her right hand and reached out toward him with her left. A foot of churning water lay between her and him. "I think if I let go, I could swim over."

"No! The water is moving too fast and I have more weight on me. I'll come to you."

"Let me..." She released the wheel and promptly disappeared beneath the raging dirty water.

"Oh, God." Drew's heart stopped. "Sarah!" His fingers cramped, so tightly did he hold onto the wheel. When her head broke the surface, he blew out a breath of relief. Once more she clung to the far wheel, her body plastered to it as she shivered. The dark green of her wet cloak blended with the muddy water. If it weren't for the glint of her golden hair, he'd have issue pinpointing her location.

"The current is too strong and the creek bottom too slippery." She adjusted her spectacles and set them to rights once more. "This is impossible."

"No, we merely need to find a different way."

"My lord, do you wish us to come in and help?" one of the drivers of his coach yelled over.

He glanced over his shoulder and spat out foul water from his mouth. "No need for us all to land in the drink. I'll have the countess out soon enough, but perhaps you can make certain there's a blanket available for her."

"At once."

When Drew regarded Sarah once more, a hint of anger sliced through him so quick he couldn't recall it. "Why the devil did you break your promise to me? You said you wouldn't leave me, yet here we are."

She snorted, ended up inhaling water and then coughed until it had cleared her airway. "You're choosing right now to take me to task?"

"It's not like you can storm away." He shook his head.

"We both seem to have a problem with running from our challenges."

Oh, he adored her, for she didn't try to hide her flaws. "You're right."

"You can vent your spleen at me once we're on safe ground."

"No, I mean you were right." Now was as good a time as any to bare his soul. "About everything. My being an arse. Finn not needing me underfoot. All of it." It was humbling to admit, but he couldn't wait to tell her everything that had transpired while away.

"For the love of God, Andrew. Let's get out of the water before we begin a discussion." Threads of annoyance cut through her voice.

What the devil had she to be irritated about? "Fine. I merely thought you might like to know." Once more he extended his arm. "Stretch out as far as you can and take my hand."

When she did as he asked, a strangled scream escaped, and she ducked partially beneath the surging water. As she regained her footing, she clung to her wheel. "I can't do this. The water is too strong, and I was never a good swimmer."

"There's no other way."

Her eyes were wide and clouded with fear as she shook her head. "I'm afraid." The sound of the rain ate up the whispered admission, but that tiny waver in her tone tore at his heart.

Perhaps everyone was indeed frightened as they went about life, and it was a matter of fortitude how they overcame it.

"So am I." That was the crux of his problems. Deep down he finally acknowledged it. Fear was the thing keeping him back, making sure other emotions held him down like a bully. *Well, no more.* "Everything I want—we want—lays on the other side of that fear, so please. You have to help me to get you to safety." Drew's pulse pounded hard through his veins. He extended his arm, his eyes locked onto hers. "Give me your hand. Let go of that wheel in faith and know that I will catch you. Always."

Archie and the other drivers stood on the bank waiting to haul him and Sarah up if they could but reach them.

Seconds went by as his muscles tightened from strain and exposure. "Sarah, now!"

"All right." She threw out an arm. Water rushed into her face, and she coughed against it. Their fingertips brushed. The creek surged and wrenched her hand from his.

He missed the connection. "Damn it." If he couldn't do this one little task, he'd lose Sarah, and there would be no opportunity to make things rights.

"My skirts are so heavy. They're dragging me down and tangling against my legs." She shook her head. "I don't know what to do."

Cold, crushing anxiety came barreling back into his chest, squeezing with tight bands to steal his breath. He shook from the force of it; would he never be free? For long, heart-stopping seconds, he stared at his wife, who looked back with a silent plea in her eyes.

I've worked too hard for this to be the end.

With all the strength of will he possessed, Drew shoved away the anxiety and the fear. Never again would he allow those emotions to rule him or shutter his life. Moving as far as he dared from his wheel, he reached out an arm to her. "Sweeting, I can't lose you. Catch my hand. You're almost there."

She slowly left the relative security of the wheel she clung to. Bit by tiny bit she came further toward the middle of the coach's frame. When she extended her left arm, it shook, from exposure or the cold, he couldn't say. This time, her fingertips touched his.

"That's it. Just a little more." He wriggled his fingers, and when she attempted the connection again, she thrust her hand into his gloved palm. With strength borne of desperation, she held on. *Oh, thank goodness.* "Now, release the coach," he urged in a soft voice.

"You won't let me go, will you?"

"I've let many things go recently, but you are not one of them. Not anymore." He might have laughed at his word choice, for that was exactly what he'd learned to do with her guidance and his father's letter.

"I believe you." Then Sarah released her hold on the wheel.

For several heart-stopping moments, the muscles in his arms strained as she hung onto him, her body battered by the rapid current, but Drew bore down, gritted his teeth, and slowly pulled her close until she clung to his body, her breath ragged in his ear.

CHAPTER TWENTY

S HIVERS RACKED SARAH'S body as she held onto Andrew. For one moment she let herself enjoy the strength of his arm around her waist, but this was no time to rest on their laurels. As she looked at him, her heart leapt. She felt the literal movement in her chest; it wasn't a figment of her imagination. Perhaps Tilly had been right all along.

"Hold onto me. I need both my arms to bring us to the creekbank." His gruff order rang in her ears, but the nominal warmth of his body was too inviting for her to protest.

She nodded and looped her arms about his shoulders. Her legs were heavy and weighted with skirting, but she tried her best to wrap them around his waist. "Hurry."

"I'm doing my level best," he replied, the words pushed out from around clenched teeth.

Inch by slow inch he moved along the underside of the coach and soon they'd cleared the wheel. When he neared the creekbank, he kept hold of the wheel, the frame, any bit of the fallen coach he could manage as he gained a foothold on the muddy bank. "Archie, help."

A man she assumed was a driver slipped down the slope. He snatched at the hand she extended, and with a mighty yank, he pulled her from Andrew's hold.

Her skirting snagged on a few sticks that protruded from the mud.

She fumbled to free them while the driver tugged on her hand and wrist. With the dull sound of wet fabric tearing, her body slid up the muddy bank. Once she was fully out of danger, the driver let go her hand to tend to assisting her husband up. Two other men held onto her arms and dragged her a bit away from the creek, away from the rushing water. When they left her to help Archie, she gasped for breath, her palms firmly against the wet grass, her mind in a whirl.

How the deuce had he appeared as if by magic when she'd needed him? Then her heartbeat accelerated as she glanced over her shoulder at the men who were retrieving him from the creek water. He'd come home early. That was the only way he could have met her on the road. Pleasure mixed with annoyance in her chest.

All too soon, Andrew stumbled over to her location. Mud covered his person like it did her. His hair was slicked back from his forehead, rain rolled down his face, but he helped Sarah to her feet and bundled her into his arms for a tight hug. "My God, I feared I'd lost you."

To the rushing water or forever? Suddenly, she desperately wished to know. Wedging her hands between them, she pressed her palms to his chest and shoved him away. Emotions surged inside her in a chaotic mix, and she let them rage. No doubt they were a direct result of reaction, but she didn't care. They'd have this argument, but at least the air would be cleared, and she would know where she stood with him.

"Of course, you'd return in time to play the hero because that puts all the attention on you. Folks won't think you're such an arse that way, will they?" She didn't care that the drivers looked on or that poor Tilly and her hurt driver were stranded on the far bank. As with each interaction with her husband, he drove her to the extremes.

"What the hell are you talking about?" Hurt jumped into his expression. "I never planned on being a hero, but from the looks of things, you couldn't wait to break your promise to me." He shoved a hand through his dripping hair. "If you wish to leave me, say it, Sarah."

In a quieter voice, he added. "I'll understand. I've been the world's biggest bastard, but I want you to know that I'm in the process of changing."

The admission stole some of her ire away. "Actions speak louder, Andrew, and I haven't seen such from you."

"That's fair." He took a step toward her, but when she held up a hand, he paused, insecurity in his stormy eyes.

"I've maintained my position all along, and I will not stay with a man who gives into his anger and temper. Nor can I live with a man who won't let himself feel. Emotions are a part of life. Good or bad, we all have them. They're a sign that we're alive, but we can't ignore him."

"Sarah."

"No." She paused for breath and to shiver again. Rain dotted her spectacle lenses, obstructing her vision. It was best to say her piece here and now, for she might not have another chance. "I won't live with a man who refuses to forgive others and himself, a man who seeks to orchestrate everyone else's life except his own."

"Sarah—"

"Let me finish," she interrupted whatever he would say. As exhaustion sank into her shaking limbs, she planted her hands on her hips. "I need *you*, Andrew. Only you, not your title, your wealth, your position, your name." After this, she'd be vulnerable for him to make jest of, but at least she would have told him how she felt. "Just you, protecting me, supporting me, *loving* me as I do you."

His lower jaw dropped then his mouth worked as if he were a caught fish. For several seconds, no sound issued from him. Finally, he apparently got himself in hand. "You love me?"

"Yes." Now that she'd said it aloud, she feared his reaction. "I'm well aware you probably don't return that regard, but I can't help how I feel and wanted you to know in the event that you..." Her words trailed off, for she couldn't remember what she wanted to say. Her attention never left his face, and the transformation was... amazing.

Never had she seen such joy or hope in his expression. A slow grin curved those impossibly chiseled lips. The gesture reflected in his eyes and he took another step forward. Two hand lengths separated them now. "Sarah?"

"Yes?" The one-word question was propelled on a wave of breathlessness. Had she concluded her argument sufficiently? Did it matter anymore?

"I love you too." As she stared, he closed the distance and took her into his arms, holding her close, rocking her in his embrace. "Don't ever do that to me again." He pressed his lips into her temple, and the shudders that racked his body transferred to hers.

"I won't." She could scarcely breathe he held her so tightly, nor could she think properly. There were so many questions she wanted to ask, but none would leave the tip of her tongue.

"I can't survive without you; I know that now," he whispered into her ear. "When I went to London, I had mixed feelings, was a different man than the one standing here." He pulled away only to hold her head between his hands. "I was an arse and a fool." His eyes bored into hers. "Finn is all right. He told me much the same thing as you did."

"That's wonderful to hear—"

He cut off her words with a quick, hard kiss that tasted of muddy creek water. "I was given a letter that my father penned before his death, meant for me on my wedding day." The joy in his countenance hadn't lessened. "It explained so many things and made me realize something above everything else."

"Yes?" Had she been reduced to uninteresting one-word answers?

"Nothing else matters except making things right between us, and showing you with every day that I'm given how much I love you, need you, want you with me always." His words tripped over themselves as he rushed on. "Once a man has that, everything will fall into place as it was always meant to."

"Oh, Andrew." Her mind reeled. "I never thought you'd say such things, that you would make your way to this point." He hadn't exploded with anger, nor had he suffered an attack, when by all rights he should have. "I don't know what to say." The change was there, and it overwhelmed her.

"I realize I'll have to work at it and that I'll most likely fail at times."

"We all will."

"But with your help I'll succeed." His eyes shone. With a wicked grin that promised equally wicked things in the future, he sank to one knee in the mud and muck, despite the rain and the servants who gawked at them. "Lady Hadleigh, will you promise to remain married to me, now and all the days of our lives?"

Tears sprang into her eyes. Her heart squeezed and overflowed with the love and affection she'd come to have for him. With a shaking hand, she drew her gloved fingers through his sopping hair. "I will." The urge to laugh welled in her chest, but instead, tears fell to her cheeks. "Oh, please get up." She tugged at his arm.

"Thank you." Once he'd stood, the drivers clapped and uttered catcalls, all of which he ignored, but he hadn't lost his grin as he looked at her. "My God, I love you." Before she could move or say anything, he caught her up into his arms and claimed her lips in a series of long, drugging kisses that had her mind spinning, her pulse racing, and heated tingles circling through her insides.

When she pulled away to breathe, she touched his cheek. "Thank you for coming back early. I missed you but was stubborn and hurt. I needed to go away before you returned because my heart was breaking. And I thought you would never love me."

"I'm sorry." His hands at her waist tightened. "Forgive me."

"Only if you do the same for me. I was wrong, wasn't thinking clearly." She shook her head. "Then everything happened so fast. The coach fell over, we were in the water... I didn't want to die before bearing you this child…" *Oh, drat.* She hadn't meant to reveal that so soon without confirmation, but she was allowed to be overwrought just now.

"What?" His eyes rounded with shock as his lips formed a perfect "O" to match.

Suddenly self-conscious, Sarah cleared her throat as her cheeks burned. "Perhaps we should discuss this matter once we're home and in private."

As if he were a man trapped in a dream, Andrew nodded. He moved slowly, the shock firmly in place throughout his expression as he turned to address the men behind him. "Everyone in this coach. Someone tell poor Tilly that we'll need to go around to the next bridge, but once we're over, we'll come and retrieve her and the driver." He held out a hand to Sarah. "Come, countess. We're going home."

Home. The word shivered down her spine. For the first time in years, she had someplace where she felt like she belonged, and it was all due to the man she'd married.

>>>×<<<

A FLEETING, GENTLE touch on her face nudged Sarah awake. The dark interior of the coach hadn't changed since they'd left the scene of the accident, but now the door had been thrown open and the servants had disembarked. For the moment, she was alone with her husband.

"Have we arrived?" When she lifted her head from his shoulder, her muscles protested the movement. Her clothes were damp and cold in places, stiff in others, and they both stunk of mud and creek muck. A quick look out one of the windows showed soft golden light illuminating nearly every window at Hadleigh Hall.

"We have." He pressed his lips to the top of her head. "Let's get you inside." His baritone, in that thrilling whisper, had the power to see her undone. Before she could respond, he stood and then vaulted to the ground, turning to offer her a hand. "You'll need a proper rest."

"I'm fine, truly." His hands at her waist sent warmth into her cold extremities, but her feet had barely touched the gravel drive when he scooped her up into his arms and carried her toward the front door. Water spots marred her spectacle lenses.

"Dalton! Mrs. Hastings!" His shouts rang in her ears, but she hung onto his shoulders and snickered at his assertiveness. "There's been an accident," he said, the second he came into the entry hall and the butler scrambled through the corridor. "Please arrange a hot bath for both Lady Hadleigh and myself. Post haste!" he shouted while the housekeeper met him at the grand staircase. "We can't have Her Ladyship catching a cold," he told the older woman with a grin that caused Sarah's heart to sing. "She's carrying a babe," he said as if imparting the greatest secret ever known to mankind.

"At once, my lord," Mrs. Hastings said with a surprised smile and a glance at her.

Sarah shrugged. There was no point in denying it now that he'd blurted out the news. The household would hear of it within minutes. "Do hush, Andrew. How embarrassing."

He merely winked as he carried her upstairs like she weighed nothing at all.

An hour later, Sarah sighed. Her bathwater had cooled, but the warmth of it had seeped into her body and chased away the chill from the rain.

"Best come out of there, my lady," Tilly advised as she entered the room holding a dressing gown of red silk embroidered with gold thread in the Chinese style. "Your fingers will prune. No doubt you're exhausted."

"I was, but right now, I'm wide awake." She stood in the bath and used a soft towel that had been draped over the end of the tub to quickly dry her skin. "I suppose that's what a near-death experience will do for a person." While she'd soaked, one of the maids had polished her spectacle lenses while another had whisked her soiled and ruined clothing out of the room. As she stepped out of the tub and allowed Tilly to wrap her in the beautiful dressing gown, she sighed again. Such luxury. Would she ever become acclimated to it?

"If you're hungry, I can ring for a tray. Perhaps some tea?" Tilly led the way into the attached room where the bedclothes had already been turned down. A single candle burned on the nightstand.

"Not yet, but no doubt I'll find a nice appetite in the morning." What she wanted more than anything was to see her husband, to assure herself that he hadn't suffered injury. To hold him in her arms while she digested the events of the evening.

"Very well, my lady. I'll tuck you in then?"

The sound of a masculine throat being cleared at the door had them both looking in Andrew's direction. The earl wore a dressing gown similar to hers, except his was midnight blue. And, oh goodness, he was so handsome!

"That won't be necessary, Tilly. I'll see to the countess' needs tonight." He flashed a smile at the girl that had the maid blushing and stammering. "You've had an ordeal the same as Lady Hadleigh. Please take the remainder of the night off and find some rest."

"Thank you, my lord." After she'd executed a curtsy, the girl fled.

Andrew looked at Sarah. His eyes were more blue than gray in the flickering candlelight. "Would you like me to comb your hair?" He roved his gaze up and down her person while she cinched the dressing gown's tie at her waist. "I've never seen it down before."

Tingles danced along her spine. "I'd like that."

Wordlessly, he moved into the dressing room. When he returned, he held the silver, ivory-handled comb in one hand. He crossed the room to stand behind her, and as he began to draw the teeth of the comb through her hair, working out the tangles with a gentle hand as if he'd spent a lifetime doing so, a shuddering sigh escaped her.

There was something both erotic and relaxing about having a man pamper her. Awareness of him rippled over her skin, and she shivered.

"Are you cold? Still suffering from reaction?" His warm, clove-scented breath skated over her cheek. Had he brushed his teeth before joining her?

"No. It's you." There was no sense in denying that she was besotted by her husband, for it was bound to come out in the next few weeks.

"Good." Andrew continued to comb her hair until all the tangles and snags had worked loose and the damp tresses fell down her back in smooth waves. "So much like gold it's unbelievable." He tossed the comb onto the foot of the bed and then moved the mass of her hair over one of her shoulders. "I'm in awe of you." When he pressed his lips to her nape, another shiver racked her body. "And you wore the emeralds."

"You said I always should." She pushed her spectacles back into place. "I'm nothing special." His words sank into her heart infusing it with joy.

"Oh, but you're wrong." He moved to stand in front of her, his eyes intense, dark with desire and shining with the deeper emotion of love. "To me, you are everything." He drew his fingertips along the curve of her cheek and his hand shook. "You peered into the soul of this Storme and found something I had no idea was worth saving."

Tears pricked the backs of her eyelids. "I knew what you could be, built upon who you are. That's all." Did every woman feel cherished and safe when a man finally realized he was in love with them?

Surprising her further, her husband dropped to his knees on the Aubusson carpeting. He held her hips in his hands, but he laid pressed his lips to her belly. As he stared up at her, he asked, "Is it true, what you let slip out there?"

"I think so." Sarah finger-combed his still-damp hair. The threads of silver glimmered in the low light. "It's too early to have a midwife confirm, of course, but I missed my menses last week, and that never happens with me." Another shiver raced down her spine, anticipation for everything she'd ever wanted culminating within her blood. "I don't want to hope in the event I'm wrong or nature takes its course, but…"

"It's a bloody miracle. You're my hope, Sarah, my salvation, and I promise to try every damn day to be worthy of you."

A tear fell to her cheek. "You are, right now, as the man I see here." The change was noticeable, in his expression, his eyes, his attitude, how he acted, and it stole her breath. "I'm so proud of you, so glad it was you who ran me off the road that day."

"When you gave me the biggest dressing down of my life?" They shared a chuckle and he tugged at the sash of her gown. "With that one meeting, I set my feet on the path I'd need to walk, for it would lead to you and a life I had no idea I wanted."

She sucked in a breath as her robe gaped open and the relative coolness of the room wafted over her skin. "When did you turn into a romantic?" How was she supposed to think when his hands were beneath her robe and gliding over her bare legs?

"You bring out the softer side of me." A wicked gleam popped in his eyes. "I'm going to show you right now how much I adore you."

As her robe slipped from her shoulders to pool at her feet, Sarah smiled. "I can't wait."

CHAPTER TWENTY-ONE

DREW TRAILED HIS fingertips up and down the backs of Sarah's legs. As gooseflesh popped on her skin, he grinned. Oh, they would have such fun together. While kneeling, he busied himself by kissing and licking a path around her naval. The adorable divot captured his attention for a few seconds. All the while, he continued to caress her silky legs. A tiny moan escaped her, and he slid his hands upward to cup the soft globes of her buttocks.

How had he ever thought her plain? He kissed her mons, dared to delve his tongue through the blonde curls between her thighs, and as he urged her legs apart, he spent the next few minutes coaxing that all-important little pearl out from hiding. At her surprised inhalation of breath, he pressed her lower half closer and buried his face in the heaven that was his wife.

With every sweep and pass of his tongue to that nubbin, his shaft hardened. As he teased the button, and tiny cries were pulled from her throat, he explored further, intent to bring her to swift release before he did anything else. He drew his hands up and down her legs, both the inside and outside, until she trembled where she stood, and still he worked that nubbin for all he was worth. It swelled from his attentions, and he increased his friction: sucking, nipping, flicking, and then soothing with his tongue.

A low keening cry issued from Sarah. Her legs shook. The hand she'd rested on his shoulder clenched, her nails digging into his dressing gown. With a smug masculine chuckle, he surged to his feet and caught her into his arms as her knees buckled. "Merciful heavens, that was quite intense. I had no idea one could... oh, my."

Yes, setting her at sixes and sevens was by far one of his most favorite games. "I'm not nearly done with you tonight, darling." Once he'd laid her on the bed, he shed his dressing gown and joined her, reclining on his side. "Are you enjoying yourself?"

"Immensely." Her eyes were wide and dark behind her spectacle lenses. She raked her gaze along his body, and he swore he felt her regard as if she'd touched him. "The first two times we came together, you were in various stages of undress." Slowly, with a timidity he found endearing, she pressed a hand to his chest. "I've never had cause to blatantly inspect your naked form."

"Ah." Wanting very much to please her, Drew flopped onto his back and tucked his arms beneath his head. "Explore at will, love." He probably wouldn't last long once she laid hands on him, for even now his length had tightened to near pain.

"How scandalous." She blinked at him.

"I don't see how. We're married." How could she sport such a blush when they'd been together carnally twice now?

"Newly married at that, given the issues surrounding our union." She kneeled at his side. When she trailed the fingers of one hand down his chest, raking through the mat of hair, he hissed in a breath. "I've not seen a naked man apart from Greek statues in the London Museum." The other hand sailed over his abdomen, untying the sash of his dressing gown, and then went lower until she brushed his erection.

"Oh, God." There was no hope that he could make this last for hours as was his want. Every touch, each trip of her fingers, all the tiny caresses she gave him pushed him closer to the brink. She was all too beguiling and intriguing, and as she'd said, their marriage was too new; he needed to bed her a handful of times before he'd have enough of her that he could finally make love slowly. "Careful, Sarah. I'm primed enough."

"Poor thing. I guess it's your turn to suffer exquisite torture then, hmm?" With a smile that promised him wicked delights—or a swift death—his wife circled his shaft over and over. Her palm barely brushed the sensitized flesh, but each time she touched him, his need for her increased and his stones tingled from pent-up desire.

Then she wrapped her fingers around him while watching his face. Drew held his breath. When that didn't stave off the acute sensations racing through him, he attempted to wriggle into a sitting position, but she pushed him back down with a palm on his chest.

"Perhaps it's time for you to learn patience." As she stroked her curled fingers up and down his impossibly hard length, he lost his focus and well as part of his rational mind. "It's so satiny and thick." She turned her head, watching as she moved her hand. A pink blush infused her cheeks. "Turnabout is only fair, don't you think, Lord Hadleigh?"

Oh, dear God in heaven. He gasped as she lowered her head and tentatively touched the tip of her tongue to the head of his member. The waterfall of her hair rasped over his chest to cultivate exquisite eddies of need and fire through his blood. Never had he been subjected to anything as exquisite as that. "Sarah, please stop, else I'll embarrass myself."

But when had his damned wife ever listened to him? With a laugh that he felt all the way into his stones, she took part of his length into the hot cavern of her mouth and swirled her tongue around it. When she came off him, she giggled. "This is quite... interesting."

He couldn't stand it any longer. Tugging on her arm, he urged her off his prick. "There is plenty of time for you to experiment and master that particular pleasure." With that small amount of breathing room, he pulled her over his body until she straddled his waist. "I need you,

Sarah." The words came out more breathless than he'd intended, and for the first time in a long while it wasn't due to anxiety. It was with him in the background, but he refused to give it power. This trouble breathing had everything to do with wanting his wife, his beautiful, intelligent, strong-willed wife, the woman who potentially carried his child.

Perhaps his heir.

"There's nothing stopping you from taking what you want." The dulcet sound of her voice washed over him in a soothing wave, but it was the twinkle in her dark eyes that sent longing coursing through him.

"Minx." Drew coaxed her down so he could kiss her lips. "I don't want to take anything. Not anymore. I'd rather share with you." When she wriggled her bottom, the sensations against his straining member nearly undid him. "Ride me." The command taxed the last of his control.

"Oh." The look of concentration on her face was adorable, and he couldn't wait to teach her everything he knew regarding delights found in the bedroom. "I don't think..." She lifted onto her knees, and once more her fingers were on his length, guiding him to where she needed him. "I'm afraid I won't be very good at this."

"It doesn't matter." He gripped her hips, showing her. "Push down when I thrust upward, and... Christ!" She'd done what he asked. White stars erupted behind his eyelids while intense sensation raced through his length.

"Oh!" Sarah dug her fingers into the skin of his chest and abdomen. Each little touch hurtled him closer to breaking. The emeralds around her neck winked in the candlelight. Was there anything more erotic than making love with a woman who wore nothing but gemstones? "This is... well awkward, but somewhat... nice." When she moved, bouncing up and down without finesse, his eyes crossed. "This feels incredible, and I... oh!" Her eyes briefly rolled back in her head behind her tilted spectacles. Pleasure lined her expression.

And damn if it wasn't the most sensual sight.

If she weren't careful, he'd spend before he was ready, for her inexperience was more arousing than a skilled courtesan. "Perhaps this is too advanced just now." He held her as his body tensed. Seconds later he flipped them both over and covered her body with his. His dressing gown slipped off his body. "Let me love you properly, as I should have done all along."

She cupped his cheek with one hand. "I won't say no."

A shuddering breath escaped him as some of the pressure eased. For long moments, he kissed and licked seemingly every inch of her soft, clover-and-violet scented skin. With tongue and teeth, he brought her, shaking, to the edge of release as he tormented her nipples and teased his fingers between her thighs. She retaliated, though, by trailing a hand down his back. She squeezed an arse cheek, and he had to bear down to stop the inevitable. How was it that a few touches from her had him needing to prematurely shoot his wad like a green schoolboy?

Perhaps this act was more powerful when the right emotions were behind it.

Drew settled himself comfortably between her bent, raised knees, and with one flex of his hips, he penetrated her as deep as he could go. Her honeyed heat surrounded him, pulled at him, and he sighed. "I adore how you feel."

"Not as much as I do you." She looped her arms about his shoulders to hold him closer. Then she bumped his hips with hers. "Now, do hurry, my lord. I am in great need."

"We can't have that." Then he set about bringing his wife to release.

Over and over he moved into her with slow, gentle strokes while he held his weight on his forearms. She watched him, canted her hips, and matched his rhythm. All too soon they fairly danced together, in a waltz as old as time itself. Then her eyes shuttered closed and she simply held onto him as he worked his length in and out of her sweet, tight passage.

Heat buzzed through him. Anticipation tingled at the base of his spine. Need roiled through his stones, pulling them tight to his body. His member pulsed with each thrust. His control shattered. Faster and faster he speared into her. Deeper and deeper he went in the attempt to join with her. Harder and harder he worked to bring her over the edge before he went too.

Heated need consumed him, and he shifted his angle, so the root of his member brushed her nubbin. A moan wrenched from her throat, and he fractured. Frenzied cries came from her as she dug her fingernails into his shoulders. Then she screamed. The walls of her passage fluttered greedily about his prick. His thrusts were frantic, and on a particular deep one, he broke into a million shards of white light as he fell into bliss and took her with him.

As he marveled over how this former straightlaced governess was a screamer during intercourse, he ground his pelvis into hers while his length emptied. With a sigh, he collapsed on top of her and wrapped his arms around her. What a novel experience feeling her heartbeat racing against his, her breathing as ragged as his own. If she weren't already increasing, he would have a wonderful time putting her in that state over the next few months.

Eventually, as his overheated body cooled and his breathing returned to normal, he rolled off her and onto his back. "Woman, you wear me out, and I'm not a young man any longer."

"That's too bad." She yawned, nestling into his side with a hand on his chest. "For I'll want another go 'round soon."

God, but she'd be the death of him. "Give me an hour or so and I'll let you have your wicked way with me." And gladly. He grinned into the darkness. Had he ever been so happy in his life? All too soon, he sobered. Turning his head, he found her gaze in the inky shadows.

"I'm glad you rescued your flute."

"I couldn't leave it behind. It's the most valuable thing I own, excepting everything you've given me." Her spectacle lenses were smudged, and they sat at an awkward angle on her nose, but it was the most adorable thing.

"Darling." He took her hand, entwining their fingers. "I've asked my mother to handle the planning for this, but I want to have a recital or musicale evening at my townhouse in London for you. Sometime next month if you agree. This way you can see if playing in front of a crowd is what you'd like to do." The surprise in her eyes gave him pause. "But only if you're willing. It'll be a good way to introduce you to society as my countess, and you can come to know my family."

"Truly?"

"Yes."

She squeezed his fingers. "You believe in my talent that much?"

"Oh, yes. You tamed this wild beast with it, did you not?"

"Perhaps." The smile she gifted him with had the power to light the shadows. "I would like that."

"Good." For long moments, he remained silent. The sound of their breathing blended with the summer insect and animal life that teemed outside the open window. As his eyelids were fluttering closed, he roused himself, for there was something he needed to say. "Before you came into my life and upended it—"

"Reordered it so you could see what mattered," she interrupted softly.

"All I had left of any of my family—Father, Finn, Brand—was my anger toward them," he continued as if she'd not spoken. "I wrongly told myself that if I let go of my anger, I'd have nothing left of them." It had taken days for him to come to such a realization, but looking at it now, it made complete sense.

"Anger is not the same as fond memories."

"I know that now." A tiny grin curved his lips. "In my father's case, nothing can bring him back. I realize that now as well, and while in London, I made my peace with that. But my brothers are still lost, not dead, but lost to me…" He would always worry about them because that's what the oldest son did. It didn't mean he wanted to manage them, it merely meant he cared. "I love them, but don't know how to say it."

"I'm proud of you." Her eyes lit with happiness. "There is time to make things right by them, Andrew."

"I don't know how." Admitting to things beyond his ken was difficult, but if she were there, he could tackle it.

"None of us do; we go by faith." She brought his hand to her lips and kissed a finger. "Yes, the war damaged them, and yes, they will need to navigate their new realities by themselves, but you can make a fresh start with them, heal the rifts like you did with me."

"How?" He was at a loss.

"Leave your ego and arrogance behind and lead with your heart. Show them that you love them but let them spread their wings." She smiled. "They'll soar if you allow them to."

After a few seconds rumination, he nodded. "Will you stand with me when that happens?"

"Of course, I will." When he pulled her close and wrapped his arms around her, the tiny squeal she uttered sent tingling awareness through his shaft. "I'll do whatever is needed, because you are worth saving too."

"I love you." His chest swelled with affection while his heart skipped a beat. "I can't wait to see where our path leads next." For now that he'd found his, he would never walk alone.

"You're learning, changing, evolving into the man you needed years ago, and that is quite an aphrodisiac." She snuggled into him and dropped a kiss to his lips. "I wouldn't have married you otherwise."

"Ha!" He snorted in mirth. "I'm fairly certain you married me to keep your cute little arse out of the gutter and away from your great uncle's children. A business arrangement, remember?"

"Do shut up, Hadleigh. It's not well done of you to bring up such unsavory things to a lady." The fondness in her dulcet tones continued to cultivate a sense of peace within him.

Sometimes, calming the storm meant suffering through it until he came out the other side into clear skies, and he couldn't be happier with that outcome, all due to the woman in his arms. Perhaps in this he'd succeeded where his father had failed. Would that there be more moments like that in his future. "Ah, but it's such fun to tease you, countess." He looked forward to more of that for as many years as they had together.

The End

About the Author

Sandra Sookoo is a *USA Today* bestselling author who firmly believes every person deserves acceptance and a happy ending. Most days you can find her creating scandal and mischief in the Regency-era, serendipity and happenstance in Victorian America or snarky, sweet humor in the contemporary world. Most recently she's moved into infusing her books with mystery and intrigue. Reading is a lot like eating fine chocolates—you can't just have one. Good thing books don't have calories!

When she's not wearing out computer keyboards, Sandra spends time with her real-life Prince Charming in central Indiana where she's been known to goof off and make moments count because the key to life is laughter. A Disney fan since the age of ten, when her soul gets bogged down and her imagination flags, a trip to Walt Disney World is in order. Nothing fuels her dreams more than the land of eternal happy endings, hope and love stories.

Made in the USA
Middletown, DE
15 October 2021